"Why are the Divines liars and thieves?"

Rosa looked earnest.

Viscount Sunley's reply consisted of a laugh and a graceful attempt to kiss her hand.

Rosa drew it away before he could complete the kiss. "You mean to have Beckwi....... ...ney one way or another, an..... ....e to the law as wel..... ....ceed. Nevertheless, ...s you say."

"If you car................., by all means tell m........

"I don't kno...... ...en enough yet to point out your redeeming qualities. I shall let you know, however, as soon as I find one. For now, I must base my judgment on what I know of myself."

Puzzled, he regarded her with interest.

"After all, I am an imposter and a pickpocket, and yet I am not so very bad, am I?"

"No, you are not so very bad at all." At that, he pulled her to him and kissed her firmly on the lips. His arms went round her so swiftly that she could not breathe.

Then, releasing her just as swiftly, he planted his hat upon his head and made his way out the door.

ALSO BY
BARBARA SHERROD

Mary Ashe
The Players

Published by
WARNER BOOKS

LADY DIVINE

Barbara Sherrod

WARNER BOOKS

A Warner Communications Company

To Neil

WARNER BOOKS EDITION

Warner Books, Inc.
666 Fifth Avenue
New York, N.Y. 10103

A Warner Communications Company

Printed in the United States of America

First Printing: September, 1988

10 9 8 7 6 5 4 3 2 1

◇ **One** ◇

Rosa noticed two elegantly dressed gentlemen elbowing their way through the crowd. The short one, a gray-whiskered old man, anxiously scanned the faces surrounding him. His companion—who was both younger and taller—looked as though he smelled a three-day fish. Whenever he was rudely pushed, he peeled the offender from his fashionable coat and set him down as far away as the crush would allow. From her vantage point under the gaslight, Rosa tried to imagine what had brought two such swells to a filthy London playhouse. After some thought, she concluded they could have only one reason for being there—to have their pockets picked.

Carefully she made her way into the throng and permitted herself to be thrown two or three times against the old gentleman's breast. All at once, she clutched her cloak at the throat, gasped loudly for breath, and crying that she would surely faint, forced the sea of ticket holders to part and let her through. At last she emerged onto the street and quickly surveyed the mob to see if she was followed. When it was clear that all was well, she ran down an alleyway and dashed through the actors' entrance.

Impatiently she waited for an answer to her knock on the dressing room door. Finally, upon hearing "Enter!" she burst into the room and waved the purse in the air. "We shall sup tonight," she declared.

Mr. Merriweather Tripple grinned at her through his powder-caked face. "Ah, you are a resourceful girl," he said. "It inspires one to greet yet another dawn, yea, to tread the boards once more and speak the speech trippingly on the tongue."

"You mean you are glad not to starve."

"I have a great aversion to starving, my dear, though I am

careful never to consume more than a roast fowl and a bottle before a performance."

"So you say, but after yesterday's bottle, you could hardly speak your lines." Rosa stood behind him and peered at the reflection of the two of them in the mirror.

"It would take more than a full stomach and a head full of wine to impair my skill." He adjusted his putty nose.

"There's a bit of treasure in this fine purse, I expect. Let's open it."

"We must wait for a better hour, my girl. Just now our public awaits. We all have our entrances on this stage we call the world, and I have mine momentarily." He rose, swept his cape about him, and strode grandly from the room.

Placing the purse in a large powder box, Rosa dashed behind a screen. There she removed her cloak to reveal a well-worn costume. She adjusted her bodice, pinched her cheeks, and with a rapid glance in the mirror, ran out to the wings.

The house was clamorous with hooters and whistlers. They were impatient for her entrance, she knew, and she drew her shoulders back with pleasure. As soon as the principal actress threw out the cue, Rosa bounded onto the stage as the sauciest of saucy maids. Shouts and handclapping greeted her appearance, and she acknowledged the reception with a humble curtsy. Rising, she looked across the row of candles edging the stage, into the face of the gentleman whose purse she had just filched. His eyes grew wide as they met hers. He pointed at her, babbling something urgent to his companion.

Rosa's first thought was to flee, but she had a line. The audience breathed in anticipation of it, and she had not the heart to deny her public. She delivered the line with an arch wink, saying, "La, madam, your father awaits abovestairs, your husband waits below; your lover awaits without, and your Fate awaits withal!" She then inclined her head in response to the foot-stomping applause and wondered how much time she would have before a constable appeared to drag her off.

When she moved downstage to fetch a prop, she availed herself of the opportunity to steal a glance at the two gentlemen. They stared at her grimly, never laughing at the farce. Although there was a good deal to fear in those grave looks, there was comfort in the fact that they neither moved nor spoke, for it signaled their intention to stay to watch the play. Apparently they meant to wait for the intermission before sending to Bow Street. Real gentlemen such as these did not leave the theater before the curtain fell, any more than they threw their hats in the air, slapped their knees, or guffawed. Consequently, she would have a full ten minutes in which to plan her escape.

At the end of ten minutes, she did indeed have a plan. She had no sooner delivered her exit speech than she ran to the dressing room and plucked the purse from its hiding place. A cloud of powder spewed in her face, making her cough. But she had no time to waste on coughing, and no time for changing her costume, either. Tripple was already halfway through his scene, and the intermission would follow his monologue. There was no time to regret the confusion of the other actors when she failed to make her appearance on cue. Nor was there time to take leave of Tripple, who would deduce that she'd got herself in another scrape and would meet her later at their Southwark lodgings. The only thing she did have time for was to quit the playhouse as quickly as possible.

Nevertheless, she could not resist opening the purse and peeking inside.

As soon as she unfastened the clasp, twelve gold guineas winked up at her. Underneath them lay a folded piece of paper, which curiosity impelled her to open. When she read the inscription written there, her hand flew to her cheek and she uttered a cry. The scrawled document was addressed to Rosalind Divine.

Stuffing the letter back into the purse, she stashed it in the pocket of her cloak and ran out the door. She ran along the cluttered hall, through the exit, and down the alleyway. She ran through narrow streets until her blood pounded in her ears. Unable to run any farther, she paused in a doorway to lean against the post and catch her breath.

Suddenly she started at the sound of footsteps echoing on the mud-wet cobblestones. Several alleys met here and she could not decide which would take her into a thoroughfare and which to a court. It was critical to decide, for she was not merely running from the law. She was in flight from sorcery itself, from a devil who knew her name and, no doubt, her crimes as well.

Choosing the darkest way, she ran she knew not where or how long. She ran past strength, wishing she dared to stop long enough to listen again for the noise of footsteps. She kept on until she came to a high iron gate and, pulling on it violently, found it locked against her. Trapped, she turned to see a tall figure approaching her. She flung herself into a nearby entrance, hoping the door would yield to her weight. When it did not, she turned to see the man behind her. He was the companion of the old man she had robbed.

With a surge of desperate strength, she flung past him and would have succeeded in eluding him had he not caught her by the arm. With a swift motion, his hands pinned hers against the wall of a building, and as she turned her head furiously from side to side, she caught a glimpse of a smile. Neatly he evaded her kicks, continuing all the while to smile, and when at last she tired of struggling in his grip, she quieted, looking boldly into his eyes.

"Now, now, my lady, this is not very hospitable of you," he said. "I mean you no harm."

She stared at him. He was not just a devil, she thought. He was a lunatic of a devil. To address her as "my lady," and to look at her as he did, with such a smile, he must be either mad or bosky, and if he were the latter, she would certainly smell drink on his breath. But, in fact, he smelled not at all; that is to say, he did not smell at all unpleasant. He regarded her with something like gentleness.

"Take it," she whispered. "The purse is in my pocket. Take it and let me go."

"Thank you, my lady, but my intention is not to rob you."

"What is your intention?" she hissed and would have succeeded in kicking his knees had he not deftly stepped to one side.

"I only ask leave to accompany you back to the theater."

He removed his hands from hers and let her free. She rubbed her wrists, still feeling the sensation of his fingers. Then, with a lurch, she bolted. Just as quickly, however, he caught her, holding her tightly by the arms.

"Will you kindly stop wriggling, my lady."

"Let me go. I will pay you, I swear."

"If you will come with me to the playhouse, I promise you everything will be explained."

"And who will explain? The old gentleman? I warrant he will explain very prettily before he has me hauled off to the jail."

"Good God! Does my father look like a jailer? He will be furious with his tailor." His voice had not a jot of anger in it. Moreover, he still smiled as though amused.

Rosa began to wonder if she might do something far more effective than running to secure her freedom. A just application of her theatrical skill, she suspected, might be the very thing, and, accordingly, she produced a shower of tears. Her hand fell heavily on her brow, her bosom trembled, and in a full voice she murmured, "My child! I must go at once to my child."

The gentleman's face grew serious and the smile was lost. "A child, you say?"

"He is only an infant, sir. I pray you, let me go to him."

"It never occurred to us that there might be a child. But it may work to our advantage. Of course, we shall go at once."

Appalled, Rosa struggled in the strength of his hold on her. "*We* shall do no such thing. What have you to do with a child of mine?"

"We must fetch the child at once. Where is he? If he is far from here, I shall call for my carriage." Firmly holding her arm, he strode along the narrow street in the direction from which they had come, and Rosa was forced to hurry next to him.

"I cannot go any further," she cried, pulling to a halt.

The expression of concern on his face made her cheeks flame. "But what about the child?" he asked. "I fear from your alarm that he is not well. Perhaps it is a daughter. Has she been fed?"

"There is no child."

His expression was so intent that she could not meet his direct look. She lowered her eyes, fixing her gaze on the moonlight reflected in his Hessians. Devoutly she prayed that she would soon wake from this nightmare.

He took her chin in his hand and lifted her face. "Do not be ashamed," he said softly, "and do not fear for the child. We will care for your boy as well as his mother."

"Devil take my boy!"

He regarded her with interest.

"There is no boy. He does not exist."

"I beg your pardon. Did you not just beg to go to him?"

"Of course I did. I thought you would let me go if you thought I had a brat."

"Let you go? Now see here. It is one thing to mistake my father for a policeman. Lord knows his tailor hasn't the least notion of style and dresses him like the worst sort of character. But to mistake me for one, that is the outside of enough. Do you really believe I mean to take you prisoner?"

"Yes, and I believe you mean to take this as well!" She thrust a hand into her pocket and produced the old man's purse.

He looked from the purse to her face, then again at the purse. His face grew grave, and he was silent for some time. All at once he burst out laughing.

As soon as his laughter subsided, he took the purse from her and placed it in the pocket of his coat. "My Lady Cutpurse," he addressed her with great courtliness, "permit me to escort you back to the theater." He offered his arm with a flourish, and Rosa, not knowing what else to do, permitted him to lead her where he would.

◊ Two ◊

Only two men greeted Rosa in the musty costume room—Tripple and the old man. She searched for a third, a Bow Street runner, but did not find him. This circumstance eased her mind not in the least. On the contrary, it was so strange and unexpected that she grew frightened. She would have turned and run out again, but the tall young gentleman placed himself in front of the closed door and leaned against it with folded arms.

"Will you do me the honor of sitting a moment?" the old man invited her.

Rosa's eyes narrowed suspiciously as she took the proffered chair. She directed a questioning look at Tripple, who moved to her solicitously and took her hands. "My poor child," he intoned.

Turning around, Rosa saw the tall gentleman lounging at the door. His arms were still folded, and he wore his customary smile.

"You are Rosalind Divine?" the old man asked. His voice was shaky as he spoke.

"So my father tells me." At this, she looked at Tripple.

"Your father?" The old man turned a shocked look upon the actor, who instantly let go of Rosa's hands.

"Allow me to explain, my lord. The poor child would have it that I am her father. It has not been in my power, seeing her homeless and unprotected, to cast her from me, for though I am but the shabby, unfortunate creature you see before you, I am the most tenderhearted of men. 'How tender 'tis to love the babe that milks me,' as it were. But, alas, she is not my daughter. Only a pitiful orphan."

"Liar! Will you disown me?" Rosa would have concluded this outburst by scratching Tripple's face had he not eluded her fingers.

"You see for yourself, sir. If she were my daughter, would she be shouting such names at me? No, indeed, she would show me the respect due my age and infirmity."

Rosa glared at him. Then, suddenly, she put her face in her hands, overwhelmed with a heartsickness such as she had never known before. Pressing her lips together, she tried to restrain her sobs, but the tears would out.

Soon she became aware of something close to her cheek. Looking up, she saw the tall gentleman. He handed her a handkerchief, then returned to his post at the door. Made of the finest linen, the handkerchief smelled sweet, and she wept more wretchedly than before.

The old man came to her chair and knelt before her. It cost him considerable effort to bend so low. Rosa paused in her weeping to see if he would tumble to the floor. When he did not, she allowed him to take her hand.

"Dry your lovely eyes, my dear," he said with a smile. "I have news for you that will cure all your sorrows."

She looked over his head at Tripple, whose stern visage admonished her. "Hear the gentleman out," he commanded.

"Aye, you must listen," said the old man, "for you are Lady Rosalind Divine, daughter of my cousin John, Earl of Beckwith. I have been searching for you these many years, and now I've found you, I declare I think my heart will crack." He let forth a sob which inspired Rosa to offer him the handkerchief.

When he'd dried his eyes, she shook her head. "You are very kind, sir, I'm sure, but you are mistaken."

"We have searched for you since first we heard of your birth. And now I see you at last, I need no further proof of who you are. Your face is the very image of his sweet bride's."

"If you knew what I was, sir, you would not talk so."

"I know everything I care to know, except the number of ways I can see to your happiness."

Rosa shook her head. "I don't know who you are, nor who this gentleman is either. What do you want of me? I am only a poor actress."

Tripple stepped forward at this juncture to say, with a theatrical gesture, "We have the honor to entertain Lord Grantley Divine and Viscount Sunley, his son."

The gentlemen each bowed. Rosa looked at one, then the other, hardly knowing what to say or do. The young one wore an expression of perfect contentment. The old one seemed so kind, so hopeful, so genuinely pleased with what he imagined to be his discovery, that it pained her to disillusion him. However, disillusion him she must. It was not her habit to let romantic notions of honor influence her overmuch, but in this case, where she had done such wrong and received such gentleness in return, she could not help but own the truth. Besides, the old gentleman would discover the loss of his purse soon enough. The young one would be sure to smile as he named the thief.

"My good sir," she said, "I beg you to listen to me." She

faltered a moment, then forced herself to go on. "It is true my name is Rosalind Divine, but you will not call me your cousin when I tell you who I am."

"Ah, it is for us to tell you who you are," cried the old man. "We have the proof of it. Moreover, we have a letter for you."

On that, he reached into his breast pocket. When he did not find what he sought, he fumbled in his other pocket. He paled and began to tremble. "I shall never forgive myself," he said hoarsely, "if I have lost her letter."

"Is this what you are looking for?" the viscount inquired, drawing the purse from his pocket.

Lord Divine's eyes grew wide. "Why, how very strange. I am sure I put it in my pocket."

"You did, father, but you must have dropped it, for Lady Rosalind found it and returned it to me."

Too surprised to speak, Rosa searched Sunley's face for an explanation of this bold-faced lie. The viscount answered her look with his usual smile.

The old man's eyes filled with tears. Turning to his son, he declared it nothing short of a miracle. "That she should have found it at the very moment we sought the letter's rightful owner—why, it is providence, William!"

"No doubt it is, father. What else but providence would have placed your purse in her ladyship's hands?" His smile was broader than ever.

"What is the sign of providence, after all," the old man cried, "but a coincidence too wonderful to be believed? My dear girl, if you only knew what this purse contains." Thereupon, he opened it and removed the document. "This is for you," he said, handing it to Rosa. "You must read it at once."

Standing up, Rosa protested. "It isn't true."

Recognizing the purse, Tripple intervened, preventing Rosa from blurting out the truth. "Her ladyship is distressed, my lord, a natural feeling, I think, given the circumstances."

"Yes, of course. We did not mean to distress you, my dear, and very sorry I am if we have."

"Perhaps your lordships would leave us alone for a bit. I fear the news of so much good fortune all at once has overset the poor girl. I will help her compose herself. She will listen to me."

"Come, William. We shall step just outside."

Silently Viscount Sunley followed his father. Before closing the door behind him, he glanced at Rosa. His smile so infuriated her that she sat down again with a cry of vexation.

As she reviewed the evening's events, she could not make sense of them. They wound around and spun themselves out of control. Everything she did to bring them back into the realm of understanding only led to further confusion.

Tripple's voice recalled her to the present. "Now, my girl, is the winter of our discontent made glorious." There was exultation in his tone.

She studied her fingernail and did not reply.

"Ah, you act the tragedienne, I see. A most unsuitable role, Rosa."

"Are you not my father?"

"You have never heard me say I was."

"Nor have you expressly denied it."

"It is impolitic to commit to a thing before you've seen all the advantage of it. The better part of valor, you know."

"Do you see no advantage to having a daughter?"

"I see the advantage of not having one at present."

"Who is my father, then?"

"Stapped if I know. Perhaps it is this Earl of Beckwith. Why should he not be your father as well as anyone else's? And you do bear his name."

"What am I to you, if not a daughter?"

He sighed mournfully. "It is an ugly tale, unfit for the telling. I shudder to repeat it, but as you insist upon hearing it, I am compelled to reveal it. I found you outside a workhouse in Surrey, begging with a gaggle of urchins. You stopped me and asked if I would pay you to sing a song."

"You are trying to bamboozle me. You invented that tale."

"Invented! You flatter me. I speak the lines; I do not write them."

"Why did you take me? Why not one of the other urchins?"

"The reason is simple—you sang me a bawdy song. Stap me, if I know where a babe of five or six years learns such a song, but you lisped it in the most enchanting manner, and I knew at once you were a lassie after mine own heart."

"Swear to me you are telling the truth."

"The only truth which need concern you at present is that Beckwith claims you, and I make no doubt he dresses his claim in gold and jewels."

"I believe I already have a father, such as he is."

Tripple regarded her with amazement. "Why on earth would you have me for a father when you might have a nob who can provide for you in the high style?"

"I do not want the high style, only the truth."

Bewildered, he shook his head. "Then you are a fool and certainly no daughter of mine."

Rosa grew pale at this. At last she stood up and paced the room. It was foolish, she knew, to argue with Tripple when he had his mind made up, and it was ridiculous to insist upon his paternity when he had no intention of owning her. He would never own her as long as he imagined it might profit him better to do otherwise. Sooner or later, she told herself, he would repent of his falsehood. The day would come when he would admit that he had fathered her and that she belonged to him. Until that time, however, she must resign herself to patience.

"What would you have me do?" she asked.

"Be her ladyship."

"But what will become of you? I cannot forget you merely because some lord fancies I have a title."

Tripple patted her head. "You are a good girl," he said. "I have not done so ill by you after all, despite carting you over town and countryside all these years to play for peasants. You have learnt loyalty, I perceive, and I would not be ashamed to own you as mine, if it comes to that."

"If it comes to that, I hope you will not forget that I've also picked a pocket here and there along the way, risking life and limb so you might eat more than three times in a week."

"Nay, I forget nothing. But you must forget a great deal, Rosa. It is imperative you forget your past career and not get any silly notions about confessing old sins. That purse you filched, for example. I charge you to keep mum about that."

"It hardly matters, I think. Viscount Sunley knows precisely who and what I am."

"Does he? Does he, indeed? Why do you suppose he says nothing?"

"I don't know. I wish I did."

"Well, his silence is all to the good, it seems to me, and we shall do well to follow his example."

"I am sorry, Tripple, but I mean to tell the old gentleman everything."

"If you give yourself up for a pickpocket, how am I nobly to step aside and allow you to assume your rightful position in life?"

"My rightful position? You are stepping out of character, I think. It is not like you to play the hypocrite."

"That shows how little you understand me. I can play any role I am cast in. So, I vow, can you. And this role you've been handed is nothing less than the greatest of your career."

"I am unseasoned. It is beyond my talents."

"It is not, I assure you. Not for nothing did I groom you for the heroine's part."

"Do you profess to believe I can carry it off?"

"Faugh! I do not profess in the least. I scoff at profession. I do, in the deepest reaches of my heart, sincerely and honestly believe that you will act the role to perfection."

"I might pass myself off as a lady's maid, perhaps, but never her ladyship."

"It is not as difficult as you may think. The only difference is that a lady's maid never deviates from good manners, while a real lady may be as rude as she likes."

"Who would believe me in such a part?"

"As to that, you see how they call you her ladyship already and bow over your hand. You have only to let them continue."

"I should be known at once for an impostor."

"And have you so little faith in me, in my judgment and perspicacity? You pain me, child."

"You pain me as well, papa. Ah, I must not call you that."

"If you will not keep your own future in view, then I beg you will consider mine." Here he assumed a mournfully pathetic visage.

Unmoved, Rosa replied, "I am well aware you mean to

profit by this charade. As for me, I prefer picking a pigeon's pocket and being done with him. I never wish to set eyes on him again."

"Picking pockets is paltry stuff, my girl. Our little scheme will do nothing less than make my fortune. It will make both our fortunes."

"How?"

Here he was caught up short. "I do not know precisely as yet, but I am confident we shall discover the way."

"We shall discover nothing, except that I am to be taken from you and set up as a fine lady among strangers who will despise me."

"The letter may tell us something. Read it. Read it aloud."

Opening the yellowed, much-creased document, Rosa read as follows:

Beckwith, November 7th

To Rosalind Divine, my only child,

God willing, you will read this one day and
forgive your father. You must believe it was
never my intention to do harm. My excuse
must be my youth—my selfish, heedless youth.
Despite what anyone may tell you, I loved your
mother, and had I learned of your birth before
it was too late, I should have acknowledged you
both and performed all my obligations toward
you with a glad heart. Where she has taken you,
I know not. I know only that if you are reading
this, you are found, you are alive, you are safe.
My blessings go with you, my beloved child,
and I commend you to the care of my worthy
cousin.

Beckwith

"It says nothing about settlements," Tripple observed in disappointment. "We shall have to fish awhile longer yet to see what we are to net."

Though brief, the letter exerted a powerful force upon

Rosa. The loneliness of the writer moved her, and she was conscious of an answering voice within her own heart. Her cheeks grew warm and she put a hand to her face. Clutching the letter, she ran to the door, pulled it open, and surprised the two gentlemen standing in the hall.

She cried, "Take me to him. Take me to my father."

The unexpected plea stung the old gentleman into silence, thus leaving it to his son to speak.

After a pause, the viscount said softly, "I am sorry. He is dead."

Looking about her wildly, Rosa endeavored to absorb this news. She permitted its effect to sweep over her until she could regain her composure. Then, raising her eyes, she asked, "May I please keep his letter?"

◇ Three ◇

"What a stroke!" Tripple said in a whisper.

He stood with Rosa before the coronet carriage while the two gentleman settled themselves inside and awaited the completion of her good-byes.

"I should never have thought of it myself. Such humility. Such a tremor in the voice. Such irresistible helplessness. 'May I keep his letter?' Gad, you have done more than learn your lesson well; you've improved upon the master."

Here he swept his hat from his head and performed an elaborate obeisance.

"I was not acting."

"Ah, that is why you were so convincing."

"I doubt Viscount Sunley is convinced."

"Nonsense. He seems perfectly content with you."

"Yes, and I don't like it. Oh, Tripple, I feel it—we ought to have no part in this scheme. If I climb into this coach, we shall both regret it. Who knows what evil may follow? Is it not better to content ourselves with the evil we know than one we cannot possibly imagine? I beg you, let us leave now, while there is still time."

"Ah, yes, time. We must make much of time, Rosalind. You are right; we must gather our rosebuds while we may."

Rosa brightened at these words. "Do you mean it? I am so relieved, and I promise you won't be sorry for it. Let us go at once to Southwark. I can pack my valise in a flash and we shall be off. To the Midlands, I think. Yes, I have a fancy to see the Midlands."

Stunned, Tripple gaped. Then he shook his fists in vexation, saying, "Is it possible you would rather go hungry, dodge landlords, and breathe the dust of a falling-down stage than drink chocolate in the morning and dance the quadrille at night?"

"But I thought you had changed your tune."

He fixed her with his most funereal look. "It appears I must make my meaning more explicit, for you are either so obtuse or so sentimental that you persist in misunderstanding me. I have only two tunes in my repertoire, my girl, and it is for you to choose which one I shall hum herein after. The first is the one in which you come upon the great world as Lady Rosalind Divine. The second is the song in which I disappear from the stage, never to be heard from again. I do not see how I can make myself plainer, Rosa."

Searching his face, Rosa concluded that he was dead serious. In a low voice, she asked, "What will you do?"

"Never you mind about that. I have impressed upon the old lord that I am wholly bereft at the loss of my ward, and he has endeavored to fill the empty space in my heart with guineas. That should see me through until our next meeting."

"Our next meeting? Then you do not mean to desert me altogether?"

"You wound me, child. I vow, you cut me through the heart. How sharper than a serpent's tooth! If I'd meant to desert you, I should have done so long before this, when you were poor and a nobody."

Rosa studied him. He exasperated her, hurt her, evaded her questions, and railed at her answers. But she had known no other parent, no other caretaker, and her loyal heart clung to him. Besides, he had a round red face and a naughty expression between his mustache and beard. She could not help laughing when he regarded her sidelong and grinned, as he did now. "I don't know why I even speak to you, you old thief," she said with a smile. "You deserve hanging."

"Well, if one got what one deserved in this life, I daresay we should all swing."

"I should not be at all surprised to see it come to that."

With a buss on her cheek and a pat on her head, he handed her into the carriage.

As soon as she was seated, she drew aside the curtain so that she might watch him as they drove off. His portly frame was soon swallowed up in the fog, and, exhaling deeply, Rosa turned to face the two gentlemen who sat opposite.

The old one leaned forward to take her hand. The young one gazed at her, abstracted.

"Where are you taking me?"

"You shall go to my sister at George Street in Hanover Square. She will look after you. Do not be afraid."

"I am not afraid, only curious. You are pleased to insist I am a member of your family, but I am completely ignorant of any particulars."

"Quite right. William, you must tell our cousin everything."

Obligingly, the viscount related the story in as few words as possible—the earl's unfortunate marriage to a tradesman's daughter, the family's insistence that he break with her, and his subsequent betrayal of the young woman. Soon after, Sunley continued, the earl discovered the existence of a daughter. He gave way to uncharacteristic guilt and remorse, which, rendering him physically ill as well as sick at heart, at last killed him. Before he died, Beckwith had begged his cousin Grantley Divine, the heir to his title, to find his wife and child and restore them to their position of respectability.

"I might have gone on searching forever," the old man said with a bewildered sigh, "if William had not employed Buffel and Buffel in the case."

"Your solicitors produced nothing for fifteen years except an annual bill," said the viscount. "I naturally concluded that we needed to hire someone who did not confine his search to the environs of Mayfair and who would not be averse to sullying his waistcoat in the less fashionable districts."

With some pride, the father said, "Quite right. And these new fellows took barely a month to find you."

"But how did they find me?"

"Ah, providence again. It is the only rational explanation, for they found you by happenstance, in a playbill lying in the street. Mr. Paul Buffel read your name there and came to us at once with the news. He advised us to go and see you, and as soon as I clapped eyes on you, my dear, I knew you were Rosalind."

"You said there was proof. What proof?"

"You must tell her about the witness, William, for that is a most interesting part of the story."

Folding his arms, Viscount Sunley said, "Mrs. Dawes, a nursemaid, accompanied your mother to the workhouse in Surrey. As your mother lay dying, Mrs. Dawes swore to look after you, which she did for several years until she fell ill. When she recovered, she found you had left the workhouse, but she could not find out where you had gone. I located Mrs. Dawes by the simple expedient of advertising in the newspaper."

"You say the nursemaid has not seen me—that is, she has not seen your Rosalind Divine—since she was a child. How is it possible she can act as a witness?"

Sunley smiled. "It is remarkable, is it not? Providential, as my respected parent might say. Mrs. Dawes, the nursemaid, has no doubt whatever that you will prove to be the Rosalind Divine she clasped to her bosom in those bygone days."

Rosa replied with a skeptical look and, attributing the nursemaid's amazing compliance to error, turned her attention to Lord Divine.

"There. You know as much as we do now," he said, "and I expect you are glad to have that mystery cleared up. What you must have thought all these years! What you must have wondered!"

This heartfelt sympathy gave Rosa pause, for it always surprised her when people were kind to her even though they had nothing to gain by it. "I remember nothing of those early years," she told him. "There are some vague memories, but they are like shadows. Sometimes it seems to me I can recall my mother singing, or perhaps she is crying. When these images come into my head, they seem very real. Later they seem like dreams. I honestly do not know if I am who you say I am."

"My child, you must be of good cheer and not look so gloomy. William, tell her she must not look as though she had been sentenced to prison."

"I cannot tell her any such thing, father."

His words chilled Rosa. She began to fear that he meant to betray her after all.

"Whatever do you mean, William?"

"Only that we are taking her to Aunt Delphia, and if that is not being sentenced to prison, I should like to know what is."

In the second sitting room, Lady Delphia Divine inspected the creature from top to toe. Walking round Rosa a full three times, her head shaking and her tongue clucking, she threw up her hands at last and exclaimed, "So this is what you bring me, brother?"

"Well, I suppose it is." Lord Grantley Divine stared down at the carpet.

"But look at the face. What can that be all over it? Why are the lids and brows that purple color and the cheeks that unnatural red? I vow you've brought the pox into my house."

"Do not be alarmed, aunt. She is an actress and has learned to augment nature with art, as you see." With that, the viscount swept a finger across Rosa's cheek and allowed Lady Delphia to view the red on his fingertip.

"'Pon my word, brother, you might have washed it before you brought it here."

"I assumed you would see to any washing, Delphia. What do I know of making young girls fit for society?"

"Nothing. You know nothing about anything, so far as I can tell. If it were not for your son, there would not be a groat's worth of sense between you."

"You must not bark so, sister. You will frighten the child to death. Why, look at her. I declare, she is on the point of fainting."

"I do not bark. I merely say what I think. And if she is to go into society, she must learn not to mind a little barking."

"Are you quite all right, my dear?" asked Lord Divine.

Rosa curtsied to the old gentleman, then addressed Lady Delphia. "You will please not speak of me as though I were not in the room."

Her ladyship's brow wrinkled and she peered at Rosa through her glass. "'Pon my word, I thought you said it was frightened to death of me. For a creature so terrified, it shows little enough respect. But it is no less than I expected, brother. You've brought me a savage."

Rosa eyed the three standing before her—the father, who gazed at her fondly; the son, whose odd smile made her lower her eyes; and the aunt, who inspected her through her glass with the supremest contempt. The first aroused her gratitude. Whenever she looked at the old gentleman, she was seized by a desire to please him.

The second alarmed her; Sunley's expression was enigmatic in the extreme. When she had pulled forth the purse from her pocket, he had only smiled. What, she would be pleased to know, did he find so amusing about bringing a thief into his aunt's house?

The third face made her bristle. Lady Delphia's contempt stirred her rebellious spirit and inspired her to summon the confidence with which she was accustomed to making her entrance onstage. In the most queenly voice she could muster, Rosa said, "If you will call your housekeeper, ma'am, I shall retire now."

Lady Delphia's jaw dropped. She turned to her brother with an accusatory expression, but before she could frame her outrage in words, her nephew interrupted with a strong laugh.

"She is a match for you, dear aunt. I daresay, we shall find this little scheme highly entertaining."

"There is nothing entertaining about it! It is necessity which drives us to these extremes and not any lack of amusement. You will wipe that maddening grin from your face and be serious, Sunley, or I shall not speak to you ever again."

"You are already not speaking to half the world, aunt. Do you wish to include your favorite nephew in the ranks of the out-of-favor? It will be your loss, I assure you."

Instead of retorting, her ladyship flounced up the grand staircase, where her resounding voice could be heard calling for the housekeeper and a bed for their guest.

Lord Divine whispered to Rosa, "I envy your courage—standing up to her that way."

Rosa, meanwhile, looked at Sunley to see what he would say, but he remained silent. For the life of her, she could not make him out. Not only did he decline to tell his father that he had mistaken a pickpocket for his relation, but he supported her high-handedness with his aunt. She recalled how he had chased her through the alleyway, how passionate his concern for her imaginary child had been, how earnestly he'd offered to take her to that child. He was utterly different now—satiric, smiling, and not a little frightening, certainly more frightening than his blustering aunt. Rosa longed to know the reason for these contradictions in the man. She longed to know why he'd kept her secret. She longed to know what his game was.

The next morning began the work of making Rosa presentable to the civilized world. Lady Delphia rose early, and her voice, issuing orders belowstairs and above, woke the gentlemen. They dressed, removed themselves as quickly as possible from the precincts of George Street, and repaired to Waiter's, where a man might be permitted to doze in blissful silence.

"Do you know, son," said Lord Divine from the depths of one of the softest club chairs, "I do not often regret the past. But whenever my sister's voice chases me out of doors, I cannot help regretting the loss of the town house."

Sunley accepted a newspaper from a footboy and replied, "It was a fine house, father, but we will have a much finer one soon."

"Fineness is not what I regret. My sister's house is as fine a one as I could wish, if I wished for fineness. A little shabby here and there and in want of repair, but still very fine. And Hanover Square is as fashionable a center as you will find in London. It is only that I prefer my own establishment."

"We will have our own establishment again and very soon, I assure you," said the viscount. "In fact, I intend to go this afternoon to Lincoln's Inn. We must lose no time in informing Buffel and Buffel that we have now restored your cousin's daughter to her family."

"Ah, will it answer, do you think? Will the funds be released?"

"I will insist on no further delay. You have endured enough, having to sell off Frampton, having to mortgage the lands, having to give up your house in town and remove to my aunt's. The court will see that we have done everything required. We've found her, restored her, and we mean to acknowledge her. In short, we've done our part. Now let the law do its part."

Lord Divine shook his head sadly. "We have a great many bills, William. My sister is a very elegant lady, and elegant ladies are amazingly expensive. She will not stint at dressing poor Rosalind. I fear it will all come to nothing and we will not be able to pay the bills."

"It is this damned search, father. It has eaten everything away, including your health. It is high time you were repaid. The estate ought to pay you something for all your trouble."

"Not trouble, son. Never trouble. It was all worth it. I thank God we have found her."

"Perhaps I will look in on her before I go to Lincoln's Inn."

Sunley had the pleasure of seeing his father smile. The old gentleman rested his head on the back of his chair. "Thank you, son. I would have done it myself, but I'm not accustomed to waking so early and would prefer taking a nap to making myself generally useful to my sister. I cannot please her, in any case. She finds fault with whatever I do." Then, after some minutes, he added, "I like our Rosalind very much, William. I think you do, too."

Before Sunley could answer, he was interrupted. A gentleman approached to greet them.

"Mr. Grahame," Lord Divine said heartily, "we are glad to see you in town again."

Mr. Grahame, a gentleman of middle age, distinguished countenance, and attractive bearing, sat down and assured his friends that he was indeed returned to London.

"And is Miss Grahame with you?" the viscount inquired.

With an arch smile, Mr. Grahame replied, "My niece is with me and is at home this minute, should you wish to call."

Sunley stood up and looked at his father. "I am afraid I am promised to my aunt."

"Go ahead, William. If you are a bit late in George Street, I am sure it will not be noticed."

This assurance was instantly belied, however, by a note which the servant boy placed in his lordship's hand.

"Good God. It is a note from my sister. Why is she writing me at Waiter's, do you suppose?"

"Open it, father, and find out."

"I think you had better open it, William."

"Very well. My aunt writes that you must come to her at once, for if you do not, she will never speak to you again."

"Ah, do you think there is any hope that she really means it this time?"

"I think I had better go to her," said the viscount. To the visitor he said, "Kindly tell Miss Grahame how sorry I am not to be able to call on her today."

"Nonsense, William," his father exclaimed. "I insist that you go to Miss Grahame this instant. I shall feel quite ashamed of my cowardice if you go to Delphia in my place and never have a moment's pleasure this entire day. Say you will please me in this."

Sunley laughed. "But we do not know what catastrophe may have befallen them. Perhaps your sister has murdered our heiress, or vice versa."

"If they are dead," Mr. Grahame observed sagely, "then there is no need to rush to them. They will certainly wait for you. In the meanwhile, my niece is very much alive."

◊ Four ◊

The butler grew red-faced and confused.

"What is it, Crouch? Is Miss Grahame ill?"

"No, sir."

"Is she at home?"

"No. Yes. I do not know, sir."

"Steady, man. You will give yourself a seizure. I take it Miss Grahame is not receiving this morning?"

"I cannot say, sir."

"Perhaps she already has a visitor and has asked not to be disturbed."

Crouch swallowed hard.

"She has asked you to deny her to all other visitors."

"Oh, but she could not have meant you, sir! I am sure she would not want me to deny her to *you*."

This exclamation brought a smile of satisfaction to Sunley's lips. "I will wait for her."

"Oh, dear."

"I take full responsibility, Crouch. Now I shall hie myself off to the library and be as patient as any man may be when he knows he will soon set eyes on the loveliest creature in Britain."

Crouch shook his head and, looking as though he were making a march to the gallows, admitted the visitor to the library.

As soon as the door closed, the viscount made every effort to occupy his thoughts. He drew several books from the shelves, turned over the pages, and replaced the volumes. When he came to *Tom Jones*, which he always enjoyed in spite of Dr. Johnson's dicta on its improprieties, he took it down from the shelf and sat down in a comfortable chair. But when he opened the volume, he found the pages still uncut, and it occurred to him that cultivating patience required considerable effort. He located a knife on the escritoire and set about cutting the first page. A noise outside the door made him pause. After listening for a time and hearing nothing, he resumed his task. Another noise—a cry—stopped him again. Setting down the book and knife, he walked to the door and opened it. In the hall stood Miss Grahame, looking white, thin, and unhappy. Holding her hands and pressing them to his lips was Fremont Dennis, Lord Pomeroy.

The two of them started at the sound of the door. They stared at Viscount Sunley for a time until, at last, Pomeroy collected himself, dropped the lady's hands, and stepped away from her. With cool politeness, he nodded to the intruder.

"Pomeroy," Sunley said with a curt nod, but he did not take his eyes from Miss Grahame. "Are you well?" he asked her. "Should I call Crouch?"

At that, Miss Grahame raised a pair of imploring eyes.

"There is no need to call Crouch," Pomeroy said coolly. "Miss Grahame will no doubt feel better as soon as I leave, which I am on the point of doing this very minute." Instead of leaving, however, he took a second to glance from the viscount's face to Miss Grahame's. He assessed the former's expression of concern, then the latter's expression of anguish, and after a moment's thought, approached Miss Grahame again. Abruptly, he put his arm around her waist, pulled her roughly to him, and pressed a kiss to her forehead. Then, pushing her away, he made his exit.

Sunley found the ensuing silence painful but hardly knew how to break it. It distressed him that she could not look him in the eye. Whatever hopes he'd nourished in his heart regarding Miss Grahame, whatever would or would not come of them, he had always been and would always be her friend. Surely she knew that. Surely their friendship had been of such longstanding that she would not doubt him. But evidently she did, for she moved her head to gaze at a portrait on the wall and when she could no longer hold her head up, bowed it low rather than face him.

"Say something," she begged. "Say anything. I don't care

what it is. You can tell me I am a fool, or worse. I don't care."

"I will say something, if only you will look at me."

"No. I don't want to look at you. You are too handsome and too generous and too good."

He laughed. "I thank you for the handsome. Unfortunately, I am not rich enough to be generous. As for the good, I am no better than I should be—considerably worse, in fact."

She looked at him, surprised. "You are joking. Of course, you are good."

It was Sunley's turn to avert his gaze. He deflected the question by saying, "I don't like to see you unhappy."

"If it were just a matter of my misery," she said with bravado, "I should not mind. But I do mind your seeing me thin and pale. I want to be beautiful for you again."

"Why? You are in love with Pomeroy, aren't you?"

She looked away again.

"A most eloquent answer."

"I hate him."

He went to her and took her by the shoulders. "Do you mean it?"

Still she kept her eyes averted. "Yes, I mean it. And I love him, too. God help me."

After a long while, he said softly, "Well, there it is. You've said it and thunderbolts did not strike us dead. Unless I am mistaken, the sky did not fall. That is to say, the roof did not fall. I cannot tell from here whether the sky did or did not fall, but I feel quite certain that if the sky had fallen, the roof would have fallen, too."

Miss Grahame smiled at him. "You have my permission to forsake me."

"I thank you. That, of course, was the purpose of my visit. If you had any idea that I came because it was important to me to see how you do, you flattered us both."

"Well, you see how I do, and you do not like it. Why should you? I do not like it."

"And because I see what I do not like, I'm to turn tail on my friends?"

Overcome by this loyalty, Miss Grahame could not hold

back an anguished sob. Sunley took her in his arms, allowing her to press her face into his shoulder.

"Don't leave me, William," she implored. "I shall die if you do. I shall die anyway, if one can die of self-loathing. But I shall die that much sooner if you forsake me."

"My poor Suzanne."

"Say it, William. Say it."

Pulling away from him, she put her hands to his cheeks. Hers were fiery red, and her eyes sought his.

"I won't leave you."

"Say it again."

"I swear I won't leave you."

She studied him closely, then threw her head back with a bitter laugh. "Ah, William," she said. "You are an even bigger fool than I am."

The viscount decided to proceed straightaway to Lincoln's Inn. It would be far more convenient to stop in George Street after his visit with the solicitors, he concluded. What was the sense in poking one's head in for barely a minute, then excusing oneself immediately, pleading urgent business elsewhere? Once he entered his aunt's door, he preferred to change his clothes, join the others for dinner, and entertain his father at a game of brag for the remainder of the evening.

Besides, he detested the house in George Street. Every day he issued from its door and caught a glimpse of the immense free-standing columns adorning Hanover Square, and every day the sight reminded him cruelly that his father had been forced to give up his fine house in Cavendish Square for want of funds to keep it. Lady Delphia ought to have given up her house as well; it was visibly and shamefully in need of repair and stood among the other houses along the wide street as a veritable scandal. She hadn't the money to keep it up, let alone repair it, and continually sought her brother's assistance. Although Lord Divine had not the wherewithal to help support his sister's expensiveness, he was incapable of insisting she give up her house. It was all she had, the old man told his son.

"I have you, William," he argued whenever the subject arose, "and you—poor fellow—have me. But Delphia . . ."

and here he would spread his hands wide in a gesture of compassion.

The upshot was that Sunley and his father compounded their debts so that Lady Delphia might live in George Street.

One might expect her ladyship to be grateful for this consideration. However, she habitually referred to her charity toward her brother and nephew. She let it be known throughout London that she had taken them in when they had so foolishly permitted themselves to become poor.

But of all the reasons for bypassing George Street, Sunley admitted, Miss Grahame was the strongest. Moments before, he had alternated between wanting to kiss her and wanting to shake her, and he had ended by doing neither. Recollecting his inaction, he grew irritated—with himself, with her, and with the entire world. Such irritation, he told himself, rendered him unfit for society of any sort.

He had no sooner enumerated all these excellent reasons for proceeding directly to his solicitors' chambers than he thought of Rosa and instantly changed his mind. On reconsideration, it was not only courteous but politic to stop in George Street, if only for a minute. The girl was going to transform that hideous portico of free-standing columns into a delightful vista. The girl promised to be the means of his father's restoration to fiscal health. The girl would not only make it possible for the old man to have a house of his own once more, but his dignity as well.

Any creature who threw so much good his father's way deserved attention, Sunley allowed, for Lord Divine was more to him than just a fond parent and favorite companion. The man was sweetness itself, a true gentleman, born with a generous and chivalrous nature, ready to extend his courtesy to all, no matter how low or how rude.

And the girl they had found was certainly low and rude. Sunley had scarcely known her five minutes before he'd found her to be a liar and a thief. She was also, he had no doubt, an accomplished schemer. She was probably in league with that unwashed price of bombast, Tripple. Somehow they meant to profit from this sudden rise in the girl's position, and if the profit derived from extortion and embezzlement, Tripple was the sort to like it that much the better. Well, no matter,

Sunley mused. Let them use her sudden good fortune to their advantage. He intended no less himself.

One thing did puzzle him about the girl, however. It had taken Tripple an inordinate amount of time to convince her to go with them. Any other starving young actress would not have hesitated a moment. Seeing the prospect of ease and comfort before her, any other girl would have seized her opportunity and never looked back. But this one had demurred, making no attempt to conceal the fact that she preferred to stay with Tripple. If this reluctance was part of a scheme, she had nearly overplayed her hands. It had struck the viscount at the time, and struck him now, as a highly unusual display of loyalty. Devotion of that magnitude and depth could not help but touch him. He admired it. More than that, he understood it. He, too, was devoted to the man he called father.

For all these reasons, he knocked at the door in George Street and waited. The wait was considerable, and it ended at last with the unusual sight of the housekeeper standing in the doorway, looking ashen.

"Thank God you've come, your lordship!" she greeted him.

He smiled. The greeting foretold of great entertainment within. Entering, he handed Mrs. Violet his hat and gloves and asked, "Where is Nunn? Why did he not answer my ring?"

"She's given him notice."

"Impossible. Nunn has been with her these hundred years at least."

"Yes, sir, but she has given him notice, for she got angry with him and said she would never speak to him again after what he did."

"What did he do?"

"He did not burn the young miss's clothes."

"Do you mean Lady Rosalind?"

"Yes, sir. At breakfast her ladyship sends Nunn to get the clothes and have them burnt because they stink worse than a fishmonger's, but the young miss says she will not let them be burnt and her ladyship says she will have them burnt or there will be the devil to pay and so they go on like that until her ladyship says that Nunn should take the clothes that very instant to be burnt."

"And were they burned?"

"Oh, yes, sir, but not by Nunn because he stands there and does not move—so amazed is he at the young miss saying what she says and defying her ladyship like that. But her ladyship thinks he is defying her as well, which I swear he an't."

"Is that when she gave him his notice?"

"It is, sir, and also when she calls me in to burn the clothes, which I does as soon as I am told, and now we're in such an uproar."

The housekeeper removed a handkerchief from her pillowy bosom and put it to her nose. "Oh, pardon me, sir," she sobbed.

"You may cry if you like, Mrs. Violet. I'm sure you will be much the better for it."

"Thank you, sir." Then, excusing herself, she hurried to the door which led belowstairs.

Sunley listened for sounds of uproar and heard none. In fact, he heard nothing at all save an unaccustomed silence. Moving through the hall, he opened one door after another, peeking inside each room to see whether it was inhabited by any sign of life. The first sign he spied was a housemaid, who dropped a vase and her feather duster upon hearing him come into the drawing room. Horrified at what she had done, the girl threw up her hands and tottered past him out the door.

The only other sign of life the viscount found was his aunt, still seated at the breakfast table. Although the cover had been removed, she sat bolt upright in her chair. She glared ferociously at a point in space and did not blink. Sunley approached and kissed her on the cheek. She ignored him.

"My dear aunt," he greeted her, "how very charming you look this morning. I daresay, your expression would peel that paper off the wall."

Slowly she turned her head to look at him, regarding him as though he were apparition.

"I have no objection to your peeling the wallpaper, believe me. It's the vilest pattern I ever laid eyes on. I give you these feathery monstrosities by way of example. What are they supposed to be, I ask you? They put me in mind of a bonnet Lady

Nitney wore just the other day. One likes to believe there is some safety from Lady Nitney's bonnets in wallpaper."

Her gaze turned ugly.

He took that gaze as an invitation to sit. "We need not discuss wallpaper, if you do not like the subject. What *do* you like to talk about, aunt? The news from France, perhaps? Mr. Brummell and the rumors of his debts? The latest cantos of *Childe Harold*? or perhaps you'd prefer to talk about Lady Rosalind Divine and how much depends on her."

"Get rid of her."

"I see. You no longer wish to live on a grand scale, or refurbish your house, or walk out of your door without fear of being dunned."

"Of course I wish to do all those things! I do mean to have the bequest, as you well know, you puppy. But you will have to get someone else for the purpose. I cannot abide this one."

"My dear aunt, I love you with all my heart, but you are the most irascible creature I have the misfortune to know. I might parade any number of candidates before you, and it would all come to the same thing in the end."

"It would not, I promise you. 'Pon my word, Sunley, do you give me no credit a-tall?"

"None whatsoever. You would attempt to frighten any girl I might bring here, and with most you would succeed. Fortunately, this Rosalind has a little backbone."

"Backbone, you call it. She is the filthiest baggage I ever set eyes on, and she returns my hospitality with rudeness. Do you know what she is doing at this very minute?"

"How could I possibly know?"

"She is marching about her bedchamber entirely naked."

"Certainly she is. You had her clothes burned."

"I gave her another dress. 'Pon my word, what do you take me for? My maid was kind enough to let me have one for her, and it cost more than a few farthings to get it from the greedy thing, let me tell you. But would she wear it, the little baggage? Naturally not. She wanted to wear her own clothes— into Bond Street! I should have died of mortification had anyone seen us together."

"You explained that, of course."

"I did no such thing. Explain? To an ignorant, filthy creature? You must have taken leave of your senses, Sunley."

"You must have taken leave of yours, aunt, to treat Lord Beckwith's daughter so shabbily."

Her reply consisted of a scornful look and a snappish "Nonsense."

Sunley shook his head and smiled his odd smile. Folding his arms, he leaned back in a chair and fixed his aunt with a steady gaze.

Lady Delphia's eyes bulged. "It's impossible!"

"Why do you think we chose this one? Why do you suppose she comes already equipped with the name?"

"I assumed you'd given her the name. That was part of the agreement—to find a girl and make her Lady Rosalind. Who would have thought that was her real name!"

"It is not just the name that is real, aunt."

"'Pon my word, nevvew," her ladyship said in horror, "I should never have spoken to her as I did if I'd known she was the genuine article."

"Well, she is—or almost. She wants polish, to put the kindest face on it. But I was depending on you to give it to her."

"And so I shall."

"I should like to know how. If she is, as you say, marching up and down in her bedchamber, refusing any clothes you offer her, she is not likely to accept your advice on matters of deportment. And if she intends to live out her life in one room, without a stitch on, we shall never convince the world —or the law—that we have found our cousin."

"You must go to her, Sunley. You must tell her that all is well and she may put on the dress. You must tell her to come down at once so that we may go and get her measured for new gowns, and you must tell her that no one will ever burn a one of them, excepting, of course, herself, if she so chooses."

"Just how am I to tell all this to a naked girl?"

"Shout through the door."

"An elegant stratagem."

"Pooh. You will think of something. Go, nevvew. Do not stand there thinking about it. Go, for pity's sake. You have wasted enough time already."

◇ Five ◇

Standing guard before the bedchamber was a stout little housemaid. She appeared frozen in the doorway, and when the viscount approached, her teeth began to chatter. Gently he bade her not to be frightened. "You must go into the room and tell miss that I extend my greetings and felicitations."

The housemaid opened the door and slipped inside. When the door closed, Sunley heard two female voices, one meek and barely audible, the other angry and strong. Then the maid came out, pulled the door shut behind her, and turned to him "Miss is not receiving this morning, sir."

He knew very well she was not receiving, for he had heard her through the door. Nevertheless, he persisted. "What did she say?"

Turning red, the housemaid declared, "I cannot tell you her exact words, sir."

Smiling, he nodded and bade her go inside once more. "Kindly tell miss that I have news and must speak with her immediately."

At this, the maid turned a look full of curiosity on him. With a little enthusiasm this time, she opened the door and went inside. Immediately Sunley heard sounds of an argument. The little housemaid's voice was still low and timid, but she had apparently summoned enough courage to plead his case. Rosalind Divine's voice was not the least bit low and timid, however, and she steadily and firmly resisted all pleadings.

When the maid came out again, she shook her head sadly and looked at the floor. Whereupon the viscount said, in a voice loud enough for the entire household to hear, "Tell miss, if you please, that I am coming inside in exactly ten seconds."

Instantly the maid poked her head in the door, from whence

issued an angry, "I heard him!" Stepping away then, she watched as though mesmerized while Sunley began to count in a loud voice.

At ten, he entered the bedchamber to find Rosa wrapped in a blanket, seated in a chair. A gleam of shoulder caught his eye, and a small bare foot peeked from under the covering. Holding the blanket tightly around her, she looked small, even fearful, but her face shone with defiance. If she felt fearful, she would die before she would show it.

He meant to address her with some inconsequential amenity, but the picture she presented chased the words momentarily from his mind. His eyes traveled from the hint of bare shoulder to her face, now scrubbed clean of powder and rouge. Her cheeks, which were drawn taut, sparkled with smooth softness. She had wrapped a cloth round her hair so that it resembled a high turban, and a few wet strands of auburn curl wound down her neck. Her eyes studied him with intensity, and her lips pressed thin.

He must have stared too long, for she became aware of his gaze. At first she seemed to be determined to return his look without flinching. After a time, though, she could not keep it up. She blushed and looked down.

Rosa scolded herself for blushing. She had never blushed in her life, although she'd certainly had reason to. Many a time she had been stared at and taunted. Many a fellow had called out to her in the street or leered and gestured rudely. What was there to blush about now in the look of a gentleman?

But Viscount Sunley was not just any gentleman. He was a man who knew what she was and had nevertheless brought her to his aunt's house. He was a man who said she was the daughter of an earl. He was a man with a fine, handsome face and intelligent brown eyes that looked at her as though they read her thoughts.

"Good morning," he said amiably.

Thankful that he made no reference to the blanket, she considered what answer it might be prudent to make. But recollecting that he was the nephew of that harridan Lady Delphia, she lifted her chin and loftily turned her gaze on the ceiling.

"I apologize for my aunt."

Surprised, she dropped her lofty air.

"She ought not to have burned your clothes."

"She might have discussed it with me first."

"Exactly."

"She ought not to be so high-handed."

"My feelings precisely."

"She is really very rude, you know, despite her title and her silk dresses."

"May I sit?"

When Rosa nodded, he drew a chair from the dressing table and placed it opposite her. "I make no excuses for her, you understand. But she had her reasons."

"Yes, indeed. She made her reasons all too clear the moment I entered her house. She despises me because I am poor. She sneers at me because I have not had her education and advantages. She speaks of me as though I were an insect instead of a human creature. She will not even address me herself but talks to me through intermediaries."

"Well, she is wrong to do that."

Rosa swallowed and found that her throat had gone dry. She would have felt a great deal more comfortable had the viscount lectured her, expostulated with her, threatened her.

"She had your clothes taken from you because you were to be measured for new ones. It was not possible for you to wear your stage costume in Bond Street. The seamstress would have swooned at the sight of it and swallowed her pins."

"It *was* a dreadful costume, and a frightfully old and rank one, too," Rosa allowed.

"You will look more suitable in a new dress."

Meeting his appraising eyes, Rosa blushed a second time.

"Now we must get something on you. I doubt you will be admitted to very many places in a blanket."

"I should like it if Lord Divine accompanied me to Bond Street. He is very kind."

"He is the best man in the world. Unfortunately, he knows nothing about dressing young ladies. You might end up wearing orange, and you ought to wear nothing but pink."

"Well, then, you could take me."

This gave Sunley pause. For a moment Rosa thought he might approve the scheme. The next moment, though, he shook his head, saying, "Much as I should like that, I must defer to my aunt's greater skill and judgment."

"But she refuses to speak to me, and I will not speak to her."

"Yes, that is a difficulty. That is why I am here."

"If you mean to try to persuade me to apologize, you may as well save your breath."

"I am sorry to hear it, for Aunt Delphia will surely never apologize to you. Aunt Delphia never apologizes at all."

"Not even when she is wrong?"

"Aunt Delphia is never wrong." His ironic smile was engaging.

"There it is then. I suppose I shall spend the rest of my life in this blanket."

"Suppose I were to tell you that my aunt repents of her behavior and now wishes to make peace. What would you say to that?"

"I don't think I would believe you."

"Then I invite you to ask her yourself."

"I could hardly do that. She would strangle me, I think."

"Not at all. She means to treat you with all politeness from this day forward. She told me so herself, not five minutes ago."

"That is too swift a turnaround to be trusted."

"Ordinarily it might be. But I was privileged to provide her with certain information. It transformed her, I promise you."

"I should like to know what information would accomplish that sort of miracle. She certainly hated me very thoroughly until now."

"I told her you were Beckwith's daughter."

"Who did she think I was?"

"An actress hired to play the part."

Rosa tried to breathe. Her eyes filled and she turned her head aside.

"It was our plan to find someone who would induce the law to execute all the terms of Beckwith's will. These terms include not only a fortune left to his daughter, but bequests to the rest of the family as well."

"Why did you not collect them when he died? Why did you have to bring me into it?"

"The bequests were very oddly settled, for their dispersal was contingent upon the appearance of the daughter to make her claim."

"So it is the money you are after. That explains a great deal." Surreptitiously she wiped her cheek with a corner of the blanket.

"When I told Lady Delphia you were in fact Beckwith's daughter, she was very sorry for burning your clothes without permission."

"No doubt she was."

"She would like to do her possible to make it right between you again."

"No doubt she would."

Rosa stood up, discomposing the blanket a little. She turned her back on him so that she would not have to see his face. For a moment she studied the London rooftops through the window glass.

The viscount saw her shoulders shudder and began to suspect that he had distressed her. In his most gently coaxing tone, he asked, "Can you forgive her?"

"I may be brought to forgive her," she said in a full voice, "but I shall never forgive you!"

Sunley rose at this and took a few steps toward her. "Now, see here, Miss Divine. You might have everything your own way, if only you would meet Aunt Delphia halfway."

She turned on him in fury. Her green eyes blazed up at his so that he was startled.

"You ought never to have done it, my lord. It was wrong of you, very wrong, to take me from my home and set me down in the midst of strangers, strangers who despise me and laugh at me. You did not even ask me. You called me 'my lady' in that satiric voice of yours and did not even ask."

"I assumed you would see what an excellent opportunity was being offered you. It's not as if we meant to sell you to white slavers, you know. We're making you the daughter of an earl!"

"Did it ever occur to you that I did not wish to be the daughter of an earl? That I was perfectly happy being Tripple's daughter?"

He looked away. "No," he said.

"No more than it occurred to you to ask if I wished to accept the role of Lady Rosalind. You are just like your aunt, you know, just as high-handed and arrogant."

This hit caused Sunley to sit down again.

Rosa watched him wrestle with his thoughts. He began to look quite miserable, a sight which softened her somewhat. She sat down again and waited.

"Do you wish to go back?" he asked.

"Yes, more than anything. But I cannot. Tripple will not have me, not as myself, at any rate, only as Lady Rosalind."

"I'm afraid you will have to make the best of it, then."

"It is all very well for you to be philosophical, sir, when you will profit mightily by my masquerade. But what about me? Do you really think that a trunk full of dresses will take the place of the only family I have ever known?"

At this question, he paled. Then he leaned forward, his head coming close to hers. "But you will have a family. Don't you see? As Lady Rosalind you will be one of us. You will be a Divine, Lord help you. My father and aunt are convinced you are their cousin. I have made sure they believe in you, and they will treat you as they would treat their true cousin."

"I daresay your father would treat me as Lady Rosalind even if he knew the truth."

"He cares for you already. The whole family will, given time."

"Not the whole family, my lord. You will always smile at me in that way of yours, as if to remind me that you know exactly what I am."

"And what exactly are you, my lady?"

"You know very well I am a pickpocket."

"Very true. You are a thief."

"Yes."

"And a liar."

"Yes."

"You are all of these, without doubt. How do you suppose I knew you would do?"

Rosa stared. "Will you do me the kindness of making yourself intelligible?"

"It wasn't until I saw my father's purse in your hand that I knew for certain you would do."

"I should think that would prove how very unsuitable I am."

"On the contrary, it demonstrated your suitability beyond a doubt. It proved that you would require only the most superficial of polishing, for you had already acquired the most notable qualities of our family."

◊ **Six** ◊

The viscount suggested to his aunt that they remove to the sitting room to await their young cousin. Lady Delphia, concluding that it was unseemly for a personage of her dignity to roost for two hours in the breakfast parlor, followed this suggestion in haughty silence. In the sitting room, she lowered herself onto a hard, claw-footed chair, folded her arms, sank her chin into her bosom, and withdrew into her thoughts. Her countenance was more pinched than usual, Sunley noted; her expression was stormier than he could recall ever seeing it, and her silence was decidedly uncharacteristic. Nevertheless, he knew precisely what to expect from her.

Indeed, the whole world knew precisely what to expect of Lady Delphia Divine—namely, rudeness and abuse. The beau monde not only expected such behavior but demanded it as well, considering it as part and parcel of her unique charm. One expected, even looked forward to, the set-downs her ladyship levied whenever she fancied herself ill-used, which she frequently did. One expected, even hoped for, the honor of being cut dead at assembly balls and card parties because one had had the temerity to laud Clementi's music or to praise *Sense and Sensibility* in the face of her ladyship's condemnation. One got used to apologizing to Lady Delphia for slights she had invented out of the air, because one understood that her vocation, her raison d'être, her sole relief from boredom was to throw herself passionately into a snit.

Surely, the viscount told himself, if the ton could tolerate these eccentricities, Rosalind could as well. Surely she could make allowances for her ladyship's advanced age, her childless state, her lonely spinsterhood. The young woman was remarkably intelligent considering her lack of education. He'd seen the intelligence in her eyes as well as heard it in her words. Moreover, he'd seen a delicacy in her features, a natural grace in her gestures which bespoke a fineness of feeling. He had seen a sweetness in her smile and a steadiness in her eye which denoted humor, philosophy, reason. Sunley's instinct told him that he could rely on Rosalind to make peace with his belligerent relation.

At the same time, he acknowledged privately, her anger went deep. He understood it now, and he was sorry for it. He was not sorry that he had prevailed on her to play the heiress; there, he believed, he had done her great good. But he was genuinely sorry to have caused her pain. He was sorry, too, for having resorted to the highly improper act of invading a lady's bedchamber, something he made it a rule never to do without an express invitation. If he were not a man of the world, if he had not seen many a lady wrapped in bedding, he might almost blush to remember the sight of Rosa in a blanket.

Sunley was beginning to think the room had grown uncomfortably warm, when Rosa came in. She wore the maid's smoky gray dress and a beribboned bonnet. Forthrightly, she approached her ladyship with a pretty curtsy and wished her good day. Then she begged to be allowed to sit a moment before they should set forth for Bond Street. She smiled demurely at the viscount, and folded her hands primly in her lap.

Lady Delphia did not deign to express a jot of satisfaction with this complaisance. She did, however, condescend to address the young woman thus: "We will dress you in white. You will always wear white, even to ride in. It will be a sort of hallmark by which you are known everywhere. *Oh, yes, Beckwith's daughter. She always wears white, you know.* We will have a white phaeton made up for you, and your ponies will be white as well. It will vindicate you, and distinguish you from your parents. It's none of your doing that your mother was no better than she should be or that your father was a perfect scoundrel nearly to the end. Your duty is to show unreasoning loyalty toward them and to be oblivious to the hideous truth. The white will do it, without our having to say or do anything."

"I believe I shall wear pink," Rosa said quietly.

Lady Delphia blinked as though a wind had blown a bit of soot in her eye.

The viscount straightened in his chair and watched the two women. Lady Delphia's chin trembled; her teeth ground audibly.

Although none of these responses was lost on Rosa, she held firmly to the complaisant smile on her lips and said nothing further.

Some minutes went by in this manner, until at last Lady Delphia burst into smiles. "Yes, of course, pink," she stated. "What better color for your hair? That auburn against a white neck and a pink sleeve, why, nothing could be better. I see I need not be entirely ashamed of you, for the exquisiteness of your taste fairly equals mine own. This is not at all to be wondered at in blood relations. My eye for color is renowned."

Breathing again, Sunley relaxed in his chair.

"You are very kind to advise me, your ladyship," Rosa said.

"You must call me aunt now. I have every intention of being your aunt and of offering you the benefit of my experience in the world. Naturally you will have opinions of your own. We Divines always feel obliged to have opinions of our own. But no matter if we do differ; we shall still always be cousins."

Sunley smiled at this unwonted amiability, asking, "May I be permitted to differ with you as well, aunt?"

Lady Delphia turned a scowl on him. "You may take yourself off; that is what you may be permitted to do. Unless you mean to come with us to the dressmaker's and carry home our bandboxes."

That was the viscount's cue to set forth for Lincoln's Inn, and accordingly, he rose, bowed, and bade them good-bye.

In the hallway, he collected his gloves and hat from the

housekeeper. As he turned to go out, he heard Rosa call his name and was surprised to see that she had followed him.

"Viscount Sunley, will you stay a minute, please? I must ask you a question."

Intently he observed her approach. Although smoky gray did nothing to enhance her hair coloring or set off her complexion, still the rustle of the dress as she came toward him made him sharply aware of her nearness. He could not get it out of his head that just minutes ago she had worn only a blanket.

"I will be glad to answer any question of yours, cousin. May I call you cousin? As far as the world is concerned, we are nearly cousins."

"I would like you to call me Rosa."

"Well, then, Rosa."

"Why are the Divines liars and thieves?"

He laughed. She looked so earnest and had evidently given the question much thought. "I don't know," he said with a shrug. "I suppose it's inborn in the race and we cannot help it."

"You mistake my meaning. You said that I exhibited the most notable qualities of your family, by which I took you to mean a penchant for lying and thievery. In what way are the Divines guilty of such things?"

"These are deep questions for a man on his way out the door."

"I beg you, sir, give me a word that will last until we have leisure to talk again." In her urgency, she laid her hand on his arm. He looked at that small hand and then at its owner's face. Conscious of his gaze, she drew her hand away.

"I will tell you this much," he replied. "In her youth, Lady Delphia was courted by a wealthy tradesman whom she had no intention of marrying. She let him think himself engaged to her, accepted many gifts from him, and then jilted him. Afterwards she brought him up on an action—breach of promise, if you can believe it. The poor fellow was too ashamed to tell the court that it was he who had been jilted and she who had breached the promise, so he paid what he was ordered and kept mum."

Rosa absorbed this gravely. "Lady Delphia does not consti-
tute an entire family."

"I've only just begun the tale of my revered family, Rosa.
Consider Beckwith, who abandoned his wife for the sake of
money—a bribe from his family. To punish him, Elizabeth
Martin stole his child and hid her away."

She continued to look serious. "Lord Divine? Is he, too, a
liar and a thief?"

"Ah, there you have the exception to the rule."

"I knew he was a man of probity. I knew I could not be
wrong about him."

"Which brings us to the last member of the family."

Rosa glanced into his dark eyes, then quickly away.

"Of course, you need not ask how the bloodline reveals
itself in me."

"I know that you are not above using all your influence and
an appearance of wealth to have your way."

His reply consisted of a laugh and a graceful attempt to kiss
her hand.

Rosa drew it away before he could complete the kiss. "You
mean to have Beckwith's money one way or another, and you
will no doubt lie to the law as well as your family in order to
succeed."

The apt summary made him smile. "You see how very
much alike we are. We might easily be blood relations."

"Nevertheless, I do not think you are as bad as you say."

"If you can find a redeeming quality in me, by all means
tell me what it is."

"I don't know you well enough yet to point out your redeeming qualities. I shall let you know, however, as soon as I
find one. For now, I must base my judgment on what I know
of myself."

Puzzled, he regarded her with curiosity.

"After all, I am an impostor and a pickpocket, and yet I am
not so very bad, am I?"

"No, you are not so very bad at all." At that, he pulled her
to him and kissed her firmly on the lips. His arms went round
her so swiftly that she could not breathe. Then, releasing her

just as swiftly, he planted his hat upon his head and made his way out the door.

The chambers of Messrs. Buffel & Buffel seemed to have gone without dusting since the time of the second Charles. Tomes, briefs, and scraps of scribbled-over paper lay scattered about the sunless room, held together in their towering heaps solely by time and habit. The disarray of the room, like the preoccupation of its occupants, gave the appearance of serious busy-ness. One had only to look at the dust on the tables and the wig hanging half crooked on the head of Mr. Peter Buffel to know that in these moldy precincts no one and nothing went forward that did not redound to the glory of English law.

Scanning the chamber, Viscount Sunley saw no evidence of the second Buffel in Messrs. Buffel & Buffel—Mr. Paul Buffel, who was as sharp-witted and tidy as his brother was vague and dusty. Because it was Mr. Paul who had directed the search for Rosalind, and because it was Mr. Paul who recalled all the aspects of the inheritance in the minutest detail, the viscount experienced disappointment at his absence.

Mr. Peter Buffel rubbed his fingertips in his eyes until the balls could be heard to swish in their sockets. That ritual completed, he invited his client to sit.

The young gentleman found a chair, removed a volume of *Quia Emptores*, and sat down. The attorney also found a place for himself in a chair behind a table. After clearing a space, he blew away a layer of dust and welcomed Viscount Sunley

"You and your esteemed brother were right," the young man said. "We found Lady Rosalind Divine at the playhouse, exactly as you said we would."

"Did we say that? Gracious me. And you say we were right?"

"Perhaps you recall our last conversation regarding the heiress to Beckwith's money?"

The old lawyer fished among his papers and came up with a yellowed one. Clearing his throat, he commenced to speak: "The estate is a freehold estate, which is fortunate for the earl's descendants, in that it can be inherited in fee simple, which is to say, by his heirs, which is to say by any of his heirs, be they male or female, which is to say, the estate is not entailed on the male heirs. You did say the heir was a female, did you not?"

"Lady Rosalind Divine."

"Yes, I thought I had heard that name before. Fortunately, the estate is not encumbered by debts, although the costs accruing to the courts over the years have depleted the original sum. It is scandalous to contemplate the expense required to keep a case alive in this litigious age. Fortunately, however, the interest on the mining stocks and capital have nearly equaled the expense."

"We know all this, Mr. Buffel. We have been over this ground before. I am come to tell you the girl is with her family now and the estate may be probated at once."

"The terms of the estate are such that the greatest number are intended to benefit, the only stipulation being that the bequests to the family cannot be made until the daughter is found. Beckwith wished to insure that his family would leave no stone unturned in their search for her."

"All of which means that my aunt and I may receive our inheritance, and that my father may receive the remainder of his."

"Ah, but this is very interesting. It appears I've made a note here. Why, yes, that is my scrawl. No doubt about it. Now, what does it say?"

"Perhaps it says that you may proceed with the settlements. I assure you, everything has been done to meet the terms of the will."

The attorney coughed and waved away the cloud of dust his breaths had stirred. "This is very odd," he declared. "The note says the estate passes to the Crown. Now, what do you suppose that means?"

"It must be an error. Perhaps that note is meant for someone else's estate."

"Your name again, sir?"

His lordship sighed. "Divine."

Buffel looked at him and then at the paper. "I believe I recall the name."

"Is Mr. Paul Buffel in? Perhaps he might recall the purport of the note."

"My brother is in court, sir, and I am sure I will recall the purport of the note in just a moment. It is my scrawl, is it not? Or do you think it looks like Paul's?"

"I am completely at a loss, Mr. Buffel."

"If you are William Divine, Viscount Sunley, then I am afraid you are at more of a loss than you know. This note does indeed pertain to you. You found the girl in a playhouse, you say?"

"Yes, just as you and your brother said we would."

"We said that, did we? Well, then, as your attorney, I am compelled to advise you to take her back to the playhouse at once and forget her."

"That is out of the question."

"It can't be very far."

"But why should I take her back?"

"Because, my good sir, we cannot prove she is Beckwith's child, and the law will have its proof before it will parcel out any funds."

"Of course there is proof. My father swears she is the image of Elizabeth Martin, and so he will testify. And the nursemaid. What about the nursemaid's testimony?"

Mr. Buffel rubbed his eyeball noisily. "Ah, I do recall something about that. Now, where did I put that paper? You see what happens—the housekeeper comes in to clean these chambers and I can never find anything." Buffel laughed at himself. "How absurd to misplace such an important document! I am quite amazed at myself." Then, finding the paper, he read for a time before announcing, "It appears that the nursemaid you spoke of has been to see me. Gracious, if the date is correct, she was here only two days ago! As recently as that, well, well. Now what else have I written here? Oh, yes, I see it now. This clears up the matter right and tight. The nursemaid, you see, has changed her mind."

The viscount stood up. "Changed her mind? What do you mean?"

"What do I mean? I suppose I mean that she withdraws her testimony. Yes, I believe that is what I mean." He held the paper up so that his client might behold the telling words with his own eyes.

"Can she do that, after swearing to all of us?"

"Well, I suppose she can; at any rate, she has."

"And she had papers, she said, papers from the lying-in hospital where Elizabeth Martin bore her child. She had promised to show us those papers."

"And now she has broke her promise. Dear me, why do you suppose she did that?"

"She was our most important witness, Mr. Buffel."

"Was she, indeed? Well, what does she say in her new deposition? It's not very long, you know, not as long as the first one." The lawyer read to himself, moving his lips rapidly. Then, having apprised himself of the contents, he reported, "She simply says she recants her first deposition. Short and sweet, is it not?"

"But there must be other documents, records from the workhouse, perhaps, that can prove our case."

"Documents and records are always excellent things to have. They prove one's case so much more effectively than witnesses. Witnesses are a dreadful nuisance, if the truth be known. I'd always rather have papers than persons to prove my case."

"Do you suppose the woman wants urging—taking care of?"

At this, Buffel frowned in puzzlement. A moment later, as the implication of the statement penetrated his understanding, he blanched. Rising from his chair, he pounded the table so that an eruption of motes veiled his face. He coughed, cleared his throat, and insisted, "I am obliged to advise you against any urging or taking care of, my lord. Bribery will land you in prison."

"She told me in tears that nothing would gladden her heart more than to find Lady Rosalind, that she had never forgiven herself for letting the child out of her sight, that she would swear to her identity readily. I have no doubt that she will take one look at the girl from the playhouse and swear without a qualm. But I cannot understand what has happened to change her mind; nor can I sit idly by while my father is deprived of his inheritance."

"Well, as long as we have none of that other sort of thing going on."

"Mr. Buffel, we must prove this girl is Rosalind Divine."

"Yes, of course we must. The *onus probandi* lies on our side."

"Perhaps we do not need the nursemaid. Perhaps we may offer other testimony in support of our claim. I assure you, Mr. Buffel, within the next several weeks, the whole world will testify that she is Lady Rosalind, for my aunt means to introduce her into London society as our cousin."

"No, no, my lord. That will not do. It is not for the world to decide who she is. That is a matter for the court."

"Will the court allow me something from the estate to pursue this matter? I should like to investigate further."

"The court cannot disperse any monies while the question is still unresolved. Gracious, sir, how does the court know whether she be the genuine article until documents or witnesses are produced?"

Sunley paced in front of his chair. This was a setback indeed. He had counted on the settlements taking place within a very few weeks, a month or two at the outside. "Does my father's testimony count for nothing?" he asked.

"Your father? Am I acquainted with the gentleman?"

The viscount reminded the lawyer of his several meetings with his father as well as his position as heir to the Beckwith title, after which the attorney concluded, "The testimony of your father is helpful, of course, but as one of the parties who stands to gain by Lady Rosalind's discovery, his statement will require corroboration."

After a moment's thought, Sunley replied, "Suppose I were to tell you I had found another witness."

"Why did you not say so in the first place? I will consult the solicitor general. If he likes your new witness, we will bring the case before the bench."

"But if my new witness cannot give us what we need, will we then be forced to give up the case altogether?"

"Ah, that is too desperate a view, sir. I am quite sure you might continue the case forever, should you wish to. Our courts are very patient."

As he shook hands with his client, Buffel dislodged a pile of books. They crashed to the floor, producing an explosion of dust. Sunley observed the cloud rise about him and thought darkly of Tripple.

There was no one on this earth he trusted less than the old thespian. At their first and only meeting he had taken his measure of the man and concluded the fellow would not know the truth if it were presented to him on a salver by a footman. And now he, as his family's representative, must apply to this man for help. He must place all his reliance on Tripple, his last hope, if he was ever to secure the Beckwith money.

The ladies' entrance at the dressmaker's caused a stir. Miss Speckles' first assistant no sooner saw Lady Delphia come in and clamor for attention than her mouth fell open, dropping a number of pins to the floor. She rose from her knees, leaving her customer only partially hemmed, and ran to the back room. There she seized her cloak and fled through the rear door, not to be seen again the rest of the day.

Speechless with terror, the second assistant stared at the beringed finger Lady Delphia wagged under her nose. As she trembled, various appurtenances of her trade tumbled from her person—pincushions, tape measures, thimbles, and buttons—bouncing to the floor with gentle tinkles.

Lady Delphia looked the poor creature up and down and declared that something must have frightened the idiot for her to behave in such an egregious manner.

Miss Speckles, the owner of the establishment, had observed the spectacle of her fleeing assistant and swiftly deduced the cause. She came out of the back room at once, affixing to her face the smile she reserved for her ladyship alone. She murmured something about the honor done to her humble shop, and as she endured the introduction to the Lady Rosalind, Miss Speckles prayed that the young one was not cut from the same bolt of cloth as the old. Meanwhile, Lady Delphia called loudly for pink. Not bloodless, timid pink, either, but warm pink, astonishing pink, the pinkest of pinks.

Rosa tried to concentrate on pink. The best she could do, however, was nod absently as the dressmaker and her ladyship thrust yards of fabric against her cheeks. Her mind was completely engaged in thoughts of Viscount Sunley and nothing —not even being hustled into a dressing room, having her clothing unbuttoned and removed, her feet set precariously upon a platform, and her body draped with silks and damasks

—could win her thoughts away from the man who claimed quite cheerfully that he was as much a liar and a thief as she was, the man who had offered her his family, the man who had kissed her in such a way that she could still feel the press of his lips against hers.

What kind of man was he really? she wondered. He'd worn an odd expression when he sat with her in the bedchamber, an expression that differed markedly from his odd, ironic smile. The expression had suffused his face as soon as he'd seen her pull the blanket round her shoulder. Was it possible that a gentleman like Viscount Sunley could ever look at her in such a way?

He had evinced much distress at the realization that she wanted to be with Tripple, her only family. His face had worn the same expression she'd seen when she had invented the ruse of the child. The compassion in that expression, the genuine concern for the sorrow of another, moved her so powerfully that she was forced to catch her breath. Was it possible that such a laconic gentleman could have such a tender heart?

And what was she to make of his being a self-confessed liar? Was it possible that she ought not to believe his kiss?

Hearing Rosa sigh, Lady Delphia vigorously nodded her head. "Yes, it is so tedious to be measured," she lamented. "But one must endure it if one is to have one's figgah shown to advantage. And you have a passing good figgah, my child. I looked exactly as you did at your age. The Divines are a remarkably handsome race, both in figgah and countenance."

Rosa regarded Lady Delphia's stern visage and nodded. When Miss Speckles left them alone to go in search of another pink, she said to her ladyship, "Viscount Sunley is very handsome."

"I suppose he is. What is more to the point, he is a very good sort of man. The Divines are known to be an honorable race."

"Perhaps, but I don't think Beckwith acted honorably by Elizabeth Martin, nor she by him, if what his lordship tells me is true."

"Certainly what Sunley tells you is true. 'Pon my word, do you doubt your own family?"

"I must tell your ladyship, I have not always been honorable." She lowered her voice confidentially. "In fact, I have been guilty of stealing."

Lady Delphia's teeth ground for half a minute. Then, putting on a determined face, she replied, "It is true we Divines may travel a crooked path before arriving at our honor; nevertheless, we always get there eventually."

"I am relieved to hear it. I should not like to think I was doomed to pick more pockets for my dinner."

Lady Delphia rolled her eyeballs and breathed heavily. "You are Lady Rosalind now. There is no need to mention your previous career." She was spared the necessity of further reply by the entrance of the dressmaker, whose fortuitous appearance allowed her to excuse herself on the pretext of inspecting a new design for a pelisse. Rosa suspected that once outside the curtain, her ladyship would call for a bottle of salts.

She stood perfectly still while Miss Speckles completed the fitting. After some time spent tightening and loosening the new gown, the dressmaker stepped back from the platform and surveyed her handiwork.

Draped in silvery pink, pinned to form a clinging, puff-sleeved dress Rosa appeared very much to advantage. The sheen of the dress caught shades of her hair, and the color heightened the loveliness of her neck and bosom. For the first time since the arrival of their ladyships, Miss Speckles smiled. "My lady does a dressmaker credit," she said with a sigh of gratification.

Rosa glanced down at her costume to see for herself, whereupon the dressmaker invited her to turn round. "There. In the mirror. Is it not a sight?"

To look like someone else had long been part of Rosa's craft. She was used to peering in the glass only to see another woman looking back. But this time she started. What she saw in the glass made her think it was just possible that Tripple might have been right after all. Perhaps she was born to play the heroine. Perhaps that elegant young woman reflected before her really might do very well as Lady Rosalind. It must be so, because that young woman bore no resemblance whatever to a saucy wench, or to a pickpocket, either.

"The young men will have to look to their hearts," said Miss Speckles with a simper.

"Which young men?"

"Why, the ones you are going to dance with, at balls and such."

"Do you mean to say they will fall in love with me?"

"That is what I mean, my lady."

Rosa's face grew thoughtful as she contemplated this prophecy.

At that moment, Lady Delphia pulled aside the curtain of the dressing room and stood in the doorway. "'Pon my word," she said with force, "you are quite presentable!"

Rosa laughed. "Oh, aunt, Miss Speckles says I look so presentable that the gentlemen must look to their hearts."

"Never mind that. Gentlemen are busy enough looking to their stomachs."

Smiling, Rosa treated herself to another glimpse in the mirror. Then, with a surge of her old stage confidence, she said to herself, "The others may look where they please. But let Viscount Sunley look to his heart."

◊ Seven ◊

In the course of the following week, Viscount Sunley's heart gave every indication of remaining perfectly safe. Preoccupied with the search for Mr. Tripple, he scarcely noticed Rosa's existence, let alone her hair cut in a fashionable crop or her figure dressed to perfection in a pale green morning gown. Early each morning he went out and did not return until well into the night. When Lady Delphia demanded to know from Lord Devine why his son neglected them all so abominably, he answered darkly that it was "the case" and said no more.

When Sunley visited the playhouse where he had last seen

Tripple, he learned that the company had left London. Because its management had run up sundry bills and debts, no telltale itinerary had been left behind. The owner of the playhouse grimly advised his lordship to give up his quest and content himself with prayers that the thieves might burn together with Old Lucifer himself in the life to come.

The viscount endeavored to locate the nursemaid who, when he had first met her, was employed in a house in Belgravia. He was received cordially by the mistress of the house and, after an interview of five minutes, came away with the information that the nursemaid had given her notice and gone away, no one knew where. Why Sukey Dawes had decided to leave, the lady could not say, but she had the impression that something might have happened to distress her. No, Sukey had mentioned nothing about any case, any inheritance, any deposition. Yes, the mistress of the house would inform his lordship if she heard further news of the nursemaid.

The search for Tripple proved as fruitless as the search for the nursemaid, until Rosa happened to mention her former lodgings in Southwark. Sunley, immediately seizing upon the clue, sought out the landlord, who took his oath that Tripple had left the company he was traveling with and taken up with another in Hampshire.

When the viscount next appeared at his aunt's supper table, he announced that he would leave London the following morning. Lady Delphia, who scrupled not to pry into any stranger's affairs, demanded to know what took her nephew from town.

"Hunting, ma'am," he said.

"At this season?"

"I hunt a man. I am told he's gone into the south, but I have little information beyond that."

Lord Divine caught his son's eye. Inclining his head in his sister's direction and rolling his eyeballs, he said, "Perhaps you would enjoy having a companion on your journey?"

"I should like nothing better, father."

Turning to Rosa, who sat next to him at table, his lordship patted her hand fondly and apologized. "My dear girl, you are too good-natured not to forgive us for deserting you."

Before Rosa could answer, Lady Delphia interjected, "I'm

sure neither of us will miss you. We will be far too busy."
Raising her eyebrows in a manner heavy with significance,
she gave them all to understand that she had plans for Rosa
with which the gentlemen's continuance in London could only
interfere.

The tedious days that followed gave Rosa leisure to recall
the promise implied in her ladyship's assertion. As it developed, she was not busy in the least, and certainly not too busy
to miss the two gentlemen. Indeed, she missed them achingly,
for Lord Divine was invariably kind to her and the viscount,
invariably interesting. Moreover, the days and evenings with
Lady Delphia hardly merited the adjective "busy," for little
transpired the whole time save a series of lessons and a
number of morning calls with severe-looking ladies.

Lady Nitney called first and stayed a full twenty minutes,
causing Lady Delphia to swell with satisfaction and to jab her
elbow into Rosa's ribs in hopes of eliciting voluble signs of
gratitude. Rosa, however, could not pretend to be overwhelmed at the attention, for it seemed to her that the lady
came expressly to scorn.

Lady Jersey, who accompanied Lady Nitney, proved far
more amiable. She spoke amusingly and quickly and was
even so gracious as to address two sentences to Rosa, whereas
Lady Nitney remained proudly silent, all the while inspecting
Rosa through her glass.

After the ladies took their leave, Rosa expected Lady Delphia to announce a plan for the remainder of the day, and
because they had already acquired an excess of dresses, caps,
bonnets, shawls, ribbons, and baubles, they might, she reasoned, look forward to entertaining themselves in any number
of ways. Rosa would have liked to see Madame Tussaud's
waxworks or the museum. Once, when she was still an actress, she had passed Hatchard's and seen in its pretty bow
windows more books than she had ever seen in her life. She
would have liked nothing better than to enter its portals, make
her obeisance to the muse of literature, and buy a book of her
own. Or, if her ladyship had had a surfeit of shops, they might
simply stroll through Piccadilly. To walk in the midst of so
much fashion, to watch as the elegant ladies and gentlemen

stepped out of their elegant carriages and into the elegant shops—these seemed to Rosa to be pleasures beyond description.

But Lady Delphia did not intend to go out. Rosa must meet with the dancing master and the French tutor, she declared. It was crucial that she learn the dances of polite society, and in particular the waltz, in case she should be granted the honor of performing it; and she must learn French—*il vait sans dire* —for though the Gallic race was known to be treacherous and forever in league with the savage Americans, still their language was the language of civilization and must be acquired. Furthermore, she must study singing with Professore Vincente. Rosa's playing on the pianoforte was perfectly execrable but she did sing with a soft, melodious voice, which put Lady Delphia in mind of the bell-like tones she herself had produced as a girl, and her ladyship felt convinced that Rosa might one day learn to accompany herself, if she did not play excessively loud. Then, after the lessons, Rosa must rest for the remainder of the afternoon, because the next day also promised visitors and instruction.

The morrow's visitors revealed themselves to be the Princess Esterhazy and the Countess Lieven. Their conversation, though spoken in hushed whispers filled with suspense, consisted entirely of gossip about people Rosa had never heard of and had no interest in. Lady Delphia, greatly honored by being made privy to the tittle-tattle, agreed to every vicious assertion the ladies uttered. To her horror she soon found herself sneering at the excesses of the prince and his brother, Cumberland. The princess, who had introduced the subject, directed a wink at Lady Delphia, saying, "One does crave reassurance that there is still such a commodity as decorum in the world. Thank heaven one knows where to look for it!"

Lady Delphia returned the wink and nodded vigorously at this reference, but it was perfectly obscure to Rosa. What, she longed to know, was this place where one could depend on finding order and uprightness? So engrossed did she become in the question that she hardly attended to the rest of the conversation.

When the visitors departed, Rosa could not help blurting out, "What place were you speaking of?"

"It is the place where all the world goes to dance," Lady Delphia answered.

"I made sure it must be a very grand cathedral, for it inspires such reverence."

"That is because it is wonderfully select. A young lady must receive vouchers in order to attend, and the vouchers must come from one of the patronesses. They do not regard their responsibilities lightly, I can tell you. One must win their favor first."

"I am sure this place must have a name."

"Almack's."

Rosa contemplated this information, then declared, "I have never heard of it." So saying, she tripped off to the music room, where she sat at the pianoforte playing a Scottish air.

Lady Sefton and her daughter were shown into the parlor the following afternoon at four o'clock, and to her surprise, Rosa found herself kindly addressed several times during the conversation.

"How very strange for you, to be discovered like that," Lady Sefton said, leaning forward on the sofa and smiling at Rosa sympathetically. "In your situation, I'm sure I should forget where I was half the time. You must often feel you are living a dream."

Rosa replied earnestly, "You have described my feelings exactly, my lady."

"It is not difficult to imagine how I should feel in your place, my dear. Half the time, I should forget where I was!"

When the good woman rose from her seat to buss her cheek, Rosa felt her eyes fill. However, silently she gave thanks for Lady Delphia, for if she'd had to live every day with the sweetness of Lady Sefton, she would be forever dissolving in a fountain of grateful tears.

Lady Sefton paid a number of visits after that, including one late in the afternoon, during which she was disappointed to learn that Rosa was occupied in the music room. Just as Lady Delphia was whispering in her ear the name of the queen's most recent Italian companion, Rosa's voice filled the house with melody.

> *It was upon a Lammas night,*
> *When corn rigs are bonnie,*
> *Beneath the moon's unclouded light,*
> *I held awa' to Annie.*

Professore Vincente took up his flute to accompany the singer, and Lady Sefton put up a hand to stop Lady Delphia in the middle of her sentence so that she might hear the next verse.

> *Corn rigs and barley rigs,*
> *Corn rigs are bonnie,*
> *I'll ne'er forget that happy night,*
> *Among the rigs wi' Annie.*

Lady Delphia set down her teacup and stood up. "A most improper tune," she said. "I shall hush her at once."

"You will hush yourself, Delphia, if you please. How can I hear anything if you gabble on so?"

Clapping her mouth shut, Lady Delphia sank back in her chair.

> *The sky was blue, the wind was still,*
> *The moon was shining clearly,*
> *I sat her down wi' right goodwill,*
> *Among the rigs of barley.*

Lady Sefton sighed deeply. Her eyes misted over and she dabbed them with a scented handkerchief.

With the next verse, her ladyship spoke the words softly to herself.

> *But all the wonders ere I saw,*
> *Though three times doubled fairly,*
> *That happy night was worth them all,*
> *Among the rigs wi' Annie.*

At the finish of the tune, Lady Sefton asked to be taken to the music room, where, as soon as she saw Rosa, she asked to hear the song again.

"Professore does not understand English very well," Rosa explained. "I did not tell him what an improper tune it is."

"Do not apologize, my dear girl. It is the loveliest tune that ever I heard."

Seeing her ladyship moved to tears, Rosa sang the song again to the obliging professor's accompaniment.

"What a happy memory you recall," Lady Sefton said with a heavy sigh.

"What a happy thing it is that she did not accompany herself," added Lady Delphia.

Shivering with emotion, Lady Sefton dabbed at the corners of her eyes with a wisp of lace. At last, having collected herself, she took her leave, after which Rosa endured for an hour the bitter remonstrances of her ladyship.

The tirade was interrupted by the arrival of a note bearing Lady Sefton's seal. Tearing it open, Lady Delphia crowed with triumph and waved the paper around her head.

"She sent vouchers. Oh, there never was a dearer soul in all the world than Lady Sefton. I had no idea anyone could be so fond of Scottish airs."

"I am glad she liked my song," Rosa said. "I have many more just like it for her to listen to."

"I have worked it out very cleverly, you will see. Once you are accepted at Almack's, your acceptance everywhere will be assured. It is foolish to bother with small private parties and work our way tiresomely through the season when we might achieve everything in a single night."

"A single night?"

"Is that not the most convenient way?"

"But I had counted on rehearsals. I never play to an audience of Londoners until I have done the part at least three times in a country town."

"You must not let the past prey on you now, my dear. Endeavor to put all that behind you."

"But you are saying my success must depend on a single performance. If I make one faux pas, I shall have failed utterly." Fear rising in her throat, Rosa thought wistfully of the theater, where if one failed on stage, the audience merely hooted and threw cabbages or eggs. But Lady Delphia could not be expected to mete out such mild punishment as that. What her ladyship would do if Rosa stumbled over her lines or strayed from her character she did not dare imagine. And Viscount Sunley. What would he think of her if she failed?

"I collect you do not appreciate the meaning of these vouchers," her ladyship said. "Otherwise you would not look like you'd just swallowed a cupful of vinegar."

"You may return the vouchers to Lady Sefton and convey my thanks," Rosa said as coolly as she could. "I shall have to decline her kind invitation."

Lady Delphia gaped.

Seeing her hostess rendered uncharacteristically speechless, Rosa took the opportunity to walk with grave dignity from the room. As soon as she reached the grand staircase, she ran up the steps to her bedchamber and would not come out again the rest of the day.

Lady Delphia condescended to plead with her through the door for a full half hour. Hearing her ladyship make noises like the grinding of teeth, Rosa deeply regretted the pain she was causing. But she could not bring herself to face her ladyship, who, when she saw that Rosa was adamant, went away and knocked no more.

The next twenty-four hours were silent, so much so that Rosa began to wonder if her only alternative to the terrors of Almack's was the boredom of her bedchamber. Thus it was that she welcomed a gentle knock on the door. The little maid curtsied and presented her with a note. It read simply; "I have come back."

When she looked up from the note, the maid begged her to come to a small sitting room, where the viscount awaited her presence.

'It cannot be the maid's clothes that have kept you to your room all this time," he greeted her, "for you're not wrapped in your blanket."

She blushed. How many times had she acted a bawd on-stage and never given it a second thought? She was ridiculous to blush now over an allusion to a blanket. Still, her cheeks flamed, and she had to sit down and huddle her arms across her bosom to keep from shivering.

"Tell me what has distressed you."

The tone of his voice made her look up at him. It recalled the concern she had heard in the alleyway by the theater. "Your aunt wishes me to make my debut at Almack's," she replied.

"Generally speaking, people spend at least one evening at Almack's before they dislike it."

"It would be an excellent plan, except that I don't know if I can pull it off. How can I perform well when I know that everything depends on one night?"

He knelt in front of her so that she could not help meeting his eyes. "You do not need to take the town by storm, you know. You need only give it the honor of witnessing the first public appearance of Lady Rosalind Divine."

"That is precisely what I cannot pull off."

"You are the only one who can pull it off."

"Please, my lord. Do not entreat me. I do not think I will be able to say no to you, and then we shall all be in a horrid pickle."

"Do I have so much influence with you?"

She remained silent.

"Then, because you wish it, I shall not entreat you. I shall ask instead if you will admit a visitor."

"Who is it? If it is one of the patronesses, I don't believe I am receiving."

"I told you I meant to go hunting. Well, I have bagged my quarry." On that, Sunley requested she would wait where she was. Then he left her alone. In another minute, Tripple strode in through the door.

Rosa bolted out of her chair and threw her arms about his neck.

"Nay, nay, your highness," he remonstrated, peeling her arms from his person. "This is 'much ado about nothing.' I told you you would see me again."

"Yes, but I never expected to see you looking so dandified."

Tripple strutted about the room so that she might inspect his new finery. He wore a fawn coat and pantaloons made entirely of superfine, a black waistcoat threaded through with shining gold, and a cravat of such proportions that his chin could not be seen. On his walk, he paused at the door, poked his head out, and looked down the hall each way. Satisfied that no one was by, he closed the door behind him. Then he turned to her and grinned.

"'Sweet are the uses of adversity,'" he declaimed, "'which, like the toad, ugly and venomous, wears yet a precious jewel in his head.' Oh, but how much sweeter are the uses of prosperity!"

"I want to know all about this prosperity," Rosa replied. "Where did you come by the blunt to dress up like a nob?"

"Viscount Sunley advanced me something so that I might attire myself more suitably. I should not like to come before Lady Rosalind Divine looking like a beggar."

"How very generous of his lordship."

"Yes, it is, for the gentleman has barely a groat to his name. But he has seen me act and admires my work."

"You have not said you miss me, Tripple. You have not said you've repented of this scheme of yours and have come to claim me."

"No, I haven't, and won't, either. But I have been brought here for a purpose, which is, in brief, to identify you to the bench as her ladyship."

"Nonsense. What sort of proof can you offer?"

"Any sort that is required."

Her face wore a skeptical look. "You don't mean to repeat that ridiculous story of finding me in front of the workhouse singing a bawdy song."

"Certainly I do. It is the truth, as far as it goes, and a story should always contain as much truth as will make it plausible. But I thought I would flesh it out a bit. It wants pathos, I think. I had a notion to add a speech or two about how small and scrawny you were and how you et up all my bread in one sitting, though it was black and hard as stone."

"I expect the law would prefer more matter with less art."

"You may be right. Nevertheless, if I am to be extraordinarily well paid, I feel obliged to give an extraordinary performance."

"Ah, we are back to money."

"Indeed we are, and just where we belong. So much more comfortable than sentiment, don't you agree? 'Nothing comes amiss, so money comes withal,' says the poet, and jolly on the mark is, too."

"Tripple, you cannot fabricate a story. You will be found out and put in prison."

"Do not take that lofty tone with me, girl. Do you know what sort of money we are talking about here?"

"I haven't the least idea."

"Ninety thousand pounds!"

"Good heavens, as much as that?"

"Nay, more, for that is only the amount of the principal."

"One can certainly wear a great deal of pink on ninety thousand pounds."

"One can wear anything one wants to," replied Tripple, "a gown trimmed with crowns and sovereigns, if you've a mind to. But here's the rub. We can't get at it!"

"I know nothing of the arrangements."

"Then I will tell you. The first step is to get our hands on this inheritance. I shall take care of the law, but you must take care of the world."

"The world never took care of us, dear Tripple. I say, let it take care of itself."

"Rosa, you must go to this place they call Almack's."

"Ah, they've told you all about it and you take their side."

"Yes, and I agree absolutely with Lady Delphia. She is a very attractive personage, is her ladyship, and speaks most mildly and sensibly."

"If you say such outlandish things, you will surely land in prison for perjury!"

"A little more deference from you, if you please. Now you must go and dance at this place. It will prove an excellent way of showing the world who and what is Lady Rosalind Divine."

Rosa sighed. "I see there is no help for it, and I must go."

"Yes, and you must turn a step or two with the viscount. I'd like to know just what he's about here."

At this, Rosa felt her cheeks grow warm. "He's not about much of anything, I expect, at least not any more than we're about."

"He's a deep one, his lordship is. I do not trust him too far."

"Why do you say that?"

"Because he is the most peculiar fellow. He goes to all the trouble of finding me and persuading me to act as a witness in the case, and then he says I must be as truthful as I can be with Messrs. Buffel and Buffel, that there will be no getting away with bold-face lies in the court."

"It's true. Should you be found out, it will be all up with us."

"What sort of actor does he take me for, I ask you? Does he rate my talents so low as to think I would overplay my scene?"

"I have a notion, Tripple, that Viscount Sunley is not so indifferent to the truth as he thinks, in spite of the Divine blood."

"Well, how does he suppose we can tell the truth and still get at the money?"

"I don't know, but if a pickpocket can dance at Almack's, I suppose anything may be possible."

Sunley rode in the carriage with Tripple to the lodgings he had taken for him in West Street. Over the noise of rumbling wheels, the actor regaled the young gentleman with tales of his many successes before the footlights. Tripple hoped by this method to reassure his companion that he would prove the most convincing witness any gentleman could hire for the price. Unaccountably, the more he spoke, the graver Sunley looked.

Piqued by this lack of faith in his abilities, Tripple said, "I do not fancy being scowled at, my lord. If you do not wish me to tell what I know to the lawyers, I shall take myself back to Hampshire and never trouble you further."

"Of course I wish you to tell your story, Mr. Tripple. I believe you did indeed find Rosa at the workhouse and that you may well recall details of the event which will appear convincing."

"You do not look as if you believe it, sir, if I may say so. And I do not think I can perform entirely up to snuff if my stage manager doubts I can remember my lines."

"You will remember them I have no doubt. What I do doubt is that you will remember them in a way which will benefit Rosa."

Recoiling in outrage, Tripple exclaimed, "Why, sir, do you believe I would hurt a single lovely copper strand on her blessed head?"

Sunley studied the old thespian who sat opposite him in the shadows of the coach. "I don't know," he said. "I know that the money means a great deal to you and that you are willing to sacrifice her to get it."

Tripple smiled. "Why, so I am, sir; so I am. In that, we are just alike, you and I, are we not?"

Angrily, his lordship turned his head and stared through the window at the cobblestones. In a steely voice he replied, "No harm must come to her out of this scheme. She must be protected."

With a sweeping gesture, Tripple declared, "Well, sir, I should think that ninety thousand pounds will protect her very nicely."

Sunley shook his head. "You do not understand my meaning."

"Oh, but I do, sir. And the money will do a vast deal to benefit her. More to the point, sir, we have our own selves to protect her."

Facing him once more, Sunley waited for him to explain.

"We—you and I—shall see to it that she is unharmed, shall we not? With the two of us to look after her and the money to boot, what more protection can she require?"

◇ **Eight** ◇

Viscount Sunley occupied himself for the next several days with scrutinizing his personal conduct in the light of Tripple's cheerful avarice. It appeared to him that the old actor was in fact more honest than he himself could claim to be, that, indeed, while he wavered and vacillated, Tripple held firm and openly to his principles, such as they were.

After a time, Sunley acknowledged that he had come to envy the old scoundrel in an odd sort of way. He wished he, too, could believe that any means justified the end. But he hardly knew his own mind, it seemed, for one moment he wanted nothing so much as to shake loose the inheritance at any cost and the next he feared to do anything that might put Rosa's safety at risk. He knew perfectly well that a few very small judicious lies would effectively yield up the bequests. At the same time, he knew the young actress would be the one to suffer if it should be discovered that perjury had been committed on her behalf. With such gloomy ideas clouding his vision of Rosa's future, it did not occur to him to notice her daily comings and goings.

He was greatly surprised, therefore, when the crucial night arrived and at ten o'clock she descended the grand staircase in her gown of pink. Happiness suffused her face, so much so that he could not forbear smiling and allowing the lines which care had etched around his dark eyes to smooth. He greeted her by taking her hands and spinning her round. Then he looked at her with such pleasure that she felt nothing could possibly occur the rest of the evening to delight her more. She bore contentedly with Lady Delphia's fussing, and gladly permitted Lord Divine, who said she was in great beauty, to lead her to the coach.

Within minutes of entering its portals, Rosa concluded that the attraction of Almack's lay entirely in its exclusiveness. Its rooms were capacious but hardly grand enough to match the picture she had conjured in imagination. The only drinks served were tea, barley water flavored with orange flowers, and lemonade, and the tables were set with bread and butter, cakes, and nothing else. Only three patronesses were in attendance—Lady Sefton, Lady Jersey, and Countess Lieven—and of these, only the countess maintained the hauteur which gave the club its power. Lady Jersey greeted the new arrivals volubly, congratulating Rosa on her enchanting gossamer gown.

The viscount then asked Rosa for a dance. Although Lady

Delphia had impressed upon her that a lady always accepted a gentleman's invitation to dance, she stammered a refusal.

"Courage, my lady," he said with a smile.

"But I am sure to forget my steps, and then we shall be frowned out of Almack's forever."

"One must dance at Almack's. There is nothing else to do here. The stakes at the tables make it hardly worth the effort to play cards, and so we have no choice." Without waiting for her to invent another argument, he took her hand, tucked it in his arm, and led her down to the set.

Recollecting the dancing master's instructions, Rosa minded her steps and did not look into her partner's face. When she did look up—to apologize for treading on his foot —she found him laughing at her.

"Well, you would have it your own way, Viscount Sunley. I endeavored to spare you, you know, but you insisted on dancing."

"My humble foot is honored, and you must call me *William*, now that we are expected to behave like cousins."

Rosa agreed to call him William and promptly missed another step.

"May I offer a suggestion? You need not follow it if you dislike to," he said.

"By all means, although I must say, I am unused to such politeness from my family. Lady Delphia does not ask permission."

"I suggest you try not to look at your feet."

"But I shall lose the count."

"Look at my lips. I shall help you count, and I shall not have to content myself with gazing at your headdress."

With that, he took her firmly by the waist and held her so close that it was impossible for her to see her feet. He guided her swiftly around the floor, and then whirled her around more swiftly yet, until she thought she would grow dizzy. Throwing her head back slightly, she lent herself to the liveliness of the dance. She kept her eyes on his lips, which mouthed the count, and felt the hypnotic rhythm draw her in. Once or twice she closed her eyes, allowing the viscount to lead around the floor.

The dance ended. Rosa opened her eyes so that they met

his. Returning his smile, she would have commented on the delightfulness of Almack's, when she saw his face grow suddenly serious. He stared intently at the entrance.

Following the direction of his eyes, Rosa saw a lady and a gentleman come into the hall. The gentleman—a distinguished personage with silver hair—was older than the lady, who was not much older than Rosa. She was charmingly dressed in yellow, which suited her blond hair, and she studied the faces in the room as though looking for one in particular. Rosa wondered if she might be seeking Sunley's face in the crush; he certainly seemed eager enough to catch her eye. A single look at his face produced a tumbling in Rosa's stomach, and she had to summon up her courage to ask, "Who is that?"

Sunley produced a tight smile. "Come, I would have you meet the Grahames," he said, and led her forward by the elbow.

By the time they reached the entrance, Lord Divine and Lady Delphia had come up to greet the new arrivals. Her ladyship introduced Rosa to them and leveled a look of disgust at her brother when he hoped aloud that the two young ladies might soon become the most intimate of friends.

Rosa sincerely doubted Lord Divine would get his wish, for Miss Grahame's attention was everywhere but on her new acquaintance. She scanned the room, not the least bit happily, and had to be asked every question two and three times. Clearly the face she sought was not Sunley's; she seemed hardly aware of his existence. He, on the other hand, seemed unaware of anyone else's.

In contrast, Mr. Grahame was both attentive and pleasant. He spent some minutes in genial conversation with everyone, and then, as the cotillion was announced, he asked Rosa to stand up with him.

She attempted to catch the viscount's eye in the hope that he would say she was already engaged, but his attention was far away. Piqued, Rosa accepted Mr. Grahame with a polite nod and lay her hand on his arm so that he might escort her onto the floor.

The intricacies of the dance did not permit conversation. Rosa wisely saved her breath for the diverse steps and frequent changes of partner. Earnestly she prayed that she gave the appearance of being a tolerable dancer. When the music paused, Mr. Grahame drew her aside to talk.

"Will you pardon me, Lady Rosalind? I have not the breath for dancing I used to have, now I am in my dotage."

"You are not the least in your dotage, sir. You are a very handsome gentleman, if I may say so."

"You may indeed say so," he replied with warmth. "It is quite some time since I have received a compliment from a beautiful young heiress. In point of fact, I have never received one. I suppose it comes of being married at an early age."

"Is your wife in town also?"

"She is dead."

"I am very sorry."

"Save your sorrow, my lady. When my wife died, she did the one thing which perfectly reconciled me to her, nay, which allowed me to think of her with the greatest affection."

"You are cynical, sir."

"When one reaches a certain age, one has a tendency to be cynical—and to hand out advice. We ancient sages like nothing better than to hand out advice."

"I refuse to acknowledge that you are ancient, for you are not. But I will allow you to hand out advice. I shall even go so far as to accept some of it, for I believe I can use all the advice I can scare up." ´

"How very perverse of you to threaten to accept my advice. I assure you, my lady, it is not done, especially by the young and beauteous."

"I am certain my aunt would tell you that the Divines are known to be a perverse race. But now, sir, as I have been so perverse as to ask for your advice, what have you to offer? You will not disappoint me, I hope, by forcing me to come to my own conclusions?"

"Let me see. Ah, here is an excellent piece of advice, from my own experience, too, which makes it one of the eternal verities, to be sure. It is this: never marry the object of your first passion."

"Ah, that is a sad bit of wisdom and emanates from a grieving heart, I fear."

"Not at all. I am out of my misery now, thanks to my wife's last and most generous act. It is my niece who pines."

Rosa followed the direction of his eyes and saw Miss Grahame locked in argument with a tall, thin gentleman. Mr. Grahame turned from the sight in anger. Bitterly, he murmured, "Why could she not love Sunley? He adores her."

Rosa felt the heat rise to her cheeks, then asked as casually as she could, "Have they known each other long?"

"She met Pomeroy only last season."

"No, I mean has your niece known my cousin very long?"

"They have known each other forever. As children they exchanged rings and promised to marry."

"Perhaps both are fortunate, then. You have said it is a great mistake to marry the object of your first passion."

Mr. Grahame smiled. "Ungrateful girl! I give you the benefit of my sagacity, and you throw my words back in my face."

"I shall endeavor not to listen so closely hereafter. Or, if perchance your wisdom does penetrate my ears, I promise not to heed it. But I must ask you this. Is it all right, do you think, to marry one's second love? I am new to town and should not like to offend by breaking any rules."

"Are you thinking of marrying, my lady?"

Rosa stared at him. The question startled her. "Of course not!" she cried. "How can someone like myself, someone with my history, ever marry?"

"But you must marry. Someone like yourself—the daughter of a great family and the heiress to a great fortune—can do nothing else but marry."

"Oh, dear. And I thought Almack's was to be the worst of my hurdles."

Mr. Grahame laughed. "Perhaps you will be more fortunate than I was in a choice of spouse. I devoutly hope so, for I should not like to see that mischievous smile of yours turn to despair. It is a sight I have seen far too often in my own house of late. But enough of this morbid talk. I banish it. You must prepare yourself, Lady Rosalind."

"Gracious. Are we going to dance again? I suppose we ought not to be seen talking too long. We shall be suspected of coming to Almack's for our own entertainment instead of the world's."

"Prepare to be chucked under the chin, little miss."

So saying he raised his hand to within an inch of her cheek. He kept the hand suspended in the air for some time, regarding her closely. "I like you very much, you know," he said, drawing his finger along the line of her jaw.

Rosa met his eyes with a smile. After Lord Divine, he was the kindest person she had ever met.

"I ought not to have done that," he said. "Either you are not as young as I first thought or I am not as old."

At that moment, an insistent fan rapped loudly on Mr. Grahame's arm. "You will excuse us, sir," Lady Delphia said severely. "There are a great many people begging to meet Lady Rosalind."

Rosa looked back at him as her hostess swept her away and saw that he followed her with his eyes. She was not permitted to dwell on Mr. Grahame's admiration, however, for she was obliged to curtsy to a succession of beaus and matrons, to remember all of their names, and to commit to memory the amount of their incomes and the bloodlines from which they descended, both of which pieces of information Lady Delphia took care to whisper in her ear. After some ten minutes occupied in this manner, a murmur began to rise through the crowd like a tidal wave. Over it Rosa discerned the phrases, "Charming girl," "Beckwith's daughter," and "Ninety thousand pounds." Lady Delphia squeezed her hand and assured her, "You will have entrée everywhere now."

This news might have pleased Rosa more if she could have spotted Viscount Sunley anywhere. Unable to find him among the dancers or talkers, though, she had to resort to asking Lady Delphia if she knew where he'd gone.

"He was dancing with Miss Grahame, I believe. I expect he will have his two dances with her and then spend the remainder of the evening fawning over her."

"You do not approve his behavior, I collect?"

"I do not approve of Miss Grahame. She is not at all the thing, you know. And her uncle is no better, I'm afraid. His touching your chin as he did was highly improper. Had anyone else seen it, I'm sure you would be obliged to die of shame."

"Why is Miss Grahame not at all the thing?"

"Because, if you must know, she spurned Sunley's proposal of marriage. No doubt she is after a rich man, but Sunley will be rich someday and she might have shown a little patience."

"I believe you are partial to him, my lady."

Lady Delphia pulled her face into a thoughtful moue. "'Pon my word," she said, as though the notion had struck her for the first time in her life, "why, I suppose I am."

"It is not unnatural, as he is your nephew."

"Nevvew, faugh! I am partial to him because he is Sunley. The whole world is partial to him. Excepting Miss Grahame. The more fool she!"

Rosa was not at all surprised to learn that the whole world was partial to the viscount, and she was enraptured to hear that Miss Grahame was an exception to that otherwise universal truth. Indeed, she was so pleased with the information that she was quite in charity with Lady Delphia and allowed her to introduce her to a young tulip of fashion who pleaded the favor of a dance.

Mr. Bonwit smirked at her persistently throughout the set. He commented without pause on the attire of everyone in the room, beginning with the countess and ending with Rosa herself, who, he suggested, might vary the highly becoming shade of pink she wore with varicolored ribands and seed pearls. He pointed out to her the exquisiteness of his own dress, and invoked the name Brummell with every third word. When he ran out of breath, he grinned and sniffed, mightily pleased with himself, until Rosa, who could bear no more, begged to be excused from finishing the dance. She was parched, she said, waving her fan briskly to cool her neck.

The tulip answered her hopes with alacrity, insisting on being permitted to procure her a glass of lemonade. He had no sooner extorted a murmur of gratitude from her than he set forth into the crush with an air of purpose.

The moment he disappeared, Rosa faded behind a curtained arch. She found herself in a cool passageway lined with rooms. Availing herself of the handiest one, she tiptoed inside and went at once to the open window half-hidden by a Japanese screen. There she breathed in the fresh air to her heart's content.

On the third breath, she heard the door burst open and two

people entered. The lady was Miss Grahame, and the gentleman was the thin one who had caused Mr. Grahame such distress.

"You are insane!" he hissed.

"You gave me your promise," she cried. "Is your word worth nothing?"

"Do you expect me to keep a promise which exists only in your imagination?"

"My God. Don't you care what happens to me?"

"How can I? You drive me away with your fidgets. I can hardly breathe, you suffocate me so, and I cannot bear the sight of you." Glaring into her eyes, he perused her face. "Why, look at you, all red with the frenzies and your skin all blotched. Do you wonder that my regard for you is put to the strain?"

At this, Miss Grahame put her face in her hands, giving Rosa the opportunity she sought to make her presence known.

"Miss Grahame," she said softly. "I do beg your pardon."

Both pairs of eyes turned on her. Miss Grahame's wore an expression of desperate fright. The gentleman's, however, were alight with interest.

He approached her and bowed smoothly. "Lady Rosalind, I believe."

Coldly, Rosa nodded.

"I have been hoping for an opportunity of making your acquaintance."

Before he could bow, Rosa turned her back on him to walk to the door.

"Miss Grahame forgets her manners," he said.

This scornful reproach forced Miss Grahame to collect herself and perform an introduction between Lady Rosalind and Lord Pomeroy. The effort this politeness cost her was exhausting, so that she sank into a chair, all color drained from her cheeks.

Lord Pomeroy meanwhile paid her no mind. He regarded Rosa from the top of her auburn hair to the silk slippers which adorned her feet. Bowing, he begged to be allowed to escort her back to the main room.

"I will see to Miss Grahame," she replied. "She does not look well."

"No, she looks weary and cross this night," his lordship agreed.

Miss Grahame sat upright to look fiercely at him, but the words of retort died on her lips.

Rosa returned his lordship's smile with scorn and walked to a chair, where she seated herself as close to Miss Grahame as possible.

"You will find it very tedious, Lady Rosalind, to cosset a fidgety female when you might enjoy a mazurka instead."

"I find *you* tedious, sir."

Lord Pomeroy's head snapped up. His first response was a glare so full of resentment that Rosa felt afraid for a moment. But he softened it immediately afterward, saying, "If you knew the circumstances, my lady, you would not do me such an injustice."

"You have my permission to retire," Rosa replied in the voice of Lady Macbeth.

He bowed to her, ignoring Miss Grahame, and left the room.

Rosa expected to see Miss Grahame melt into tears at this juncture. To her surprise, the young woman darted from her seat and made as if to follow his lordship.

"No!" Rosa cried before she knew what she did.

Miss Grahame froze with her hand on the doorknob. She turned to face Rosa, then stared down at her trembling hands. At last she managed to say in a low tone, "I can't imagine what I was thinking, to try to follow him like that. You must think me very foolish, Lady Rosalind."

"I entreat you to sit awhile before you go back. You are very distressed. Perhaps I can send a footboy to fetch you something to drink."

"I am not thirsty. Will you sit with me?"

When Rosa nodded, she resumed her chair. "Oh, what am I going to do?" Miss Grahame wept.

"I will go and find Mr. Grahame. He will take you home."

"No!"

"But he will want to know if you are in trouble. He is the kindest of gentlemen and will look after you well."

"He disapproves of me. And he hates Lord Pomeroy. Do not fetch him, I pray you."

For some minutes the two women remained thoughtfully silent while Rosa mustered the courage to suggest an alternative. At last she said, "Very well. I will try to find my cousin William."

This suggestion brought a light of gladness into Miss Grahame's fevered expression. It was a look that answered all of Rosa's worst fears.

"Yes, William," said the distraught young woman. "He does not judge me. He only loves."

Rosa swallowed and rose. Stepping just outside the door, she located a footboy. Having whispered instructions in his ear, she sent him off and returned to Miss Grahame, who exchanged not a word or a look with her but waited in tense anticipation of a knock on the door.

When it came, she shivered, but it was only the footboy, who told Rosa he had not been able to locate the viscount anywhere. She was at a loss for a moment until she hit on the idea of sending for Lord Divine. The boy went off on his new mission, and Rosa turned to Miss Grahame once more.

"William despises Pomeroy," said that young woman with feverish intensity. "He will call him out."

"Do you mean that he will go so far as to fight Lord Pomeroy?"

"That's exactly what I mean. William will call him out and kill him." Her voice resounded with exultation.

"You are very angry, Miss Grahame. You don't mean what you say."

"I mean every word of it."

"But suppose it is William who is killed!"

"If William dies, then I suppose I shall die as well. What does it matter? In any case, I trust William. He has never disappointed me, not ever."

Rosa looked down at her hands to inspect the sapphire that winked on her finger. It had been a gift from Lord Divine, a trinket of his wife's, he had said, one of the few mementos remaining of the viscount's mother. "I doubt it is necessary to embroil William in this affair," she said as calmly as she could.

"You do not understand, Lady Rosalind. Lord Pomeroy has made me promises. He must be made to keep them."

"Forgive me, but I believe you are speaking rashly. On reflection, I am sure you will consider your reputation. To cause a duel, and to do nothing to try to prevent it, must damage a lady's reputation beyond repair, and if it should result in the death of the worthiest of men, your own conscience will torment you the rest of your life."

"I do not give a farthing for my reputation, or my conscience."

"But you would not demean yourself by taking the least notice of such a man as Pomeroy."

"And why should I not? I have no dignity or pride left. Nor does it matter what happens to me."

"Apparently it does not matter what happens to William, either!"

The energy in Rosa's voice caused Miss Grahame to study her companion. She took her in completely—the intentness of her eyes, the tilt of her chin, the quick rise and fall of her bosom. An arch look stole across the young woman's lined face as she said, "But it matters to you, I see."

Rosa met her direct look without flinching.

Lord Divine entered at that moment, escorted by the foot-boy. "My dear Miss Grahame, I am so sorry to hear you are ill. Allow me to call your coach and see you home. Oh, Rosalind, my dear, I did not expect to find you here. William told me Miss Grahame was with Lord Pomeroy. I'm afraid he has gone outside for a breath of air. He quarreled with his cards and declined to have anything further to do with such vile luck. In any case, I am glad to be able to be of service to my good friend's niece."

Miss Grahame rose and thanked him. Turning to Rosa, she said, "You will allow me to call on you, Lady Rosalind? I am delighted to find we have so many interests in common. I should be desolate if we could not continue this conversation."

Upon which she marched from the room on Lord Divine's arm.

"There you are!" exclaimed Mr. Bonwit from the doorway. "I could not imagine where you'd gone to. Here is your drink."

He handed her a nearly empty glass, which she stared at without comprehension.

"Gracious, it must have spilled out while I was looking for you. There is not a drop left! But, my lady, how did you come to be in here?"

"Allow me to answer that, Mr. Bonwit," said Lord Pomeroy. "The lady was looking for me. *N'est-ce pas*, Lady Rosalind?"

Rosa stood up, meeting his challenging look with coldness. *"Allez-vous en, monsieur,"* she said. It was one of the few French expressions she knew.

Lord Pomeroy, interpreting this command as artful banter, sauntered into the room. "Mr. Bonwit," he said, "you are a perfect dolt. You have spilt the drink and there is none left. I shall entertain the lady while you fetch another glass."

"The devil you will!" vowed Mr. Bonwit.

"Softly, there's a good fellow," soothed his lordship. "Do not take on so, Bonwit. You will wilt your cravat. It is well known you would perish with mortification if such a fate should befall that lump you wear at your throat."

"I say, Pomeroy, this is the outside of enough. I have half a mind to teach you a lesson."

"It is true you have half a mind."

Rosa's attempts to put a period to this quarrel were fruitless. She therefore moved to leave them both, when a distinguished figure appeared in the open door to say, "Lady Rosalind, is it true, my niece has gone home?"

"Yes, it is, " she told Mr. Grahame, "but Lord Divine will look after her."

"It is my place to do that."

"Lord Divine was happy to fill that office."

"Yes, he is the very gentlest of gentlemen." At that, Mr. Grahame looked directly at Lord Pomeroy, adding, "My niece has not always been so fortunate as to meet with such kind gentlemen."

Pomeroy laughed out loud at this sally. "You ought to watch her more closely, Mr. Grahame. A headstrong girl such as your niece, so careless of her reputation, might lose it altogether should the wrong sort of fellow choose to take advantage of her."

"If there is such a fellow," said Viscount Sunley, walking into their midst, "he will not go unpunished."

Lord Pomeroy's hand flew to his side, but as he had removed his weapon upon entering the sacred precincts of Almack's, his gesture was impotent.

The viscount gave him a look of contempt; then with a smile he turned to Rosa. "You must excuse his lordship," he said. "He has a reputation to maintain. When he grows weary with cheating at cards and seducing young women, he must swagger."

The fury on Pomeroy's face terrified Rosa. She was sure he was on the point of attacking Sunley. To avert such a catastrophe, she cried out, "Stop it! Stop it, all of you. I insist you behave yourselves," and to emphasize her insistence, she stamped her foot.

The four gentlemen gazed at her. One by one, they bowed their acquiescence. She read embarrassment on Mr. Bonwit's face, and admiration on Mr. Grahame's. Lord Pomeroy took pains to mask his vengeful expression, while Sunley smiled at her, amused.

And thus they were found by Lady Delphia, who bustled into the room with the patronesses trailing behind her.

For some time the whole world had wished to know where Lady Rosalind had hid herself. The question had disconcerted Lady Delphia, but she had dissembled well, answering that the young lady could not be seen for the crowd of courtiers which surrounded her. It had never for a second crossed her mind that such a statement could possibly be true. Yet there stood Rosalind, surrounded by a lord whose blood was known to be the purest, a widower whose income was known to be the highest, a pink of the ton whose taste was known to be the finest, and her very own relation, whose smile was known to be the handsomest. All four of them were lavishing attention upon the Lady Rosalind and wearing expressions on their faces of consummate stupidity.

Seeing Lady Rosalind in the center of such a circle, the patronesses held a conference on the spot and voted to grant the young woman permission to waltz. They then returned to the main hall, where they regaled everyone within earshot with the tale of Lady Rosalind's heroism in preventing any-where from two to four duels of honor.

Rosa stood in the center of the room wishing she might be taken home now. She felt the absurdity of her position more poignantly than her success. She had spent an evening en-gaged in thoughts of Viscount Sunley, who thought only of Miss Grahame, who thought only of Lord Pomeroy, who, it now appeared, thought only of Lady Rosalind Divine. If it were not so painful, the situation might be comical.

Each of the four gentlemen begged to be allowed to dance the waltz with Lady Rosalind. Lord Pomeroy would be hon-ored, he assured her with an insolent smile. Mr. Grahame had not yet had his second dance with her, he reminded her gently. Sunley claimed that as she was his cousin-or nearly so-, he thought it his duty to lead her down to the dance. Only Mr. Bonwit remained silent, evidently feeling the uselessness of articulating his modest claims against such daunting rivals.

Rosa turned to the dandy as the one who would make the fewest demands on her attention. Favoring him with a lumi-nous smile, she put her arm on his and allowed him to escort her back to the hall. Lady Delphia, nodding approval, fol-lowed on Mr. Grahame's arm. Lord Pomeroy, looking neither to the right nor the left, stalked after them.

Alone in the room, Sunley leaned against the mantel and smiled. He contemplated Rosa's success. He hoped she took as much pleasure in it as he did. And he concluded that of all the shades in nature, pink was certainly the loveliest.

◊ Nine ◊

Well before Rosa awoke, several gentlemen called in George Street and left their cards. Among them was Mr. Bonwit, who, in fact, called twice, each time to say he would return later. During breakfast, Lady Delphia turned the cards over and over and recited the roster of callers between bites of buttered toast. Glowing over the large number of cards, together with the murmurs of approval she had overheard the night before, her ladyship concluded that her niece's debut had been nothing less than a triumph.

"Now you see how it is, Rosalind!" said Lord Divine with a chuckle. "And you were so reluctant to come with us—as though we were carting you off to prison."

Rosa had to acknowledge that the world of Hanover Square was not a prison, or if it was, at least it was a gilded one.

"Lady Jersey is in raptures over you," said Lady Delphia.

"And Miss Grahame, too," added his lordship. "She did nothing but ask me questions about you through our entire ride home."

"Miss Grahame recovered quickly, it seems," the viscount said. As it was the only thing he had said the entire morning, they all looked at him.

"Oh, yes," said his father. "She was quite lively, in fact. I could not see any evidence of the illness which took her away so early."

"Perhaps it was only a temporary fit," Sunley replied, a little sharply.

"Very likely, for she did not complain in the least but only wanted to know where Lady Rosalind had been all these years and how we had found her at last and what you, William, intended to do for our cousin."

"I hope you told her I intend to get our cousin the inheritance her father left."

"Why, yes, I did tell her that, and she said she thought you would end up very rich—nay, that we all would."

"Not as rich as Lord Pomeroy, I'm afraid," said Sunley.

"He is rich indeed," Lady Delphia chimed in, "and the son —the only son, I might add—of a marquess. I perceive he was much taken with you, Rosalind."

At this, Sunley looked full at Rosa. He kept his eyes on her, even as he sipped his coffee.

She returned his look forthrightly, saying, "I do not like Lord Pomeroy, aunt."

"That is nothing to the point, foolish girl. The point is he likes you."

But Sunley seemed to think it very much to the point, because he set down his cup and smiled at Rosa. Then he stood up, saying warmly, "I am very sorry to have to leave you, especially as the conversation has taken such an interesting turn, but Mr. Tripple and I have an appointment in Lincoln's Inn." Then he said good-bye and left the room.

Rosa sighed. She guessed he would be gone the entire day. Visits to Lincoln's Inn had lately taken him away entire days, and evenings as well.

But it was only a moment before he was back.

"What, you here again, nevvew?"

"I thought perhaps Lady Rosalind would like to view an exhibition of paintings this afternoon."

"I should like that very much."

"Impossible," said Lady Delphia. "We must not forget our lesson with Professore Vincente."

"On the contrary, we must do all we can to forget it," the viscount replied. "After last night's success, his pupil deserves a rest."

So it was agreed that Sunley would return in the early afternoon to escort Rosa to Spring Gardens.

Lord Divine set out for Waiter's, while the ladies adjourned to the sitting room and took up their embroidery. Soon Mr. Bonwit's card was brought to them, and after Lady Delphia marveled for a moment at the ornateness of the lettering, the gentleman was admitted.

It appeared that Mr. Bonwit had been transfigured overnight. His mouth, which had been ready enough with a smirk when she had first set eyes on him, now curved down in a pout. His cheeks were pale, owing to an excess of white powder and an absence of rouge. His eyes grew large as they stared at her abstractedly.

"Are you ill, Mr. Bonwit?" Rosa asked.

"Yes, yes, I am," he said hoarsely.

"You ought not to have come, in that case," said Lady Delphia. "No one wants to catch your cold, Mr. Bonwit. You must go away and come back when you are well."

"I do not have a cold."

"You do not have the sore throat, I hope. My grandmother died of it, you know."

"I suffer from a sickness of the heart, ma'am."

Lady Delphia regarded him through her glass. "Oh, well, it does not signify, then."

Unruffled, the gentleman seated himself on the sofa next to Rosa. For a time he watched her draw the needle in and out of a hoop, which held a flowered footstool cover. Then, in a whisper, so that Lady Delphia might not hear, he said, "I hope that Lady Rosalind will take pity on me."

"Why should I pity you, Mr. Bonwit? You are a gentleman with the freedom to do exactly as you like. I should think you might be envied, but never pitied."

This produced a radiant gleam on the gentleman's countenance. "Oh, my lady, it is good of you to say so." Here he reached out his hand to her and pricked it on the needle. Instantly he brought it to his mouth with an exclamation.

"Oh, let me see your hand."

"With pleasure."

"I believe you will not have a scar. Indeed, there isn't a mark anywhere."

"My poor hand is healed by your compassion."

Rosa dropped it at once and said coolly, "What do you call that manner of tying a cravat, sir? Is it the Canal?"

At this question, Mr. Bonwit suddenly grew serious. Slowly he rose, walked a few steps away from the sofa, and bowed to the ladies. "I believe you mean the Cascade, my lady." Shedding his lovesick air, he expostulated for ten minutes on the tying of cravats.

There were those, he said, who went in for the plain style, which to his eye was meager-looking but perfectly acceptable, if one did not mind looking like a Dissenter. As it happened, he did mind and consequently had made it his business to learn the way of constructing something more flowing, with folds of silk and an edging of lace. There were those who regarded his attention to matters of fashion as an excess, nay, an affectation. There were even those who used his eye for fashion as a pretext for calling him a dandy. (He was well aware of what was said, despite its being said behind his back.) But there were those—and they were in the majority —who said that Finster Bonwit, Esq., knew nothing else, but he did know the tying of cravats!

Lady Delphia objected, "Surely, sir, you must know something else."

This gave the young gentleman pause. He screwed up his face in thought until he came up with a reply, "Why, yes. I know gigs."

"I knew there must be something, even if it is only gigs."

"I have bought a new one. It is standing outside this very minute. I wonder, would Lady Rosalind favor me by taking a drive in it?"

"You are very kind, Mr. Bonwit, but I am engaged to ride out to Spring Gardens with my cousin Sunley."

"Never mind Sunley," Lady Delphia said. "If you would like to have a drive in Mr. Bonwit's new gig, I'm sure you may. When Sunley comes back and finds you gone, he won't think a thing about it, I'm sure."

Rosa would have protested, except that the footman entered to announce Mr. and Miss Grahame. The former wore his usual distinguished, agreeable air; the latter was greatly improved. She had a spot of color on her cheeks which looked to be quite natural, and she smiled at Rosa. They were invited to sit, and after making polite pronouncements on the great success of Lady Rosalind's debut, Miss Grahame said she hoped to induce her new friend to ride out with her.

"She's engaged this afternoon—to Viscount Sunley," Mr. Bonwit informed her.

"Oh, if it's only William, he will never mind if I steal her away."

"If I were the gentleman in question, I should mind very much," said Mr. Grahame.

Rosa gave him a grateful look.

"I know William a great deal better than you do, uncle. Indeed, I think I know him better than anyone else in the world, and I know he would not mind. Were you aware, Lady Rosalind, that I am so long and so well acquainted with your cousin?" Miss Grahame asked.

"I was aware that you have known him a great deal longer than I have."

"Oh, ages longer. I will tell you how well I know William. I know him so well that I know his weaknesses. Are you very shocked, Lady Rosalind?"

"Yes, I confess, I am a little."

This produced a frown from the uncle and an arch look from the niece, who said, "You are shocked to know he has weaknesses?"

"Not at all. He is a human creature. It does not shock me to know that a man is not a god."

"Ah, but it must disappoint you. Intellectually, one does not expect godliness from a mere man; but in one's heart, my lady, oh, in one's heart it is a very different matter, I think!"

"You do not speak for her ladyship's heart, I hope," said Mr. Bonwit, who took umbrage at Miss Grahame's quizzing tone.

"No less than you do, Mr. Bonwit. But I cannot help asking Lady Rosalind what there was in what I said to shock her."

"I am shocked that you would use your friend so in his absence," Rosa said.

"How do you imagine I use him?"

"You speak for him, saying what he would and would not mind, and in your reference to his weaknesses, you hint that he is not what he seems."

Lady Delphia nodded approval Rosa's way. "Rosalind is right. My nevvew has no weaknesses. The Divines are amazingly free of that sort of thing."

Mr. Bonwit interposed here, saying, "Perhaps Lady Rosalind would be so good as to come out to see my new gig."

"Or perhaps she is curious to know what are William's weaknesses," Miss Grahame said. "I should think William a much more interesting subject than gigs."

"You have not seen my gig, Miss Grahame, and so you cannot tell, if I may say so."

"I have seen it. I saw it as we drove up, and a very handsome gig it is too. I congratulate you, Mr. Bonwit."

Mollified, Mr. Bonwit got off his high ropes and thanked her, whereupon she returned to the subject that consumed her. "Now what were we speaking of? Ah, yes, William's weaknesses. You are curious, are you not, Lady Rosalind?"

Rosa wished to answer no, but as she was dreadfully curious she did not answer at all. Lady Delphia came to her rescue, however, declaring, "I should like to know what you imagine his weaknesses are."

"Well, then, I will tell you. The gentleman is sentimental."

" 'Pon my word, he is not!"

"You will pardon me, I hope, for contradicting you, ma'am, but he is. He is so sentimental, in fact, that he makes it his career to be the champion of every poor unfortunate creature who comes his way."

"That bespeaks chilvalry, not sentiment," said Rosa.

"As one who has, in a manner of speaking, benefited from ths pecularity of his, you naturally feel obliged to turn his weakness into a virtue, but the truth is he melts at the least display of helplessness. He has been known to take orphans off the street and bring them into his household. Is that not so, Lady Delphia?"

"I do believe we have several superfluous footboys and maids on his account."

Rosa felt her cheeks grow warm and could not trust herself to make a civil answer.

"I give you myself, by way of example. I had once thought William my particular friend. He vowed his eternal fealty with such frequency that I began to find him tiresome. Now, it develops, he only feels sorry for me. You must not make that mistake, my lady. You must not take his charity for genuine regard."

At this, Mr. Grahame rose from his chair and endeavored to turn the conversation. "Suzanne, I'm sure you do not wish to tease your new acquaintance with your odd humor. Lady Rosalind does not know you well enough yet to know when you are joking."

"Well, that is what we were talking about—knowing William, knowing people in the general way. I hope with all my heart that Lady Rosalind and I will get to know one another better."

A pause ensued, during which Miss Grahame beamed a glittering smile at her new friend and Rosa fixed her eyes on her hoop. Then Mr. Bonwit ventured to ask Rosa, "Do you wish to see the gig now, my lady?"

Rising from the sofa, she answered, "I should like nothing better!"

After some minutes spent walking around the sturdy little gig, Mr. Bonwit induced Rosa to climb in and permit him to drive out of the square a short distance. Refreshed by the air, Rosa took advantage of a quiet moment to think. What, she kept asking herself, was Miss Grahame's purpose in making such pointed remarks about Viscount Sunley? Why did that feverish young woman .want her to think he merely pitied his newfound cousin? If Miss Grahame was in love with Lord Pomeroy, what difference did it make how Sunley felt about his cousin? And why on earth did Miss Grahame wish to tease her and wound her when she had done everything in her power to be her friend?

These questions had to be put aside for the nonce, however. Mr. Bonwit stopped the gig in front of the house and seized her hand. She expected him to kiss her fingers and was disconcerted to find him nibbling at her wrist.

"Stop that," she said.

He smirked and laughed heartily.

"Do not laugh at me, Mr. Bonwit. I am perfectly serious. You will stop nibbling my wrist this instant!"

"Shall I nibble your neck, then?"

"There will be no nibbling, sir! How dare you."

"So you say, my lady, but I know better."

"If you do, then I beg to disabuse you."

"You made your intentions perfectly clear last night, Lady Rosalind. It was I whom you singled out from among the distinguished company. Naturally, I was humbled to be so greatly exalted. I return your affection a hundred, nay, a thousand fold, my lady, and am yours to command."

"I command you to hand me out at once."

He obeyed with alacrity, then stopped dead in his tracks. Before him stood a coach of the most luxurious mahogany and glass. A signet emblazoned on the door gleamed in gold and scarlet. The coachman and footmen wore purple livery and stared ahead with blind arrogance. "Now that is a rig!" he cried in awe. All at once his face fell. He looked at his modest equipage with despair, then moodily followed Lady Rosalind inside the house.

Lord Pomeroy came forward to greet Rosa and to say, "You here too, Bonwit?"

Mr. Bonwit seemed to shrink. With his hands in his

pockets, he sulked at the window, looking out at the magnificent coach and four standing beside his little gig.

"I am come to ask you to ride out with me, Lady Rosalind," announced his lordship.

Miss Grahame answered from the sofa, "She is engaged to William this afternoon."

Pomeroy turned around, peered at Miss Grahame angrily for some time, and with a shrug, turned back to Rosa. "I should be very glad if you would say yes. I have something of a particular nature to say to you."

"Miss Grahame is correct. I am engaged." Rosa crossed the room to sit next to Miss Grahame.

"I wish to speak with you about last night. I beg you to permit me to explain," said Pomeroy.

Rosa saw the color fly from Miss Grahame's cheek.

"Another time perhaps, my lord."

"Lady Delphia, will you not plead my case for me? Your niece has taken offense at something I said to her, and she will not hear my apology."

Rosa heard Miss Grahame inhale quickly.

"You ought to hear him out, Rosalind. It is not good to carry a grudge. You have heard the expression, To err is human; to forgive Divine. Our family is referred to here, of course. The Divines are known to be a forgiving race."

Lord Pomeroy turned a victorious smile on Rosa.

"Certainly I forgive his lordship," she said. "I need no explanations. Indeed, I prefer not to hear any."

"Nonsense. You must hear them," Lady Delphia said firmly. "I insist on it. And if Lord Pomeroy wishes to drive you out, I insist you go."

"But I am engaged to my cousin."

"I assure you, he will not mind your going out."

"But Mr. Bonwit and Mr. Grahame, I should not like to leave them now, when they have been so kind as to pay me a visit."

"Very true," said her ladyship. "Well, then, they must go with you."

Lord Pomeroy's smile vanished. Miss Grahame seemed on the point of weeping. Mr. Bonwit, still dejected, gave out with a pathetic sigh. Mr. Grahame directed a look of sympathy at Rosa. And Rosa herself wished she might run up the stairs, lock herself in her bedchamber, and wrap herself in a blanket until the viscount came to fetch her.

But she had come too far for that. She was Lady Rosalind now. Her triumph at Almack's had seen to that, a triumph which, until this moment, had been perfectly sweet. Now Rosa dreaded being dragged out of George Street willy-nilly to spend the remainder of the day, not with Viscount Sunley as she had hoped, but in the company of those who vexed her.

"I have solved your difficulty, Rosalind," Lady Delphia barked. "Why do you insist upon looking so gloomy?"

"There is only one thing lacking in the scheme, Aunt Delphia. You have not said you will come, too."

"Considerate child! Of course I shall come. What a delightful party we shall make. A message will be left for Sunley. I know he will not mind."

Sir Virgil Thwaite, the renowned lawyer, who had kindly agreed to give Viscount Sunley the benefit of his advice, did not like the witness at all. He found the fellow sly. Accordingly, he pulled the Messrs. Buffel and Buffel aside to tell them so. Mr. Peter Buffel, brushing a smudge of dust from his lapel, agreed that the man was certainly not a gentleman, to which Sir Virgil replied that he did not see how he dared to bring such a witness before the bench. Mr. Paul Buffel then invited the viscount into the private chamber to give him their opinion. Sunley had to agree that the witness's bombastic style cast doubt on his testimony. At the same time, he reminded them, Tripple was the adopted parent and was in a greater position to forward the case than any other witness.

"Except, perhaps, the nursemaid," said Sir Virgil.

"Ah, there was a nursemaid in the case, was there?" remarked Mr. Peter.

"I've hunted for her all over London," Sunley said.

"Mr. Buffel has put a man on it to locate her, haven't you, Peter?"

"If you say so, Sir Virgil."

"It is imperative we find her," declared Mr. Paul. "It is hardly likely the court will believe Mr. Tripple without corroboration."

Sunley remained hopeful, having, in his view, no other choice. "Perhaps Mr. Tripple does have something to say something to the purpose," he suggested. "Perhaps it is only a matter of patience."

The gentlemen returned to the outer chamber, where Tripple sat by a table, idly drawing circles in the dust. He grinned as the four approached and brushed his hands together to cleanse them.

On seeing them, he declared, "Now let us make our case, good sirs; I beg you will not delay further. My poor Rosalind merits justice. 'For as I urge justice, so shall we have justice.' I have taken some liberties with the allusion here, but you catch my drift."

"I regret to inform you, Mr. Tripple, that we find your testimony inconclusive," said Sir Virgil. "And if we find it so, you have only to imagine how the court will find it."

"What more do you require? I shall say anything you tell me to say."

"We do not propose to fabricate testimony for you," said Sir Virgil with distaste. "But we require more than your rambling recollections."

"What more?"

"We require nothing less than solid evidence connecting this young woman with Beckwith and his bride. So far you've given us nothing but a sorrowful tale."

Here Tripple grinned again. "Solid evidence, is it? Why, there is nothing easier!"

Mr. Paul Buffel interjected here, "If you know anything, you must tell us now."

"Well, there is a locket." He looked into each face as though their expressions of skepticism ought now to vanish.

"What sort of locket?" Sir Virgil asked.

"A very pretty sort. It contains a portrait inside, of a young man, a young man who looks a good deal like this gentleman." He shot out his arm, at the end of which a knobby finger pointed at Viscount Sunley.

All eyes turned on the young gentleman.

"Proceed," invited Sir Virgil.

"The front of the locket contains a monogram—a *B*, as

luck would have it. It is full of curlicues and leaves and such. And on the back of the locket, there is an inscription."

"What does it say?"

"Now, I must think a moment. I want to be sure and get it exactly right. It says, 'To my dearest Eliza. Beckwith.' I believe that is correct."

"This is excellent!" cried Mr. Paul Buffel. "Where did you find this locket?"

"Why Rosa was wearing it when I found her. She used to suck on it until I was forced to take it away. She nearly broke a tooth on it."

Sir Virgil nodded his head. "I believe we have what we've been looking for. Very well, Mr. Tripple, we will accept your evidence. When can you bring us this locket?"

"Bring it? I cannot bring it."

"Well, then, we shall send someone to fetch it. Where is it?"

"Goodness knows. I pawned it years ago."

"You pawned a locket that was not yours?"

"I only did it to feed the child. She was too young to sing for her supper then."

"You pawned the only piece of evidence?"

"If I had known it would turn out to be evidence, I daresay I should not have pawned it."

"Do you have the ticket, Mr. Tripple?" Sunley asked.

"I shouldn't think so. Do any of you fine gentlemen continue to hold tickets for the things you pawned more than a dozen years ago?"

Screwing up his face in thought, Mr. Peter replied, "I believe I may have saved one or two."

Dejected, Mr. Paul asked, "What are we to do, alas?" to which Mr. Tripple answered, "Do not distress yourselves, gentlemen. I shall swear to the locket's existence. I shall swear it was real gold, too, which I warrant it was. And I shall swear that it proves my little Rosa is entitled to the ninety thousand and all the rest of it."

He sat back in his chair, pleased with himself, and waited for the others to replace the black frowns on their faces with grins.

But the frowns remained, as though etched on the worried

faces with acid and ink. When it was brought home to Mr. Tripple that the story of the locket would not fadge without the locket itself, he wept and confessed that there had also been a ring. It had been found on Rosa's person along with the locket, he sniffed, wiping his nose with his hand. In fact, it had hung from the very chain which had held the locket. And it, too, had borne an inscription, the very letters contained on the lost locket. Unfortunately, he could not produce the ring any more than he could produce the locket, because it, too, had been pawned.

As the implications of these revelations penetrated the old actor's brain, his air of confidence dissolved utterly in sobs. He then proceeded to contribute more than his substantial share to the general gloom. "What are we to do?" he cried to the viscount. "My poor dear Rosa is surely lost."

Sunley could not invent a reply that was encouraging. He, therefore, kept his peace. It did strike him, however, that Tripple had unexpectedly betrayed a note of real sorrow for the young woman in question. It was not the money he had mourned the loss of; he'd said only that Rosa was lost. Clearly Tripple cherished a germ of sentiment somewhere in that mercenary heart of his.

But there was little comfort in knowing that, for, Sunley feared, Tripple was right—their poor dear Rosa was about as lost as it was possible to be.

◊ **Ten** ◊

Sunley did not go inside when Nunn opened the door. He stood on the step, thinking.

"May I take your hat, my lord?" Nunn inquired tactfully.

Recalled to the present, the viscount went into the hall and handed the butler his beaver. "I am glad you have come back to us, Nunn," he said. "Lady Delphia was wise to ask you to return."

"Her ladyship did not ask me, sir. Her ladyship isn't speaking to me."

"Of course. By the way, who did ask you?"

"Lord Divine. He delivers all her ladyship's commands to me now."

"Nunn, you have the patience of Job."

"Yes, sir."

Closeting himself in the library, Sunley sat down to think again, and the more he thought, the more convinced he grew that every way one looked at it, the case was disastrous. Instead of providing testimony implying Rosalind's right to the inheritance, Tripple cast doubt on the claim; so much so, in fact, that the only sensible course now was to withdraw.

Looking back, he saw that he had been foolish to set Rosa up as Beckwith's daughter. He had been precipitate and rash to bring her forward publicly before the actual testimony had been secured in private. He ought to have waited until the nursemaid had sworn her oath in court and the judge had declared Rosa the bona fide heiress. He ought to have waited before allowing his aunt and father to present her to the world as Lady Rosalind. In point of fact, he ought never to have lied to them about her in the first place.

But perhaps it was not too late to put everything right. He might confess the whole and take the consequences, not the least of which included the icy silence of his aunt, the heartbreaking sorrow of his father, and the censure of the world. But once he'd done the deed, and a considerable time was allowed to elapse, the worst would be over and even his aunt would speak to him again. All he had to do was send Tripple and the girl away, then lie low until the ugliest hour of humiliation was past. Afterward he would return to his life as it was before.

But what sort of life would he return to? Dangling after Miss Grahame, who cared no more for him than for the puppy that chased her carriage through the streets? Living in his aunt's house, exposed to constant reminders of the family's near proverty and loss of dignity? Watching his father grow worn and oppressed with care?

No, he could not turn back now; things had gone too far. His father would refuse to send Rosa away. He had grown inordinately fond of her in the short time of their acquaintance. He liked her singing, her forthrightness, and her refusal to cower before Lady Delphia.

And Sunley could understand his father's fondness for the girl. For an actress, she was remarkably free of artfulness. One could easily like her. If Sunley should suggest sending her away, Lord Divine would point out—and he would be right—that Tripple had no means of supporting her now that he had left the company of traveling players. His father would tremble at the thought of what lay in store for Rosa if she tried to support herself as an actress. Such women generally became some rich man's bird of paradise in order to survive. Lord Divine would not permit Rosa to enter into that sort of life, even if he did learn that she was not the daughter of his noble cousin. Indeed, Sunley did not see how he could permit it himself.

It would be cruel to send her back to her former life. She had gone along with the scheme in good faith. She had triumphed at Almack's, playing her part with all the hoped-for success. He was the one who had failed, not she. Why should she have to suffer because he let the witness get away? Moreover, he liked having her here. Why should he send her away just when their friendship seemed to be blossoming apace?

On the other hand, it was probably a kindness to let her go. The real cruelty was to keep her here. Once her true identity became known, she would be forced to submit to the contempt of his aunt, the pity of his father, and the scorn of the world which had lauded her. Clearly, the best thing for Rosa was to return to her former life, where she had begged to stay in the first place.

The best thing for him, of course, was to resign himself to the world as it was—a world in which bequests accrued interest to the benefit of the courts instead of the beneficiaries, a world in which witnesses swore to stand up for you one minute and the next they vanished into the air, a world in which a young lady could cling to your love one minute and carelessly toss it away the next.

Yes, it was kinder to let Rosa go, and that is what he would do. Of course, he would do it gently. His gentleness seemed always to rouse a like feeling in her. And he would do it gradually. She did not need to leave right away, and when she did leave, he would visit her from time to time with his father and they would see to her welfare. And he would tell her today, at Spring Gardens, as they looked at the pretty pictures and strolled the pretty park, so that she might prepare herself.

Having thus decided, he bade the footboy tell Lady Rosalind he was ready to take her to the gardens. Minutes later the boy returned to say that Lady Rosalind had already gone out. Surprised, Sunley sent for Nunn, from whom he learned that her young ladyship had ridden out in Lord Pomeroy's coach, accompanied by a large and merry party. She had not said when she expected to return. No, Lady Rosalind had not left a message for him, but Lady Delphia had. The message read: "Sunley, we have gone out."

After the butler closed the door softly behind him, the viscount poured himself a glass of Madeira from a decanter. Leaning against the mantelpiece, he sipped the wine, then held up the goblet to examine its color in the gray light. When he finished the draft, he swore an oath, spun around, and flung the glass into the fire, shattering it to splinters.

Rosa's ordeal began as she waited to be handed into Lord Pomeroy's carriage. Mr. Bonwit, not content with nibbling her fingertips, progressed to her ear. When her snubs failed to stay his traveling lips, she was forced to slap his cheek with her bare hand, an act of violence which caused her much shame because she enjoyed it excessively. Seizing the hand which had just left five red welts on his face, the tulip kissed it and implored the heavens to let it be his throughout eternity. He might have continued to bedevil Rosa in this manner if Lady Delphia had not poked the young man's chest with her forefinger and conferred upon him the honor of driving her in his gig to Marylebone Park.

When the party at last alighted, Mr. Bonwit flew to Rosa's side and would attend to none of the others. Variously, Mr. Grahame, Lady Delphia, and Miss Grahame walked on her right side; Mr. Bonwit adhered to the left like a shadow. At every opportunity, he whispered endearments in her ear. Finally he breathed that he would, with her permission, announce their engagement.

So incensed was Rosa at this impertinence that she cried out. Hearing her exclamation, Lord Pomeroy, who walked just ahead with Lady Delphia, stopped in front of Bonwit and warned the man to take himself off or be sorry for it. Aware of Pomeroy's reputation as an accomplished duelist, Bonwit did not stay to argue the matter. With a self-righteous air, he marched forward to join her ladyship, only looking back once to throw Rosa a delicate kiss.

Lord Pomeroy walked silently by Rosa's side for some time, until finally she snapped, "Have you nothing to say for yourself, sir?"

"I do not wish to irritate you by speaking. I believe you said earlier you did not wish to hear me speak."

"I wish Mr. Bonwit would heed me as well as you do."

"Do not distress yourself over Mr. Bonwit. I shall make short work of him, I promise."

"You will do no such thing, my lord. Any short work to be made I shall make myself."

"Yes, I believe you will."

They were silent again until Rosa thought to observe, "Why are you suddenly gallant, *monsieur*? I vow, I do not like your being so contrite."

"Do you prefer me rude, then?"

"I do, indeed. If you continue this way, I shall be forced to think better of you, and I do not wish to think better of you."

"Whatever I do, it seems, will put me in your black books."

"You have been in my black books almost from the moment I set eyes on you."

He colored. "I wish you would not dislike me. I like you very much."

"You, sir, are not a gentleman. I heard what passed between you and Miss Grahame at Almack's."

His thin face grew stormy. "You do not understand. If I sounded to you like a villain it is because she drives me to it."

"She is unwise, sir, but that need not make you so. In fact, if she cannot be prudent, it is even more incumbent upon you to be courteous."

He stopped and regarded her. "I do not hold my temper

easily. When anyone—woman or man—demands that I act and say and feel a certain way, I am likely to balk. I have done it all my life."

"Nevertheless it is wrong."

"I suppose it is."

"You must endeavor to curb your temper."

"Yes, I suppose I must."

"Oh, Lord Pomeroy! Do not say so!"

"I am sorry if I have distressed you again."

"If you are going to take my advice so readily, I shall be forced to like you."

"That is my plan, Lady Rosalind. I hope to make you like me, and I hope to profit by your advice."

"Even if you have to mend your manners?"

"I am prepared to go to any lengths."

"You will not end by sounding like Mr. Bonwit, I hope."

"I would do anything to avoid sounding like such a fop, but I must allow, in his preference for you, Mr. Bonwit shows great discernment."

Rosa silently prayed that this politeness would not culminate in any nibbling.

"You are the gentlest woman I have ever met," Lord Pomeroy said warmly. "Your kindness to Miss Grahame, your dislike of me on her account, your tact, your graciousness—indeed, I do not know when I have met a lady of your quality before."

Rosa colored bright red at this. "You flatter me, sir. You make me out something I am not."

"At the risk of sounding ill-mannered, I must differ with you. I have lived in London all my life and never, until now, have I met with a female who shows such a ready sympathy, such a willingness to defend the troubled, such a genuine disregard for the impression she may be making on others, a female, in short, whom I could truthfully call a lady."

Rosa's heart beat in her ears, and she could not look him in the eye. "You will excuse me, my lord. I must attend to Mr. and Miss Grahame. I should not like them to think I neglect them."

Pomeroy smiled an ingratiating smile. "And you are modest, too."

She hurried ahead to catch up with the Grahames, thinking that Lord Pomeroy could not have chosen a better method of defending himself to her than the one he had just employed, namely, not defending himself at all. It had been the work of a moment to resist his flattery and his sudden contrition. But there was a note of sincerity in his tone which persuaded her that he might not have all the evil on his side, and that Miss Grahame did not have all the good.

With Mr. Grahame on one arm and his niece on the other, she strolled at a leisurely pace, allowing the gentleman to point out statuary here and there along the path. She admired several Greek gods in athletic postures and varying degrees of undress until Miss Grahame demanded to know, "What has Pomeroy been telling you, Lady Rosalind? Whatever it was, I hope you did not believe it."

"Suzanne!" her uncle remonstrated.

Ignoring him, Miss Grahame went on, "Lord Pomeroy is wonderfully charming when he proposes to insinuate himself into a lady's favor. But beware, my lady. When he tires of her, he is abominable."

"I consider myself duly warned," Rosa replied. "I thank you for trying to save me from making a mistake."

"That was not my intention," Miss Grahame said. "I do not care a jot whether you make a mistake. I care only that you not allow yourself to be much in company with his lordship."

On that, she turned around and waited for Pomeroy to catch up with her. Mr. Grahame and Rosa watched as his lordship turned down a side path to avoid her, and they continued to watch as Miss Grahame made fists of her hands and ran to follow him.

"I will not bother to apologize for my niece," Mr. Grahame said. "I know I can rely on your kindness to forgive her and place the blame where it belongs." He offered her his arm so that they might continue their walk.

"Please do not give me compliments, Mr. Grahame. I have had a surfeit today."

"Very well, I shall refrain. But do not ask me to insult you, Lady Rosalind, for I cannot do it."

"Can you speak of the weather?"

"Not very intelligibly. But I know something of Viscount

Sunley, with whom you were engaged to ride out this afternoon."

"Ah, I wish you would not remind me of it. He will think I deliberately ignored his invitation. I don't know how I shall face him."

"May an old man offer you advice?"

"An old man may not, but you may."

"My wife and I began as the most loving and agreeable pair in all the world. We had only one fault—we never spoke to one another—about anything important, that is. I believe we felt it was impolite to address matters of moment, and from that stemmed all our years of unhappiness. Take a lesson from my pitiful error, Lady Rosalind. When you return to George Street, do not let a minute go by without explaining the circumstances which took you here against your will. Tell him everything."

"What do you think he will do?"

"I know what I would do."

"Will he be very angry, do you think?"

"Perhaps it is as Lady Delphia says; perhaps he will not mind at all."

"Mr. Grahame, I do not know which I dread more—his anger or his not minding."

Lady Delphia followed Rosa into the hall, where Nunn was permitted to receive her bonnet.

"Are you well, Rosalind?" her ladyship inquired. "You look horrid. The morning air ought to have given you more color."

"I shall be fine as soon as I have seen my cousin."

"Before you do that, please ask Nunn to tell cook we will dine early this evening."

Rosa turned to Nunn, who stood stiff as a ramrod by the door. "Nunn, you heard her ladyship?"

"Yes, ma'am."

"And Rosalind, tell Nunn that the silver in the drawing room is tarnished."

"You heard her, Nunn?"

"Yes. I shall see to it."

"One more thing, Rosalind. Have Nunn tell Sunley that his father dines at his club tonight."

"Where is Viscount Sunley, Nunn?"

"In the library, Lady Rosalind."

"Will you ask him if I may have a moment with him?"

"Certainly." The butler bowed and walked a few steps down the hall.

Without thinking, Lady Delphia called after him, "Tell him Lord Divine will not sup with us."

Nunn stopped in his tracks. He looked round to peer at his mistress, who had clapped her hand over her mouth as soon as she realized what she had done.

"You did not hear that, Nunn," Lady Delphia said.

"No, ma'am."

"I am not speaking to you."

Throughout this exchange, the butler tactfully refrained from changing his expression, apart from a small gleam in his eye. "Yes, ma'am," was all he said and then marched forth to the library.

On his return, he found Rosa alone in the parlor, anxiously awaiting a reply.

"His lordship sends his felicitations to Lady Rosalind and hopes her outing was pleasant. He is occupied just now and regrets he is unable to entertain her ladyship in the library."

So saying, Nunn made as if to leave the room. Rosa called him back. "Nunn, please tell Viscount Sunley that I must speak with him. It is urgent."

Nunn blinked, then moved off to deliver the message. He returned moments later to say, "His lordship is excessively sorry, but he is still occupied."

Brushing past him, Rosa hastened to the library. She knocked on the door and called out, "You must let me explain. Please, my lord!"

She put her ear against the door but heard no sound.

"I shall count to ten," she announced in a voice calculated to penetrate the gallery of the grandest theater.

Slowly she counted. At three, Nunn poked his head round a pillar. At six, she waved him away. At nine, she took a deep breath. And at ten, she burst in the door.

Sunley stood by a tall shelf of books. His back was to her.

Standing in the open doorway, Rosa recited the speech she had rehearsed: "My lord, your aunt insisted I go out. I told her

I was engaged to you but she said you would not mind. And Miss Grahame agreed. She said she knew you better than anyone else in the world and would take her oath that you would not mind."

He turned around, smiling. "But, as you see, I did mind."

"Thank heaven."

"That pleases you, does it? Well, then, it should give you enormous pleasure to know that I broke a goblet on your account."

"Oh, yes, that is very pleasant. Thank you."

He came near to her. "Rosa."

"Yes?"

"Is it too late, do you think, to go to Spring Gardens?"

◊ Eleven ◊

Although the early afternoon sun had abated and gray clouds bulged in the sky, the journey to Pimlico proved a delight. Viscount Sunley had had the top rolled down on the curricle and he drove at a leisurely pace. Along the way he explained Mr. Nash's plan for the new Regent's Park. When Rosa asked if he would take her there when it was finished, he paled and grew silent.

Upon their arrival at the gardens, he led Rosa past a trio of musicians to the fountain. There she sat on the marble at the water's edge, trailing her hand under the spray and looking at the spacious grounds. Before entering the exhibition hall, the viscount warned her not to expect to view any of the works of Sir Joshua Reynolds or paintings of a similar quality. As Rosa had never attended an exhibition at all, she was able to assure him that she would not level too critical an eye at the works.

Inside the hall, they bent their concentration on a crowded array of pictures mounted so closely together on the walls that they could hardly distinguish one from the other. Their tastes were similar, they found; both preferred fruit and flowers to raging seas and meandering streams. Best of all, they liked portraiture. One portrait in particular, which hung in a small room off the main hall, arrested their attention. It was a study of a young woman looking almost ghostly with sorrow. As the painting seemed to act powerfully on the viscount, Rosa refrained from remarking on its resemblance to Miss Grahame.

Outside again, they found an ice vendor and a small tent under which to eat their cool refreshment. Owing to the weather and the lateness of the hour, most of the visitors had already left the gardens. Alone under the canopy, Rosa and Sunley watched a light drizzle fall, making a haze of the trees and lawn.

"It looks like one of the paintings," Rosa observed.

"Yes. Did you mark the lady who looked like Miss Grahame?"

"It did not look so very much like her. The hair was not yellow enough."

"Oh, but the expression. It was Suzanne to the very life— so pale and helpless, so despairing in the eyes."

"It is possible, you know, that Miss Grahame is not so very helpless as she seems."

Sunley regarded her thoughtfully as he held his ice.

Coloring under his stare, Rosa ventured to explain, "I'm afraid Miss Grahame is not always careful of her own interests."

The viscount looked severe. "It is Pomeroy's influence. She did not used to be headstrong."

"The fault cannot be laid entirely at Lord Pomeroy's door, I think. She may have acted imprudently."

"I suppose Pomeroy told you that. How charming of him to blame the lady in the case."

"Yes, he did say something, but even if he hadn't, I have witnessed enough of what passes between them to know it for myself."

"How long have you been in Pomeroy's confidence? I understood you to say you did not like him."

"I like him better after today. At least I understand him better."

"I see. And now you are ready to take his part against Miss

Grahame, about whom you know nothing. Let me tell you, Rosa, you would be wise to defer judgment until you have known Lord Pomeroy more than two days. As it happens, I know Miss Grahame my entire life."

"I shall remember your wise words of caution, my lord. In your turn, you would be wise to admit to a certain partiality for those whom you have known your entire life."

"I believe I am as objective as the next fellow."

"More objective, I would guess, except where Miss Grahame is concerned."

Finishing his ice, he set the cup on a wooden table with a loud noise. Then he scowled at the rain. "I warrant I am as objective about Miss Grahame as you are about Lord Pomeroy."

"I must disagree with you there, for I am not in love with Lord Pomeroy."

This caught him up short only for a moment. "I am glad to hear it. He is a blackguard."

Rosa waited for him to say more, but he did not add anything to that pronouncement. She stood next to him, staring as he did at the rain until the silence grew intolerable. Stealing a look at his profile, she declared her intention of going back to the exhibition hall.

"You will get soaked through," Sunley objected.

"Nothing appeals to me more at this moment than a good dousing." So saying, she lifted her skirts and ran through the shower to the exhibition hall.

Pushing open the door, she paused in the entrance until she caught her breath. Her shoes were brown with mud. Her cloak fulfilled Sunley's prophecy that she would be soaked through.

The viscount came up behind her. He took her hand and led her into a small room filled with paintings. "Come, it is warm in here."

"Yes, it is," said Rosa, her teeth beginning to chatter. She shivered and looked up to see Miss Grahame's likeness peering down at her.

"You are cold," he said.

"Where has everybody gone? There is no one here but the two of us and Miss Grahame."

Sunley looked briefly at the portrait. Then, hearing Rosa's

teeth chatter, he removed her cloak and wrapped his own around her. "You are right," he said. "It does not look as much like Suzanne as I thought."

Rosa huddled inside the cloak and endeavored to master control of her teeth. "A few moments ago, I implied that you were in love with Miss Grahame. You did not deny it."

"No, I did not. I could not."

"Oh."

"The truth is, I don't know how I feel about her."

Rosa gazed at the portrait, and when she was sure Sunley was not looking, she made an ugly face at it.

"I certainly don't feel toward her as I once did."

Rosa clenched her teeth to stop the chattering.

"I am not sure I would want to marry her now."

Inhaling, Rosa began to feel a little warmed.

"I want to continue to be her friend. I want her to know she can rely on me anytime and for whatever reason."

The sound of chattering teeth echoed round the hall once more.

"But I do not want to fawn on a woman who is in love with another man."

"You want a great deal," Rosa said with a shudder.

He looked at her and moved closer. "A very great deal," he said, slipping his hands under the cloak and around her waist. Pressing her to him, he softly brushed her lips a dozen or so times with his. Then he looked at her as though a new idea had occurred to him. "Perhaps I am beginning to know what I want," he said, kissing her a long time.

Rosa, who had known all along exactly what she wanted, caressed his face with her hands. After some minutes spent in this manner, she concluded that the viscount's kisses were the best cure she knew for an aching heart and chattering teeth.

As the top had not been put up, the curricle had gotten wet in the rain. Sunley found a boy at the exhibition hall to wipe up the puddles on the seat and do what he could for the horses. When all was in order, they set forth for Hanover Square under an uncertain sky. Clouds and sunlight teased one another, as though playing a game of tag, but at last the sun prevailed. Rosa felt the rays penetrate her chilled skin and make her sleepy with their warmth. Sitting by the viscount's side, watching his hands expertly start the horses forward, she thought she had never been so content in her life. The ever-strengthening sunlight nurtured her happiness like a rosebud. Unaccountably the sunnier the sky grew, the gloomier the expression on Sunley's face.

She watched him closely as he stared straight ahead at the road, deep in thought. By the time they reached George Street, he looked so stern that Rosa felt certain he had repented of his kisses. Silently he handed her out of the curricle and followed her into the house. Silently he accompanied her into the parlor and poured her a glass of hock. When she came close to take the glass, she put her hand gently on his. Silently he withdrew it. Sitting down, he gazed at the sunbeams pouring in the window. Unable to swallow, Rosa put down the glass untouched.

"Tripple told some story of a locket," he said. "I don't suppose you remember anything about it."

"Yes, I did wear a locket for some time. It was much too handsome for a little beggar girl to be wearing, and I used to bite on it."

"Was there a portrait inside?"

"Yes, a very handsome gentleman, if I recall."

"And a *B* inscribed on the front?"

"I'm not sure—there were flowers, though."

"Where is that locket now? By any chance, do you have it or know where it can be found?"

"It was so many years ago. Perhaps Tripple sold it. We were always selling whatever we could put our hands on in order to eat. That was before I learned to pick pockets."

The ensuing quiet put Rosa in mind of the rain that had chilled her blood earlier in the day. She would have given much to know how to approach Sunley now. He seemed distant, rigid. If Mr. Grahame had offered her advice at this moment, she would have accepted it gladly.

"We have to give up the charade," he said at last.

She sat down opposite him. "Very well," she said, having no idea what she was agreeing to but hoping her willingness would smooth the tension in his forehead.

Looking at the carpet, he said, "There is no use going on

with it. The nursemaid cannot be found and Tripple will not do."

"I am sorry. Will you be very poor?"

"Yes, very."

"Lady Delphia will be unhappy. I hope she will not think I failed the family. You have all been so kind to me, as much as any family I have ever known."

Sunley looked at her. "But you never wanted to come here from the first. You wanted to stay with Tripple, and with your company of players."

"Yes, I did, but I am glad you persuaded me otherwise."

"Nevertheless, it was wrong of me to take you away from your home. I did not even do you the courtesy of asking permission."

"Ask it now and I will give it to you, with all my heart."

He closed his eyes. "You cannot stay, Rosa. You have to go back."

She tried to absorb this.

"I am sorry," he said.

"I can't go back now. I can never go back."

"I realize you've known certain comforts here which you were unused to before, and I will not pretend they are meaningless. But you are hardy and will not let the absence of luxuries depress your spirits for very long."

She stood up and said angrily, "I spit on your comforts!"

He rose, too, and as he watched her pace in front of the sofa, he said, "Do not for a moment think you are being sent away in disgrace. If there is any disgrace, it is all mine. I should not have taken you from the playhouse. I should not have set you up as Lady Rosalind. I should not have kissed you. I had no right."

Rosa stared at him. In her happiness, it had not occurred to her that their kisses might be wrong, that it was a disgrace for a nobleman to kiss a pickpocket. Now he mentioned it, however, she saw it was so. It was one thing for a titled gentleman to be a liar and a thief, quite another for a nameless beggar found outside a workhouse. The titled thief could no more love the poor one than the onion could smell like a rose.

Rosa's emotion fairly crackled. She felt ashamed.

"It will be better for you. You will see. Just now it may

seem hard. And it is hard. But when the truth is brought to light, it would be better if you were out of the reach of my aunt's tongue and the world's scorn."

This allusion to Lady Delphia shook Rosa. It appeared that she was to lose everything with the snap of a finger. Her triumph at Almack's counted for nothing. Her convincing portrayal of the Beckwith heiress was wasted time and effort. And as for loving Viscount Sunley—that was merely more of the same.

"What funds we have, we will share with you and Tripple. You have, after all, done everything you were asked to do. It would be wrong of us to send you away empty-handed."

"Yes, you ought to pay, and pay handsomely!" She crossed to where he stood so that he was forced to face her. "It ought to cost you dearly to have us off your conscience."

"I will never have you off my conscience."

"I am glad to hear it, and with your kind permission I will add that you will live to regret this." She thrust her angry face close to his.

"It is true. I regret it already." He leaned forward and she caught her breath. It almost seemed as though he meant to touch her.

"Very well. Go ahead and marry your Miss Grahame. Try and lock her up against Pomeroy. Much good it will do you."

"Miss Grahame? What has she got to do with anything?"

With a proud turn of her chin, Rosa swept to the door. "Pray, will you be so kind as to allow me to borrow a dress before I leave the house? As you may recall, Lady Delphia had mine burned."

"We are not barbarians, Rosa. We do not mean to turn you naked into the streets."

"It will not take me long to pack my belongings, as I have none. When shall I be ready?" She stared at the brass door pull as though she intended to yank it out.

"I don't know."

"I should think you would want me to leave as soon as possible."

"That would be best, I suppose, but I have made no arrangements as yet."

"Well, then, perhaps it would be best if I simply went of my own accord."

"No. You will do no such thing."

"And why not? If I am to go, why am I not to decide when and where and how?"

Sunley did not answer immediately. At last he said in a low voice, "You would not go without saying good-bye to my father? Please wait until I have spoken to him. I will let you know as soon as it's done. If you leave before I have explained the matter to him, I'm afraid it would quite literally break his heart."

At the moment, Rosa cared nothing for Lord Divine's heart, but there was that in Sunley's voice which stilled her protest.

Inhaling deeply, she said, "Very well, I will refrain from breaking his heart." Then, suspecting her own was on the verge of cracking, she escaped from the room.

◊ Twelve ◊

Rosa waited in her bedchamber all morning. By noon, there was still no word from the viscount regarding her departure. She took her luncheon on a tray in her room, fully expecting a note from him at any second. She heard nothing, however. At last, a knock on the door before dinner promised to answer her anxious anticipation. The timid housemaid at the door handed her a note. It was from Lady Delphia and summoned Rosa to the dining room at once.

Candelabra and chandeliers brilliantly lit the room. As soon as Rosa entered it, she saw the highly polished table set for three. Viscount Sunley was absent, his chair as empty as a beggar's purse.

Lord Divine greeted her with his customary kindness, showing no sign whatever of having been told any alarming truths concerning her identity. Lady Delphia complained of her neglect, saying, "First Sunley deserts us, then you. If you mean to keep to your room, my brother and I will be reduced to talking to each other."

"I am sure we should find some entertainment in one another's conversation," said Lord Divine, "if only we took the trouble to look for it."

"You are wrong, brother, as usual. We discovered at an early age that we had nothing in common, for you always liked the country while I preferred the town, and you liked climbing trees and falling into mischief, while I preferred pursuits of the intellect. I am sure that maturity has served only to widen the chasm which yawns between us."

Lord Divine sighed heavily.

"Sit down, Rosalind, and please contrive to smile a little. Brother, you may tell Nunn to serve up the dinner."

The meal—a ragout of beef with pudding—was the first of many shared by the three of them together. A full week passed without any of them so much as setting eyes on Viscount Sunley, and at the end of the time, Rosa allowed herself to relax somewhat. She wondered why the gentleman did not get on with the business of her removal from his aunt's house, but, grateful for every moment she was allowed to stay, she did not dwell on the question. It did occur to her that the longer she stayed, the more difficult her departure would be, but she did not let herself dwell on that, either.

Lady Sefton called a number of times to hear the ditty about the corn rigs and barley rigs. Her ladyship went so far as to press Rosa's hand in hers and confess the tune recalled her very first beau, a soldier who chanted Scottish airs to her and nearly convinced her to elope. Not content with concerts and confidences, her ladyship took Rosa with her on numerous morning visits, one of which was made to Carlton House, where Rosa was presented to the prince. Wherever Lady Sefton introduced her, Lady Rosalind Divine was ogled, fawned over, and pronounced the prettiest-behaved young maiden of the season.

Lord Divine, perceiving Rosa's unusual lowness of spirits, determined to cheer her. He bought her a mare, which she knew was dreadfully expensive but which she knew not how to refuse, and he took her to the park each morning at six to teach her to ride. When this gift did not restore the bloom to her cheeks, he took her to the subscription library, whence she emerged with several novels about lovesick females. He even took her to visit the Grahames in hopes that their company would elicit a smile. Escorting her home again, he was forced to admit that even half an hour spent with the delightful Suzanne did not revive the poor girl.

Lady Delphia did her part to enliven her niece. She took her to the Italian opera and informed her which were the singers and songs she might safely admire. She refrained from conveying her messages to Nunn through Rosa. And she invited Mr. Tripple to tea, in the hope that such condescension on her part would jolt Rosa out of her dejection. As it developed, Mr. Tripple and Lady Delphia spent the hour conducting a lively discussion on the Elizabethan drama, and specifically examining the question of whether Shakespeare might be counted as one of the ancients or as one of the moderns. Leaving them to solve the contention themselves, Rosa crept quietly away to her bedchamber, wondering for the hundredth time if she would ever set eyes on the viscount—or his message. She dreaded both; yet she would have given much to catch a glimpse of his fine profile in the corridor or on the staircase.

Another week passed without Sunley's showing his profile in George Street. His popularity with his acquaintance suddenly exceeded all bounds. He felt obliged to accept an invitation to stay with an acquaintance in St. James's, then another in Belgravia, and when he tired of that, he slept in a chair at Waiter's. He frequented a gambling house, where he forgot to place his wagers unless his companions exhorted him to stop moping about like a rain cloud. He accompanied a merry group of gentlemen to a mill outside of Hornchurch, where he was privileged to meet the great boxer Mendoza, but even that did not eradicate the grave expression from his face. No manner of diversion, in fact, succeeded in doing that, for whatever Sunley was engaged in at the moment, his thoughts were always on Rosa—Rosa and his need to act soon, Rosa and his abominable inaction, Rosa and her future, Rosa and her blanket—always Rosa.

Such thoughts were filling his mind one evening as he strolled in Piccadilly, hands behind him, head bent low. A familiar voice called out to him, startling him out of his brown study.

"Your lordship!" Tripple greeted him heartily. "I have not seen you for ages. I'm afraid we 'fleet the time carelessly,' as the poet says."

"As there is no further need for us to meet at Lincoln's Inn, I see no reason why we should expect to meet at all."

"But I have been to your house on a number of occasions —your aunt's house, that is. (It was kind of her to take you and your father in after your money was squandered away.) Now I think on it, you have not been there once in all my visits."

"Business takes me out a good deal these days."

"Beware of business, sir. It saps a man's vitality. Why, look at you. Lear himself after the storm looked more robust than you do."

"Thank you. And now I bid you good evening."

Before he could leave, Tripple caught him by the sleeve. "No, no, my lord. We must do something about you."

"I am afraid I am quite hopeless, Mr. Tripple."

"Perhaps so. You look almost as peaked as poor Rosa. I daresay, the two of you contracted colds at Spring Gardens. The girl told me all about it."

"All?"

"Well, that you were caught in the rain and got wet through."

"She said nothing else?"

"I recall nothing else."

"Then good evening to you, Mr. Tripple."

"Wait! I have the perfect remedy. We will go to a play. Now, what do you think of that?"

"Not a great deal, to tell the truth."

"Nonsense. There is a performance of *Tom Thumb* in Covent Garden and I am longing to see it. I will permit you to buy me a ticket. It will cheer us both."

So to *Tom Thumb* they went, and not once did Sunley laugh. Little Tom's cries of "Oh, Huncamunca, Huncamunca, oh!" sounded merely forlorn and piteous in his ears.

At the end of the fifth act, as the gentlemen filed from the playhouse, Tripple scolded him for his insensibility. "Odds fish, man! I should think you would have sniggered a bit, especially at the end, with all those corpses littered about."

"It was very amusing, really."

"Perhaps it was the lead actor. He lacked subtlety, I think. His gestures were overdone, which will always spoil a comedy. Perhaps I will go in and give him a private word in his ear about it. I expect he will be grateful."

"Then good night to you, Mr. Tripple."

"Hold! Not so fast. One more word, sir. Where are you bound? You will pardon my interference, I know."

"I do not see that it is any business of yours."

"I am impertinent—I allow it completely. I merely want to say, I hope you will not go to George Street."

"And just where do you suggest that I go?"

Tripple lowered his voice in a conspiratorial manner and whispered, "To visit a lady."

"What lady?"

Tripple rolled his eyeballs and affixed a look full of meaning to his face. "Any lady."

"It is a lady who put me in this state to begin with."

"Well, do not see that lady. See another lady."

"At this hour?"

"You are young, sir, young and frisky. At least you ought to be frisky. I, who have nearly twice your years, am still frisky, and so should you be, too."

Sunley smiled for the first time in eons. "Yes, I should, shouldn't I?" he said.

"I mean to see a lady myself this evening."

"Well, then, I will not keep you, Mr. Tripple. I will be off and I will endeavor to be frisky, on your recommendation."

The viscount apologized for the lateness of the hour.

"No matter, sir," Crouch replied. "Lord Pomeroy used to call at this hour quite frequently."

"He does not call any longer?"

"No, sir. Not for some time."

"Is Miss Grahame still awake?"

"Oh, Miss Grahame never sleeps."

Sunley followed Crouch to a sitting room, where a fire blazed and where Miss Grahame paced before it with a shawl pulled tightly around her. She started violently when a visitor was announced. Then, seeing who it was, her face fell.

He noted Miss Grahame's look of disappointment and nearly turned on his heel and walked out again. Then, taking a few steps inside, Sunley noted the many books lying open and unread about the chairs and tables. It occurred to him that she had lacked concentration enough to finish any of the books, and his initial irritation with her turned to something softer.

"You are up late, William."

"No later than you are."

"Then there's a pair of us. Come in."

He walked to a chair and sat. "Were you expecting someone?"

"I do not expect any longer."

"But you still hope?"

"I try not to, but I cannot help it."

"I wish you would try harder."

"I am weary with trying. It's easier to give myself up for lost."

"Stop pacing, Suzanne. Sit down."

She sat on the sofa, close enough to him that he was able to take her hand. "Look at me," he said.

"I don't think I've been able to look you in the eye since I met him."

"I don't judge you, Suzanne."

"You *are* a fool."

"Why do you sneer at someone who wishes to help you? Is the only love you value one that spurns you?"

She laughed acidly. "How clever you are, William, clever and, oh, so very sage. I do not dare attempt to pull the wool over your eyes. You see right through me."

"Enough."

"It is not enough!"

"Save your venom for Pomeroy, but spare me. I am your friend, if you recall."

"Is that what you call yourself? I happen to know better."

"I have never been anything but a friend to you. I would have been more, if you had let me."

"Is it the part of a friend to betray me, to dash all my hopes forever?"

"Good Lord, Suzanne, I never did anything of the kind."

"You did, you did, you know you did. When you brought her into his life, you put an end to mine."

"You mean Rosa? You must be dreaming."

"You did not see her at Marylebone Park. You did not witness her flirtation with him. She is very sly, you know, always careful to remain prim and coy, but always careful to let her eyes flutter and her hand brush up against his. She does not fool me for a moment."

"Nothing passed between them. I am sure of it."

"Did she recount their conversation to you?"

"No, and I would not have been so rude as to ask her to. But she did tell me they had talked, and all that transpired was that Pomeroy said something to make her think a little better of him."

"There, you see!"

"'Better of him' does not mean 'in love with him.' It merely means she does not dislike him as much as she did before."

"Where is your good sense, William. Why do you suppose she does not dislike him?"

"I don't know. I suppose he takes pains to make himself agreeable to her, and she knows him so little that she allows herself to be taken in."

"There you have it in a nutshell." Miss Grahame looked at her hand as Sunley held it. Her lips trembled. "He used to take pains to make himself agreeable to me."

Impatiently, he took a breath. "Suzanne, could we not make a pact, you and I? Could we not comfort one another and be the sort of lovers who are friends first? Could we not protect each other from the extremes of emotion that romantic attachment inflicts?"

She stared at her white hand as he lifted it tenderly to his lips.

"Yes, I should like that."

Swiftly, he moved close to her on the sofa. "So would I."

Allowing her head to fall on his shoulder, she murmured, "It sounds restful. I should be grateful for some rest."

"I suppose restful is something, at any rate."

Tears streaming from her eyes, she put her face on his chest and wept. He stroked her hair as she repeated, "I shall belong to you always, and I shall never forget your patience and loyalty."

"Perhaps we may be married, Suzanne."

"Yes, as soon as you've sent her away."

She felt his body tense.

"Leave Rosa out of this," he said.

"How can I, when she sets her cap for Pomeroy?"

"What difference does it make, if we are to be married?"

"Exactly. What difference does it make whether she is with us in London or far off somewhere in the country? Send her to the country, William, I beg you. Send her and I will marry you."

He pushed her away and stood up. "I will deal with Rosa in my own way and in my own time."

"She's fooled you, too, hasn't she? It isn't enough that she bewitches that fop Bonwit and my poor besotted uncle. It isn't enough that she has stolen Pomeroy's love and brought me low. She must have you, too!"

"Pomeroy had cooled before he ever laid eyes on Rosa. You know it as well as you know your own name."

At this, Suzanne shrank into herself.

"You are trying to blame someone else for what you've brought on yourself by the most wild imprudence."

She retaliated by saying, "You have not the heart to hear of Lady Rosalind's preference for Pomeroy; you think to deflect the truth by attacking me. Very well, you play your game, whatever it is, and I shall play mine. We shall play it out and see who wins."

"It was a game to you from the start, wasn't it? You never had any idea of marrying me. You merely wanted Rosa out of the way so that you would have a clear field with Pomeroy."

She smiled and gave a little shrug. "You are really very sweet, William," she said. "Your loyalty to your cousin is every bit as touching as your loyalty to me."

He walked to the door. Without looking round at her, he said, "Good night, Suzanne."

"Good night," she replied, smiling tensely at his back. "I do believe one day I shall regret misusing you so."

A rheumy cough confined Lord Divine to his bed. The loss of her riding teacher meant that Rosa went some days without exercising her mare. At last, Tripple was enlisted to ride with her to the park in the morning. He sat in his lordship's coach, availing himself of pears and biscuits from a basket, and watched Rosa put Queen Mab through her paces. When she had finished, she climbed into the carriage beside the old actor and accepted a pear. Looking at it without appetite, she said, "I ought to have warned you earlier. We must be on the look-out for an acting company."

"Nonsense, child. That sort of thing is unbecoming your new station in life."

"My station is due to sink."

"You ought not to ride at so early an hour. I fear it knocks your brains about."

"Viscount Sunley told me himself—we will be leaving his aunt's house momentarily."

"Impossible. Why, I saw him just the other night and he said nothing about it."

"You saw him? How did he look? Is he well?"

"He looked like the ghost of old King Hamlet who, having taken a wrong turn on the road to paradise, now wanders the battlements in perplexity."

"Perhaps if I were already gone, he would not feel the need to avoid his own house."

"It is his aunt's house, and I have prescribed a remedy for him that he assured me he meant to follow."

"What remedy? You have not sold him some elixir, I hope?"

"Lord, no, I've done with that. Not a very lucrative vocation anyway, selling elixirs. No, I advised him to visit a lady."

"What lady?"

"Any lady."

"And he said he meant to follow your advice?" Here Rosa let her shoulders sag, as though she had heard the last piece of bad news she could sustain.

"Exactly, and once he has refreshed himself, he will return

to his aunt's house, take up the case with new vigor, and present us with ninety thousand pounds."

Rosa shook her head. "The case is hopeless. His lordship is determined to pursue it no further. He has told me you failed to persuade the attorneys to put forward my claim. He therefore considers it useless for me to continue my masquerade as Beckwith's daughter. We are to leave George Street as soon as he tells his father the truth of who I am."

"Well, we certainly can't have that, can we?"

"I should like to know how we can prevent it."

"Stap me if I know either."

"I am afraid it is hopeless, Tripple." Her eyes filled and she bowed her head.

In wonder, he watched teardrops spill onto her gloves. "I have not seen you cry since you were a babe," he said. "You cried then because someone called you a filthy little ragamuffin and chased you with a broom."

"I have not come very far since then."

"Blast it, Rosa, I was wrong to make you come. I ought never to have been so greedy. I ought to have listened to you."

"No. You were right. I am grateful for the time I have had. It is not your fault the situation turned out hopeless."

He took her hand and patted it. "I do not accept that it is hopeless. Today puts forth 'tender leaves of hope.' Tomorrow, my girl, they will blossom."

Rosa could not bear the thought of breakfast and begged to be allowed to have a cup of coffee in her room. As Lord Divine also kept to his room—breakfasting on hot water with honey and spice—and as the viscount continued to avoid the precincts of George Street, Lady Delphia might have suffered a gloomy meal in solitude had not Tripple kindly offered to keep her company.

"You are welcome, sir," she said. "You may tell Nunn to bring you some sausage."

"My dear lady, I should not presume to give your butler orders."

"It is not presumption, Mr. Tripple. You see, I am not speaking to him. Someone must therefore speak for me, and as my brother thinks only of himself and deserts me, you must do it."

Tripple scrutinized Nunn, who stood by the sideboard poised with a tray. The butler's impassive expression implied that he heard nothing. "How long has it been thus?" Tripple asked.

Her ladyship thought, then replied, "Many, many weeks. Possibly months. I forget."

"That is a very long time."

"I am possessed of great strength of character, Mr. Tripple, and have been known to stop speaking to someone for a decade."

"As much as that! Well, I do not know what offense your butler committed, but I believe you have done an excellent job of punishing the fellow."

"I hope so. We Divines believe in punishing offenders. If one did not take umbrage at an insult and punish the insulter, what would become of polite society?"

"But I should hate to see you wear yourself to a frazzle for a want of intermediaries to deliver your orders."

"How astute you are, Mr. Tripple. I do not think anyone else quite appreciates how wearing it is on one's nerves to speak continually through intermediaries."

"Having punished the fellow, my lady, I think you have done your duty to family and decency and may now address him directly without damage to your dignity."

"Why, I believe you are right, sir!" She directed her wrinkled visage at the butler. "Nunn," she intoned, "bring Mr. Tripple a plate of sweetbreads and rolls."

"Thank you, my lady," Nunn said with only the veriest trace of a grin.

When the butler had served the delicacies and Tripple had consumed three hearty portions, he wiped his eye, shook his head in sorrow, and turned down the corners of his lips. He sighed heavily six or seven times until Lady Delphia took notice of his oppression and inquired, "Do the sweetbreads give you dyspepsia, Mr. Tripple?"

"I have no quarrel with the sweetbreads, my lady. It is the young people who trouble me."

"What young people?"

"By young people, I refer to Viscount Sunley and Lady Rosalind. I do not include your ladyship, though well I might, because your wide travel and experience puts you quite beyond their reach."

"I have traveled extensively on the Continent, and for some time have been intending to see India and Africa. How I shall manage among all those naked savages I cannot imagine."

"As to the young people, Lady Delphia, I am afraid they have borne a terrible burden on their tender shoulders."

"I never heard of any burdens."

"But I know you can be depended upon to bear your share. You see, it is the case. That is to say, it is not the case, because there is no longer any case. The attorneys refuse to accept my testimony, and the nursemaid, who was to be the witness, has run off."

"How very perverse."

"Until now, the young people have shielded us from the knowledge so that we should not be put to any anxiety. They wished to spare us worry over the money, you see."

"And most considerate it was, to be sure, but now that we do know, we must lose no time in worrying over the money. There are heavy bills to be paid. How do they propose to pay them?"

"Stap me if I know, my lady. I thought, however, if you and I could put our heads together, we might come up with a solution."

"You and I, Mr. Tripple?"

"The very same."

"Put our heads together?"

"I can think of no pleasanter way to worry, can you?"

Lady Delphia, blushing from her cheeks to her bosom, was saved the necessity of a reply by the entrance of Sunley.

He stopped short, just inside the door and returned the surprised looks of his aunt and Tripple before swiftly scanning the room. When his eyes fell on Rosa's empty chair, his anxious expression turned to alarm. "Where has everybody gone?" he asked.

◇ Thirteen ◇

Rosy-fingered dawn stretched her arms across the sky and gave a great yawn. Waking at the same time, Rosa quickly donned her dark green velvet riding habit and plumed hat. She then seized a box from the dressing table and left the room. The box—a gift for Lord Divine—contained a verse, some dried rose petals, a handkerchief she had monogrammed herself, and a written promise that she would sing to him as soon as he was well enough to come downstairs. In the corridor she stopped before his lordship's door to lay the box in front of it. Just as she was rising, the door opened and the viscount came out.

Rosa stepped back. Sunley did not move from the doorway. He surveyed her from top to toe, observing in a carefully controlled voice, "You are going riding."

It was a moment before Rosa could answer. She was struck by his pallor and could hardly keep from reaching her hand to his cheek. At last she spoke. "Perhaps it would be better if I returned to my chamber and awaited your instructions."

"My instructions are that you will go riding as planned."

"Now you have returned, you will want to make arrangements for my departure."

"What I want to do is quite irrelevant. I will let you know when I have made arrangements. For now, please go on as before."

Before, Rosa repeated to herself. Did he mean before they had quarreled? Before they had kissed? Before they had ever met at all? Each of those events seemed now to belong to a far-off time.

As she could think of nothing further to say, she moved toward the stairs.

"Rosa," Sunley said. He walked to her. "I would prefer that

what little time is left be spent in as comfortable a manner as possible."

Fixing the carpeted step with her eye, she answered, "I would not willingly upset any other member of the household."

"That is my meaning exactly. It seems to me we ought to be able to behave with commonplace courtesy toward one another, at least when we are in the presence of others."

"Of course. Your aunt tutors me in the ways of politeness, and I have learned that fine ladies are expected to dissemble their true feelings as well as actresses. I will try to do as you suggest."

Although he had won her agreement, he did not appear very pleased. "There is one more thing."

"Yes?"

"I hope you have a pleasant ride."

Mr. Tripple, who had tired of waiting for Rosa in the carriage and had already consumed all the pears and biscuits, greeted her in the hall.

"Viscount Sunley is back," she told him.

"I saw him last night. I'm afraid my advice did not help him a great deal."

"Oh, Tripple, I wish you had not offered him advice. He looks as though he has been following a vast deal of bad advice."

"Now, that is unjust. I offered him excellent advice, and why should I not? I have lived in the world. I have seen a great many young men in his condition. And I know the cure."

"But what if he went to see Miss Grahame?"

"Am I acquainted with the lady?"

"Suppose he asked her to marry him?"

"Marry? Why on earth would such a frisky young fellow as his lordship shackle himself to a wife?"

"For one thing, her uncle is very wealthy and she is his heiress. If the case is not to produce money for the Divines to live on, then Viscount Sunley must find another means."

"What a very interesting idea—if the law refuses to let him

put his hands on his own blunt, he may marry someone else's."

"And for another thing, he entertains certain tender feelings toward Miss Grahame."

At this, Tripple's eyes went wide. In a moment, however, he shook his head. His face took on an expression replete with doubtfulness. "I ask you, Rosa, if he had heeded me and gone to see this young lady and won her hand and heart, would he look as dreadful as he does?"

"He does look awfully pale."

"He caught his death of cold, I expect, just as you did. The two of you ought never to have gone to Spring Gardens in such weather."

"Very true. We should never have gone to Spring Gardens in any weather." Then, shaking off certain painful recollections, Rosa said, "Oh, let us hurry to the park. This may be the last ride I shall ever take on Queen Mab."

They returned from the outing to find the viscount and Lady Delphia in a wrangle. Her ladyship's voice could be heard throughout the house as it boomed from the parlor, while Sunley declared quietly that the idea his aunt proposed was out of the question. Accustomed to having her way, Lady Delphia maintained that the idea perfectly answered their need for a little pleasant society.

She applied to Rosa and Tripple, as soon as they entered, for their votes on the matter. It was explained that a note had come, a very kind invitation from Miss Grahame—and heaven knew she was not in the habit of issuing kind invitations—requesting the honor of their presence on an excursion to the Tower. Miss Grahame had delivered the note in person, which was a courtesy unlooked for in that sour-faced young woman, and, in truth, the invitation was as tempting as it could be.

The outing was to begin with a lavish dinner at the White Hart. From there the party would ride in open carriages to the river, from whence it would be rowed to the Tower. Mr. Grahame would act as their guide, for he had studied the history of the site and would like nothing better than to tell Lady Rosalind of its wondrous past. Miss Grahame expressed her hope that Lady Rosalind longed to hear the bloody tales asso-

ciated with the fortress, and in particular, to stand on the very
spot where Lady Jane Grey had been separated from her head.

"It sounds highly interesting," Tripple said with a yawn.

"You have not heard the rest," Sunley said. "There is a
stipulation."

"It is nothing!" Lady Delphia assured them. "It is only that
Rosalind must ask Lord Pomeroy to join us. Miss Grahame
has already obtained Mr. Bonwit's acceptance."

"Why did not Miss Grahame invite Lord Pomeroy herself?"
Rosa asked.

To which Lady Delphia replied readily, "She explained that
as he is your particular friend, he would be glad of an invitation from you."

"I scarcely know Lord Pomeroy. I cannot ask him."

"Miss Grahame has paid you a great compliment, my dear.
I should think you would be pleased."

"I have no desire to see the Tower," Rosa said.

"'Pon my word, Rosalind. You've been harping on it for
weeks. You declared there was nothing in the world you
would rather see!"

"Is that true?" Sunley asked, looking at her for the first time
since her entrance.

A little abashed, Rosa admitted that it was. "But I never
expected there would be such a to-do over it."

"I suppose we might go if you would really like it," Sunley
allowed.

"Excellent!" his aunt cried. "Mr. Tripple will accompany
us. Miss Grahame said he might, if he cared to."

Hearing his name, Tripple started and endeavored to replace his bored expression with a smile.

"Come, Rosalind," her ladyship barked. "We must write to
Lord Pomeroy this instant."

Rosa followed her ladyship to the desk. As she sat with a
newly mended pen poised over a sheet of paper, she said, "It
may be that Lord Pomeroy is engaged that day and will be
forced to decline."

"What a bleak thought. Of course he will come, Rosalind.
Do not despair. The Divines are a sturdy race. They never
despair."

As directed, Rosa did not despair. She continued to hope

throughout the week that Lord Pomeroy would not accept the invitation.

Everyone at the White Hart was mightily pleased.

The keeper of the public house was pleased because the soft curd cheese had been cradled to perfection. The fresh oysters were succulent, and the sweet pineapples ran with nectar. The ladies and gentlemen at his table consumed every one of the dovecote pigeons in roseate pastry he had ordered from the chef. Moreover, they set up a cry of pleasure when the footman appeared at the table with a whipped syllabub topped with angelica and crystallized cumin.

Although the still-ailing Lord Divine had been forced to remain at home, Miss Grahame was pleased that everyone else—to wit, Lord Pomeroy—had consented to make one of the party.

Mr. Bonwit was pleased to be included in the noble company and to sit in a place of honor at Lady Rosalind's left hand.

Mr. Grahame was pleased to be seated on her right. It relieved him to discover that she was not in the least devastated by the news that there would be no viewing of the mint owing to its recent removal from the Tower.

Lord Pomeroy was pleased to have an opportunity to show Lady Rosalind how courteous he could be to Miss Grahame, even going so far as to converse amiably with the yellow-haired young woman through the first two courses.

Lady Delphia was pleased to see Lord Pomeroy looking at her niece every so often as if to extort a murmur of approval from her. She was even more pleased to see him jump up and come fully to the other side of the table to retrieve a napkin Lady Rosalind dropped. The gentleman might properly have let the footman take care of the napkin, but he evidently meant to seize any opportunity, even such a humble one, so long as it might afford him a soft word with the lady.

Mr. Tripple was most pleased of all. Dressing, traveling, and dining in luxury never failed to please him.

Viscount Sunley, if not precisely pleased, was at least grateful for the chance to justify his procrastination in the matter of Rosa's departure. He told himself it was not possible to send her from George Street before she had been granted her wish of seeing the Tower. Once she had tasted the joys of tourism, he reasoned, he might send her off into the world with a quiet heart. He might bid her good-bye in the knowledge that he had done everything for her that could possibly be done. Naturally, he would have been more pleased if Lord Pomeroy did not continually seek out Rosa's eyes and approbation, but for the moment the avid attentions of Mr. Bonwit and Mr. Grahame sufficed to protect her.

As for Rosa, even she was pleased. Since becoming Lady Rosalind, she had seen nothing of the town except Spring Gardens, Almack's, and the exquisite drawing rooms of several town houses. She ached to see more of the sights of London. A day at the Tower answered her longing and promised that she would be able to leave George Street with at least one of her hopes realized.

The party journeyed in two carriages to the river. There the cries of the boatmen so offended Lady Delphia that she threatened to drive back to Hanover Square on the spot. Happily, Mr. Tripple discovered the cause of the offense and explained that the boatmen were only calling, "Oars! Oars!" They had no idea, he assured her, of implying that she was a woman of sullied reputation.

Owing to the large size of the party, they were rowed upriver in two boats. From her vantage point in the second, Rosa could see Miss Grahame in the first, feverishly radiant, surrounded by Mr. Bonwit, Lord Pomeroy, and the viscount. Miss Grahame looked back at her, tossing her head in triumph. Rosa, content in the undemanding company of the others, wished the lady joy of her companions.

They debarked at the wharf, where Mr. Walwart, a lieutenant of the Tower, greeted them cordially. He evidently knew Mr. Grahame and displayed to him the keys he had in readiness to open all the rooms to viewing. He led them through the Traitors' Gate, where they were stopped by Mr. Grahame and exhorted to imagine London Bridge dotted with the heads of traitors set on pikes for all the town to view. Having duly entertained themselves in this fashion for some minutes, the party then made haste to the menagerie.

Mr. Grahame's introductory remarks on the leopards, lions, and elephants succeeded in fatiguing his niece.

"We want to see the crown jewels, uncle," Miss Grahame said. "What is it to me if each lion eats a quarter of a sheep a day?"

Thereupon she put her arm through Lord Pomeroy's and swept from the zoo.

Rosa, however, listened closely to the distinguished Mr. Grahame's history, and nearly wept with fury at his description of King James's bear baiting. So long and enthusiastic was the lecture that when the two of them emerged from the menagerie, they could not find the rest of the party. Mr. Walwart had apparently been persuaded to grant their wish of seeing the jewels. Mr. Grahame, therefore, took it upon himself to show Rosa his very favorite view, from Lady Jane Grey's room in the Gentleman Gaoler's Lodgings.

It was a bare, simple, dim room. A beam of light filtering through the window drew Rosa to look outside.

"Through here Lady Jane watched her husband mount the scaffold on Tower Hill," said Mr. Grahame.

Looking toward the hill, Rosa tried to imagine what it was like to be the young Jane, doomed to follow her husband to the next world. The actress in her empathized so completely that she soon lost all sense of the present.

Seeing her rapt in contemplation, Mr. Grahame tactfully withdrew from the room.

Rosa was not aware he had gone. She was wholly engrossed in seeing herself as Lady Jane. She saw her lover torn from her and put to death before her very eyes. She anticipated the bloody end to her young, innocent life. She saw a future which held in store nothing but the chopping block. Oh, it must have been more horrible than she could ever imagine, even worse than being banished from George Street.

"My dearest Lady Rosalind," said an ardent voice.

She turned to look at the intruder. It took her some time to absorb the fact that she was in the present once again and that Mr. Bonwit was smirking at her as was his wont.

"You are alone!" he breathed.

"Not at all. The ghosts of the place keep me company."

"Do you believe in that sort of thing? I hear that the ghost of some queen or other—I think it's the one that had her head lopped off—does haunt the place."

"I'm afraid more than one young queen lost her head here. And I am certain the ghosts of all of them do haunt the place. If I were permitted to haunt a place, I should certainly choose these picturesque grounds."

"Not I. The menagerie smells dreadfully foul."

"Yes, but think of living for all eternity with the crown jewels."

"I did not see the jewels. I came looking for you."

On that, he moved to her and clasped her hand in both of his. Drawing it to his lips, he cried, "Lady Rosalind, do I reach too far above myself in declaring that I love you with all my heart and would cherish you forever if only you would say you would be mine?"

"Mr. Bonwit, as I've told you repeatedly, I detest nibbling."

"You would find in me the most considerate of husbands. You would have an ample allowance out of your inheritance, I swear it. And I should never interfere if you wished to go to the opera or the play with Lord Pomeroy."

"It is beyond my power to answer you as you deserve."

"I realize it is unconventional for a husband to be so generous. However, I am a forward-looking fellow, if I may say so. You see, I have even abandoned the striped cravat. It is decidedly outré."

With that positive declaration, he began to move his lips and aim them in the direction of her cheek. He slid his hands up and down her arms so that she was forced to back toward the window to put him at a distance. When she could move no farther, she shook off his hands.

"We must join the others," she said firmly.

"A pox on the others!"

"You will want to see the jewels, sir."

"I have all the jewels I crave right here."

"If you do not stop this, sir, I shall be forced to take action."

"Your protestations become you prettily—and fire me all the more."

With a deep breath, Rosa said, "I do beg your pardon, Mr.

Bonwit, for what I am about to do," and then she tweaked his nose until he howled.

"Good God! What is that noise?" Mr. Tripple cried, coming inside. "It makes my blood run cold. Have you seen a ghost that haunts this place?"

"She has broke my nose!" Mr. Bonwit whimpered.

"Is that true, Rosa?"

Rosa sighed. "I believe the gentleman has been shot by one of Cupid's arrows."

"Is that true, Mr. Bonwit?"

"She has murdered me," he repeated, gingerly patting his nose.

"Well, 'murder will out,' as the Bard says. Allow me to show you the way, sir."

Having deposited the moaning suitor in the hall, Tripple returned to Rosa.

"Has that puppy been making love to you?"

"He evidently thinks so. He asked me to marry him."

Mr. Tripple's brows rose at this. He had noted Lord Pomeroy's attentions to Rosa. Now it appeared that this other young fellow had formed an attachment as well. His little Rosa was apparently a heartbreaker. Well, well, he thought.

A delicious idea took root in the old actor's head, and as the fertile soil contained therein was nurtured by dreams of wealth, he questioned Rosa closely.

"Do you wish to marry him?"

"Beheading would be preferable," she replied.

"He seems a decent sort. Surely you could like him a little."

"In forty or fifty years perhaps, if he does not become my husband."

"It would answer everything, you know. If you married well, we would never have to give up a thing. We would not need the nursemaid or any other witness to insure your position."

Rosa looked at him intently, then bowed her head. "I wish it would answer," she said regretfully. "But much as I dislike Mr. Bonwit, he does not deserve to be married to a wife who is in love with someone else."

"My dear girl! Are you in love? Why, how perfect. I vow,

the gentleman returns your affection, for I have seen him making spaniel eyes at you all day."

Her eyes filling, Rosa said angrily, "I will not hear another word about him. And if you are not careful, Tripple, you, too, will have your nose tweaked!"

Gathering her skirts, she left the room, leaving her former guardian to marvel at her excess of emotion. Such irritability denoted love of a very deep, lasting, and miserable sort, the sort that guaranteed pliability and persuadability in the lover. It guaranteed that, in the end, Rosa would be brought to marry her gentleman. It meant that in the end she would thank her funny old Tripple for persuading her. And, in the end, she would make them all rich.

He found Lady Delphia in the museum, examining a suit of protective plate worn by Henry VIII. The proportions of the armor attested to the monarch's girth and caused her ladyship to pronounce the founder of the English religion a veritable sybarite.

"My lady, the time has come for us to put our heads together," he said.

"Here, Mr. Tripple? Surrounded by all this weaponry?"

"What better surroundings for the campaign we are about to wage?"

"I am sure your metaphor is very literate, sir, but I do not catch your meaning."

"Lady Rosalind will marry Lord Pomeroy and we shall all be as rich as old King Henry was plump. Now, that is a three-barreled pistol for you!"

Her ladyship turned to contemplate the weapon he pointed at. It incorporated a mace and battle club as well as a pistol with three barrels, and it promised fairly to dispatch anyone who came too near it.

"What has Lord Pomeroy to do with a three-barreled pistol?"

"One, that our girl loves him as much as he clearly loves her. Two, that they will be married and his money will set us all up in style. Three, that we may dispense with the law and the lawyers, the nursemaids and the documents, and direct our attention to our single purpose here on this earth, namely, to amuse ourselves."

Lady Delphia's countenance contorted into a smile. She turned to Mr. Tripple, overcome with admiration and respect, and warmly shook his hand. "My dear sir," she crowed, "you have done no less than save the family. The Divines will never forget this, I assure you. We are known to be a grateful race and will generously reward such ingenuity as yours."

"Naturally you will reward me, dear lady. But we must plan our strategy. It would be impolitic to be obvious. Nothing is more certain to prevent a match than to be caught forwarding it."

"Very true, and I have just the solution. We will enlist the aid of someone who will know exactly how to proceed, someone who will be as glad as we are to have a way out of our pickle."

"Excellent. You must talk to him at once. I saw him not a half hour ago on the battlements. I'll wager he will be glad to be relieved of his burdens."

Sunley gazed at the horizon from the battlements. The fine weather afforded him a view of the town, the river, and the grounds of Smithfield. Below lay Tower Green, where he could see various members of the excursion party assembling in leisurely fashion. Directed by Mr. Grahame, the party formed a circle. Mr. Walwart entered the center of the circle carrying a large wooden block niched on top so that a neck would fit in it most snugly. He set it down on the lawn as Mr. Grahame began his exposition. Leaning forward, the viscount tried to hear what was being said.

A tug at his sleeve made him look round into the glowing face of his aunt.

"We are saved, nevvew!" she said.

"I am glad to hear it, aunt." Peering over the battlements again, Sunley saw Mr. Grahame signal Mr. Walwart to leave the circle. In a moment, the lieutenant returned wearing a black mask. He had armed himself with a gargantuan axe.

"Mr. Tripple has found the answer to all our difficulties."

"Has he, indeed?" Sunley saw Miss Grahame step forward toward the block. The murmur of voices from below had quieted to a dead stillness. Laughing recklessly, Miss Grahame suddenly threw herself prone so that her head lay on the

wooden block. She turned toward Lord Pomeroy, imploring
him in words the viscount could not hear. He could, however,
discern the embarrassment of Mr. Grahame, who attempted to
persuade his niece to rise.

"Rosalind must marry Lord Pomeroy!" Lady Delphia announced.

Whipping around, Sunley stared at her.

"Isn't it perfect? What does it matter whether a hundred
nursemaids desert us if Rosalind can marry well? And then if
you can do likewise, we may consign Beckwith's ridiculous
will to oblivion. I daresay Miss Grahame may be brought to
appreciate your superior character. She has a great deal of her
own money and stands to inherit her uncle's."

Sunley turned again to look at Miss Grahame. She now
clung to the block, crying and moaning. It appeared that she
was imploring Pomeroy to save her. The viscount saw that
neither Mr. Bonwit nor Rosa could prevail on her to stand.
Lord Pomeroy stood frozen, then turned his head away. To
Sunley's eye, he appeared disgusted.

"The idea fills me with disgust!" Sunley said.

Lady Delphia was surprised. Nevertheless, she was not de-
terred. "I had no idea you had changed your mind about Miss
Grahame," she said. "Very well, then. We shall forget her. I,
for one, shall be glad to forget her. In the meanwhile, Rosalind will have Pomeroy and we will leave it at that. I shall
speak to her at once, as I know the news will delight her."

She turned on her heel and was well on her way down the
stairs before Sunley realized what she proposed to do. He saw
her emerge onto the lawn and march toward the party gathered
at the block. He saw her push her way into the circle and
heard her booming voice exclaim, "Get up, Miss Grahame.
You will stain your dress. If you meant to roll on the grass,
you ought never to have worn white!"

Shamefaced, Miss Grahame rose. Sunley did not wait to
see what she would do. At this moment, he could not spare a
thought for Miss Grahame. In a flash he ran down the steps
and made for the party on the green.

◇ Fourteen ◇

When he reached the others, the viscount found them standing in awkward silence, trying not to notice Miss Grahame's torrential sobs. That young lady stood apart, beside an ancient tree, her face in her hands, crying to break her heart. Rosa was at her side, endeavoring to calm her with gentle words. She reached a soothing hand to the trembling shoulders. Violently, Miss Grahame shook her off. "You!" she cried. "Oh, can you not leave me in peace?"

Facing the others, Rosa perceived that it would be best to let the distraught young woman collect herself and to do what she could to distract the onlookers. Accordingly, she declared to Mr. Grahame that his lecture on executions of the Tudor period—lately interrupted by Miss Grahame's sudden attack of hypochondriasis—had been vastly illuminating and she, for one, would be thankful to have him go on with it. As soon as his niece could have a private moment to herself, without eight pairs of eyes staring her to mortification, she would be sure to recover.

Nodding at this wise prescription, Mr. Grahame stepped forward and addressed the company at large. He said that he had copied some words of Anne Boleyn's on a paper, words that had been recorded at the time of the queen's beheading. He had thought it would be amusing to read them to the party as they gathered about the block and imagined the poor lady's head lying upon it. Desolately, he scanned the faces of his listeners to learn whether he should proceed with the scheme.

None of them appeared to find the idea the least bit amusing, especially as it recalled Miss Grahame's late display. With a pained look at his niece, the gentleman crushed the paper he held in his hand and let it drop to the grass. He walked some small distance from the company and stopped.

Picking up the paper, Rosa uncrumpled it. She smoothed it as best she could and perused it for a brief minute. Then, addressing her companions, she said with a ring of authority in her voice, "The king does this to prove me!"

Recognizing the words, Mr. Grahame looked at her in astonishment.

Rosa walked with quiet dignity to the viscount. "Mr. Kingston," she said, "I hear say I shall not die before noon, and I am very sorry therefore, for I thought to be dead now and past my pain."

"Is she raving?" Lady Delphia whispered to Tripple.

"She is Anne Boleyn," he whispered back. "And a devilish fine heroine she is, too."

Sunley met Rosa's impassioned gaze. "The pain to come will be felt by all of us, my queen," he improvised. After a pause, he took one of her hands in his.

Lady Delphia leaned toward Tripple once more. "Who is Sunley supposed to be?"

"Stap me if I know. The jailer, perhaps. I vow, he does very well for a novice."

Rosa looked at the strong hand enfolding hers. Then, recollecting herself, she looked at her paper and smiled wistfully. "I have heard say that the executioner is very good. And I have a very little neck." She put her free hand to her neck and laughed. In another moment, she was laughing hysterically, frightening all the onlookers out of their wits.

"'Pon my word, Mr. Tripple," said Lady Delphia, "Who is she supposed to be now? Miss Grahame?"

"She is still Queen Anne, I believe."

"What on earth ails her?"

"She is about to lose her head."

"Well, it is very distressing to see her carry on about it in such a noisy fashion."

Lord Pomeroy, who had observed the drama with fascination, now started forward and took her hand from Sunley's. The instant he possessed himself of it, he cried, "Oh, my queen. Do not speak of death."

She stopped him from speaking further by pulling her hand

away and gesturing wide. "I have seen many men, and also women, executed," she told him softly, "and they have been in great sorrow, but this lady has much joy and pleasure in death. I ask only one thing, my lord."

"Anything!" Pomeroy swore.

"Oh, I like that," Lady Delphia whispered, a sentiment which Tripple echoed with a wink.

Miss Grahame, who had watched this last exchange in suspicion, now turned white.

"I beg you to take my baby daughter Elizabeth into your paternal care," Rosa said.

Lord Pomeroy swallowed, flushed red, and promised.

Then Rosa slowly glided past each member of the party. Lady Delphia and Tripple, after taking in Lord Pomeroy's look of admiration, beamed upon her indulgently. Miss Grahame looked as though she would willingly see the blood spurt from Rosa's severed head. Sunley could not tear his eyes from her; nor could the rest of them.

Rosa came to a halt at the block, glanced at her paper, and looked up to address the assembled. "Good people," she proclaimed, "I come hither to die according to the law. I praise the king's mercy and pray he will protect my relatives and dependents, for a gentler nor a more merciful prince was there never."

"I should not have called the king 'merciful,'" Lady Delphia said. "It is my understanding that he was the one who gave the order to take her head off."

"I suppose she must say that or the fellow will chop up her whole family," Tripple explained.

Rosa continued: "I take my leave of you and the world, and I heartily desire you all to pray for me."

Mezmerized, the audience watched Rosa remove her pelisse. She dropped the garment to the ground as though it were the most regal of ermines. Taking a handkerchief from her reticule, she begged Tripple would come tie it across her eyes. When he had blindfolded her, an act he performed with a sweeping flourish, the actor handed her down to a kneeling position and resumed his place in the circle beside Lady Delphia.

Rosa felt for the block, and when her groping fingers

touched it, she cried, "Bring me the sword!" Slowly she lay
her head upon the niche in the wood.

Mr. Walwart, stunned by Rosa's performance, came close.
Hearing his steps, Rosa looked up toward the sound and said,
"I forgive you for what you are obliged to do."

The Tower lieutenant ripped off his black mask, revealing a
face covered with wet streaks. "I cannot!" he exclaimed.

Here Lord Pomeroy stepped forward and knelt by the
block. Swiftly he untied the blindfold so that Rosa might look
at him. "My queen," he said, "rise and come with me. I repent of all the wrongs I've done you, and if you can forgive
me, I beg you will consent to live with me as my wife, for I
cannot live without you."

"Oh, well done!" Lady Delphia applauded. "It ought to
have happened just that way."

"London is full of actors!" Tripple exclaimed.

Rosa, charmed by his lordship's eloquent improvisation,
allowed him to hand her up. Brushing off her skirts, she said,
"Very well, sir, I shall live if you like. Only you must promise
never give me such a scare again." Looking up into his face,
she laughed, and he laughed with her.

Sunley turned away from the spectacle, not the least
cheered by the laughing finale Rosa and her ardent King
Henry had invented. The others blew their noses into their
linens and opined on the sweetness of happy endings. That is
to say, Lady Delphia and Tripple thought it a happy ending.
Mr. Bonwit and Mr. Grahame were not quite so satisfied.
They fidgeted and looked bleak. Miss Grahame stormed away
in a fury. And the viscount, taking himself off to the Chapel
of St. John, soon found himself in the Dungeon of the Little
Ease.

Entering a comfortable dining hall, recently restored and
modernized, Lord Pomeroy urged Rosa to sit, saying, "We
have been walking and standing for hours, and you must be
fatigued after such a performance."

"I will sit, if you will, for your performance was nearly as
flawless as my own."

They shared another laugh, after which Pomeroy, growing

serious, said, "It wasn't a performance. I meant every word. I want you to come live with me as my wife."

Coloring, Rosa shook her head. "I am very honored, my lord, but I cannot accept your offer."

"You do not mean to have Bonwit, I trust."

"You are right there."

"Mr. Grahame, perhaps?"

In astonishment, Rosa repeated the name.

"Do not undervalue your claims, my lady. Mr. Grahame is in love with you. You ought to have seen his expression as you knelt at the block."

"He is in love with Anne Boleyn, not me."

"Well, I am in love with you, not Anne Boleyn."

"You are very kind, my lord, but I cannot marry you."

"I do not expect you to love me yet. You are too used to seeing me behave in an ungentlemanlike manner. But I am changing, you will see. Perhaps you've noticed already."

"I've noticed that you take pains to be polite to Miss Grahame."

"Ah, you did notice! Then the effort was not wasted."

"The effort ought to be made for its own sake, because it is the right thing to do, not because it will please me or anyone else."

"You are right, of course, but until such time as I can do it for its own sake, can I not do it to please you?"

"No, my lord, you cannot. I do not wish to be responsible for your manners, or the want of them."

"If you marry me, I shall have cause to be thoroughly polite to all the world."

"It's as much as I can manage to look after myself, sir, and therefore am not competent to oversee your behavior to all the world. But even if the idea were not so silly, I should still refuse you. You see, I have no money at all. The court will not acknowledge my claim and the inheritance will never fall to me."

Surprised, Lord Pomeroy stood up and paced in front of a long table of polished mahogany. His footsteps echoed on the stone floor. No other sound could be heard for some time. At length he paused in front of Rosa to ask, "What will you do?"

"I shall leave London."

"No!"

"I'm afraid it's best."

"I do not care about the money. Marry me."

He looked as though he would take her hand, but with a manful effort of control, he refrained.

Rosa bowed her head. "That is the kindest thing I have heard in a long time."

"It is not kind, damn it. I want you and I mean to have you!"

Rosa looked at him, half startled, half amused. "Am I some plaything, sir, demanded by a spoilt child?"

"You are no plaything, but I am a spoilt child. If you have any heart, you will spend the rest of your life unspoiling me. You say I have been kind to you, Rosalind. Will you now return the favor?"

"No, my lord. Besides, you cannot very well marry a beggar. Your family would throw you off."

"My family would see what I see—that you are a lady of genuine quality. Such refinement comes only with the blood of an old and noble lineage. It has nothing to do with money. Miss Grahame has a great deal of money, but her father earned it in trade, and you see the result!"

This line of conversation discomfited Rosa, so that she stood up. Lord Pomeroy, thinking she meant to leave him, took her hand. "Hear me out," he said.

She would have left without reply, but Lady Delphia's entrance on Tripple's arm prevented her. Seeing Pomeroy caressing Rosalind's hand, her ladyship stopped and said, "We shall turn around and go right out again, my lord. Please, go on with whatever it was you were doing."

Rosa would not let them go. Shaking off the hand, she said, "Please stay, aunt. His lordship has finished speaking."

"Lady Delphia, Mr. Tripple," Pomeroy said, "plead my case for me with Lady Rosalind. She will not listen to me."

"I believe young ladies have grown too elegant for their own good," Lady Delphia declared in pique. "First it is Miss Grahame who will not have Sunley. Now you, Rosalind, will not hear his lordship. Well, my dear. That other young lady should stand as a lesson to you. Sunley has changed his mind. He will have none of her now."

"That is a highly interesting lesson, indeed," Rosa replied. "Now I beg you will excuse me. I am promised to Mr. Grahame in the White Tower."

To the distress of the others, she hurried out of the hall.

Tripple, looking first at Rosa's departing figure and then at Lord Pomeroy, vowed he would not let her get off so easily, and after her he went.

Lady Delphia, not knowing whether it was more incumbent upon her to soothe the frustrated suitor or to press the reluctant lady, rocked back and forth on her feet.

"Do not vex yourself, madam," said his lordship. "I am confident she will love me in time."

"I believe you are right, sir," said her ladyship, relieved that he had not given up on her niece. "She no longer hates you as she did before. Indeed, I do think she finds you quite tolerable now. It is only a step from that to love."

His lordship laughed. "I should not respect her half so much if it were that easy. I much prefer the challenge of an unwilling bride."

"Oh, if that's the case, I shall tell her to take her time—as long as she submits in the end." On that, Lady Delphia took her leave and went in pursuit of the others.

Rosa's reluctance had served to raise her in Pomeroy's esteem, and as he rated his own attractions highly, he viewed the recent proceedings in the dining hall with rather more pleasure than pain. One recollection in particular—her admiration of his acting performance—gave him profound satisfaction, and he congratulated himself on winning the lady's approbation. He took it to mean that she would not long be proof against his charms. Naturally, it would prove an anticlimax to win her acceptance. Boredom was certain to follow hard upon it. Nevertheless, the sweetness of his triumph ought to cause his love for Rosa to flame longer than ever it had done in the past.

Such sanguine thoughts produced a smile of satisfaction on Pomeroy's lips. It faded, however, when he saw Miss Grahame appear from out of the shadows. Her white skin was flushed and she wore an air of weariness.

"I did not hear you enter," he greeted her irritably.

"I have been hereabouts for some time."

"Spying on me, I've no doubt."

"I do not need to spy on you, Dennis. I know exactly what you are doing, even when I am miles and miles away."

"If you are so perspicacious, then I warrant you know I wish you would go away."

"You are a fool. She will never love you, not as I do."

"I certainly hope not. I much prefer a civilized woman, one with sufficient breeding to keep loose reins on a fellow."

"She will not love you at all. She is already in love."

"Your stratagems, Suzanne, grow tiresome."

"Scoff at your peril, Dennis. She loves Sunley and will refuse you on his account."

Although this piece of news vexed his lordship, he replied calmly, "Even if she does love him, she will not refuse me. The family cannot lay hands on their inheritance. They will need money. Sunley will need it as well as the others and will come round. He will see where his best interest lies."

"I think you like her the better for loving someone else."

"It would not do you any harm, you know."

"You made me promises, Dennis. You know you did."

"There, you see. It is just like you to hold me to promises made in a moment of rashness. A fellow ought not to be held to account for every silly thing he says. Lady Rosalind would not throw promises in my face. As a lady, she would know how to behave."

"A gentleman would not renege on his promises."

"It will be time enough to turn gentleman when she is my wife."

"You mean to marry her?" she asked.

"As soon as I can talk her into it."

Anguished, she whispered, "What is to become of me?"

"Whatever you like. I might still call on you late at night, as I used to do, if you are pleasant to me and do not complain of me at every turn. Naturally, I should need to let a decent time go by after my honeymoon, but afterwards, we can still be as we were before."

Miss Grahame paced on the echoing stone floor. When she faced him, it was with wild, streaming eyes and a voice that quavered. "There will be no wedding. I will prevent it."

"You will not do that, Suzanne."

"I will. I will go to her and tell her everything—your love-making, your promises, your treachery."

"You would brave her contempt just to frustrate my plans?"

"How little you know her. She would contemn you, not me. She would pity me."

Angrily, Pomeroy turned his back on her and made as if to leave. Thinking better of it, he stopped and faced her. "I warn you," he said.

"Oh, Dennis, you can stop me if you like. You can stop me with a word."

Seizing her shoulders, he shook her. When she felt his hands on her, she threw herself against his chest and closed her eyes. In another moment, she was holding his cheeks and kissing his lips. He pushed her away.

He took a moment to glare at her, then said, "I have a letter." Reaching into his pocket, he drew forth a paper and unfolded it. "Perhaps you recall the letter."

She would have snatched it from his hand, but he pulled it away in time. "No, no, Suzanne. You must look at it from where you stand. We are, after all, in a museum. One may look at the artifacts but one must not touch them."

"That is my letter," Miss Grahame said.

"As you sent it to me, it is now my property, and not for anything would I part with it. Such language! Such feeling! I daresay just thinking about it makes me warm about the collar."

Miss Grahame blushed.

"I had an idea you would threaten me," he said. "All women are dreadfully predictable, and you are more predictable than most. You can always be relied upon to make threats if you don't get your way. Fortunately, you can also be relied upon to write love letters—and to be sorry for it afterwards."

"What do you mean to do with it?"

"I thought I would show it to Mr. Grahame. I am certain he will take you from London at once when he sees it. Then I shall be rid of you."

"I should refuse to go. I should find a way to stay and prevent your marriage."

"In that case, I should be forced to show the letter to my very large acquaintance in London and, in addition, to my

friends at the *Clarion*. I don't know whether the *Times* would
see fit to print the item, but the *Clarion* is certain not to scru-
ple at a violation of taste."

The lady stifled a gasp. Seeing that he'd got the better of
her for the moment, she murmured, "Very well, Dennis. What
must I do to get it back?"

"You will not get it back, as it is my security that you will
leave London at once. Your choice is very simple, Suzanne.
You may leave London under your own power or be driven
from town in humiliation. I believe you understand me now."

"I understand that she has wrecked my hopes for all time."

Laughing, he shook his head. "Blame Lady Rosalind, by
all means. It is certainly better than hearing your recriminations against me. And now I bid you a safe journey from
town." With that, he bowed and headed for the door.

As Miss Grahame followed him, her eyes spilled over with
tears of desolation and spite.

◊ Fifteen ◊

Rosa entered the White Tower at the east door and had not
taken many turns through the rooms when she abruptly
stopped. She could not remember from which direction she
had come. As the hour was late and the other tourists had
gone, no one appeared to show her the way. Instead of the
murmurings of sightseers echoing through the halls, she heard
only an eerie quiet.

Weary and hungry, she frowned at a rusted ship's cannon
and scolded herself. She had been so anxious to make her
escape from Lord Pomeroy that she had not stopped to consider where she was headed. She had been so intent on evad-
ing the blandishments of Lady Delphia and Mr. Tripple that
she had paid no attention to the route she took. And this was
the result: she was lost.

From far off, a clock tolled the hour. The touring party was scheduled to gather on the green in half an hour to meet the boatmen at the wharf. She must find her way out quickly or Miss Grahame would row back down the Thames without her. That bitter young woman would like nothing better than to leave her to spend the night with the ghosts of headless queens.

Gathering her spirits, Rosa walked slowly and thoughtfully for some time until she came to an ancient stairwell. Dark and cold and walled with crumbling stone, it could have been the very one Mr. Grahame had earlier described to her—the one under which two skeletons had been discovered centuries earlier. Mr. Grahame was convinced that the discovery represented nothing less than the remains of the two little princes imprisoned by their scheming Uncle Richard, who now appeared in Rosa's imagination as Shakespeare had portrayed him—hawk-nosed, humpbacked, and lame. Feeling a sudden chill, she strengthened her resolve to resume her search for the entrance. Then she saw a dim figure come toward her up the stairs.

The figure moved slowly, skirts smacking lightly against the steps. Head bowed, shoulders hunched, the figure loomed black and hazy as it passed through a ray of light. When it emerged, it revealed itself as Miss Grahame.

"I thought you might be a ghost," Rosa said.

"I am. Suzanne Grahame is dead. All that is left of her is this ghostly form."

Rosa shivered. Althought she had spent the better part of her life in the theater, Miss Grahame's theatrics unnerved her. "Will you help me find the door? I'm afraid I am lost."

"Yes, I will help you, if you will help me."

Rosa faced her. "If it regards Lord Pomeroy, I promise you I have not accepted him and do not mean to accept him."

"Oh, I want far more than that from you, Lady Rosalind."

"I have nothing you could possibly want, Miss Grahame."

"You underrate your charms, my lady. In any case, I want my letter back. Dennis carries it in his coat and he means to use it to drive me from London. You must get it from him."

"I know nothing of any letter, and I cannot interfere. This is a matter between his lordship and yourself."

"He will not give the letter to me, but he will give it to you. I am certain you will know how to ask him in just the right manner."

"I do not wish to see Lord Pomeroy again," stated Rosa.

"Odd, is it not? I do wish to, but I will not. You do not wish to, but you will. Unfortunately, I do not have the heart to savor the irony at present. You must choose a moment when he is warm with ardor. He generally will give you anything you ask for at such moments as those."

"I have told you, I do not propose to involve myself in your dealings with his lordship."

"And I have told you that you will. It is a compromising letter, one which will hurt my uncle as much as myself if it should be made public."

"I should not like to see your uncle hurt. But perhaps it would be best if you told him the particulars of your difficulty. I am sure he would find a way to retrieve the letter for you."

"Lord Pomeroy despises him almost as much as he despises me. No, my lady, you must and will get me my letter. The reason is that William stands to suffer if you do not." Miss Grahame had the satisfaction of seeing Rosa pale.

"What has William to do with it?"

"Simply this: that if I have to resort to asking him to obtain the letter, he will call Pomeroy out and be killed for his trouble."

Rosa quieted herself before replying, "William would not be so foolish as to call out Lord Pomeroy. He would go to the law first."

"The law will not help him; the letter legally belongs to his lordship. Moreover, William is used to being foolish on my account. The knowledge that he will be shot will not prevent him from being foolish again."

Rosa retorted, "What will that solve? Why should you send William to his death? It will not get your letter back."

"I rather fancy having my honor defended."

"Therefore, you will allow your friend to be killed?"

"Perhaps he will only be wounded. Pomeroy is an excellent shot and has killed two men already. But he only wounded the last one he fought."

Rosa closed her eyes a moment. Miss Grahame was poised,

serious, and firm. Nothing in her manner and tone betrayed the wild obsession driving her. She was as calm as death. Then Rosa asked, "You do not care for him at all, do you?"

"Not really—certainly not as much as you do. Besides, I do not care for my own life. Why should I care for his—or anyone else's?"

"Suppose Lord Pomeroy will not give me the letter?" asked Rosa.

"Do not be coy, my lady. He imagines he is in love with you and intends to make you his wife. Surely you can make use of that."

"Suppose I do manage somehow to get the letter? What then?"

"I will trouble you no further. I swear it."

"And you will say nothing to William?"

"You must hurry, Lady Rosalind. We are due to depart very soon. Who knows when you will have another opportunity to get the letter?"

"I must have your pledge first."

"Very well, I will say nothing to William. Why should I, after all? I would not distress him for the world, unless it was absolutely necessary. There is not that much malice in me—yet."

They found the exit by dint of following the echoes of Lady Delphia's strident voice calling for them throughout the ancient corridors. As soon as they reached her, her ladyship scolded them for nearly missing Mr. Walwart's tour of the Bloody Tower—the final event of the afternoon. "As it is near the Traitors' Gate, he says we may embark on the river directly from there."

"Have you seen Lord Pomeroy?" Miss Grahame asked.

Lady Delphia turned a lofty frown on her, then looked indignantly away, not deigning to answer. "We must hurry or we shall miss Mr. Walwart. He will be mortally offended if we do not hear his lecture."

"Lady Rosalind wishes to speak with Lord Pomeroy immediately," said Miss Grahame.

Her eyes narrowing with suspicion, Lady Delphia asked Rosa if that was true. At Rosa's nod of the head, her ladyship smiled broadly. "Oh, if that is the case, why, he is sitting on a bench on the green. He is dog tired, he says, and would not climb up another tower if Mr. Walwart promised him a sackful of rubies from the crown jewels."

"Kindly make my apologies to Mr. Walwart, if you please, aunt. I shall be sorry to offend him mortally and to miss his lecture."

"Never mind him. I daresay he is offended regularly and is quite used to it. It's much more important that you speak to Lord Pomeroy," said Lady Delphia.

Making her way toward the green, Rosa wondered how she could ask for the letter in such a manner as to inspire the gentleman to hand it over. He was smitten with her, or so he would have her believe, but how far would he go if asked to prove it? And would he expect her to give him something in return?

Before Rosa could analyze the question further, Sunley called out to her. She stopped and saw his brown eyes looking at her gravely. Glancing toward the green, she saw Lord Pomeroy lounging on a bench.

Following the direction of her glance, the viscount seemed as though he would say something angry. Instead, however, he took Rosa by the elbow and led her round the corner of the White Tower, where they could not be seen.

"You are going to meet Lord Pomeroy, I collect."

"Yes. I mean, *no*. That is, there is no meeting, but I am on my way to meet him."

"Rosa, do not meet him."

She inhaled and said as lightly as she could, "How very serious you are, Cousin William!"

"Do not pretend with me, Rosa. I know exactly what has happened these past hours."

"How could you know?"

"Aunt Delphia. She told me a match is being made between you and Pomeroy. I am telling you—and I take my oath on it—you do not need to marry him. You may stay in George Street as long as you wish. I shall not send you away if it means sending you to him."

She bowed her head. "I should very much like to stay in George Street. Thank you."

"Then you will not meet him?"

"I have to meet him."

"You have to? I believe you mean that you want to."

She looked at him. "I don't want to at all."

He smiled and took her hand. Never taking his eyes off her face, he put the hand to his lips.

"But I have no choice," she said and, repossessing herself of her hand, ran toward the bench before the viscount's kiss could send Miss Grahame's letter flying from her mind.

Rising to welcome her, Lord Pomeroy vowed he was bored senseless and had been ready to jump into the boat for the past age. "But now you are here," he said, "and the others are not, I am content." On that, he moved close to her on the bench.

Rosa clasped her hands together on her lap, smiled, and tried to think what to say. Gritting her teeth, she told herself that she was merely going to act a part in a play, that the performance would be over after the first act, and that she must take heart. She wished she could think of a line from one of her former roles, or, saving that, one of Tripple's vast store of quotations. The best she could do, however, was to fasten an ingratiating expression on her countenance and glance side-long at his lordship. "I am content, if you are," she said.

"Are you, indeed?" he said with a laugh. "You look perfectly bleak."

"I do not! I vow, I look as content as you do." Never in Rosa's life had her acting abilities been so impugned.

"Then I look perfectly bleak, too. But I certainly do not look as lovely as you." On that, he raised her hand to his lips.

As it was the very hand Sunley had so lately touched, she stared at it. For a moment, she feared it would slap his lordship roundly. It behaved itself, however, and she was able to return it to its place in her lap.

Lord Pomeroy moved still closer and whispered, "Damn me if I ever saw a woman so doleful in my presence. Should I go away? Would that make you happier?"

Lifting her chin, she said archly, "Then you should truly see me doleful."

He regarded her seriously. "Come with me into the White Tower," he said. "If I do not kiss you, I think I will not sleep tonight." He took her hand and pulled her to her feet. She would have found herself inside the Tower in another moment if she had not immediately summoned the force and wit to pull away, saying, "No, my lord. I wish to tell you why I look so bleak and doleful."

She had his full attention now. Taking advantage of it, she gestured for him to sit down again. Sitting next to him in the primmest manner, she prepared to speak. He turned all his concentration on her and waited.

"You profess to love me, sir."

"I do not care for your phrasing. It implies my professions are empty."

"You *say* you love me, then."

"That's a little better. But I prefer 'You love me.' It's the truth."

"I don't think so."

"Marry me. That will prove it. I have never before offered marriage to a woman, at least not so sincerely and so persistently. You ought to be flattered."

"I would be more flattered if you entrusted me with Miss Grahame's letter."

Lord Pomeroy gaped, rose, and swore an oath. He paced for a moment, looking enraged, then walked toward the Bloody Tower as though he meant to drag Miss Grahame from its dungeon and strangle the life out of her. Halfway there he stopped. He seemed to Rosa to debate with himself. At length, he made an about-face and returned to her. Taking his place beside her on the bench, he asked, "Why should you care about the letter?"

"I do not like to think our happiness depends on your threats against Miss Grahame."

"Is this more gentlemanlike behavior you are requiring?"

"If you like."

"I wish I could oblige you, Lady Rosalind. There is nothing I would rather be than a worthy gentleman in your eyes. But you see, if she stays in London, she will ruin any chance we have of happiness. This letter will prevent her staying."

"I cannot think well of you while I know Miss Grahame is thus threatened. How do I know you will not threaten me when you tire of me?"

He grew white. She thought he was on the verge of falling into a towering rage when suddenly he changed his mind.

"You are right, of course," he said between thin lips. "I suppose I could tell you that my treatment of Miss Grahame has nothing to do with you, but you would have no reason to believe me, would you?"

"I would have every reason not to."

"Then here is what I propose to do: I shall have a contract drawn up. We will go to my solicitor in Gray's Inn—tomorrow, if you like—and I will put all my promises to you in writing, signed and sealed, and the lawyer will stake his life that the paper is legal and binding or I will run him through. Will that satisfy you?"

"No. I must have the letter."

Drawing close to her, he touched her arm. "You still insist on that?"

"I would not marry a gentleman who carried another woman's letter with him and could not bear to part with it." She looked at the hand on her arm but did not shake it off.

"Do you mean you will accept me if I give it to you?"

Rosa did not reply.

At her silence, he withdrew and sat back, arms folded. "Apparently you do not care either for me or the letter as much as I had hoped."

"Do not press me, sir. You must give me time."

"Oh, but I will press you," he said and pulled her to him so that he might bury his mouth in her hair.

Rosa permitted him to murmur into her curls for a brief time. Then, stroking his ear with one hand, she felt for his pocket with the other.

It had been some time now since she had filched anything and she felt sorely out of practice. Even if she could find the opening to the pocket, she could not trust that her dexterity was still what it had once been. Her fingers might betray themselves as they eased through the coat.

Lord Pomeroy stirred as though an itch or some other sensation distracted him. Before she could withdraw her hand, he looked down and saw it sliding along his waistcoat. In another moment, she feared, he would pull away and she would lose her opportunity for good. But he did not pull away. Seeing her graceful hand on his chest, he gave out with an amorous cry and sank his face into her neck.

To prevent his noticing the hand again, she traced his ear provocatively with the fingers of her free hand. The writhing and grunting this produced told her she had succeeded in directing his thoughts elsewhere. As she boldly moved her hand inside the coat, she moved her head so that her lips brushed his. He kissed her then, but so continuously that she could hardly gasp for air. In her effort to breathe she ended by biting his lip. At this he held her more tightly than ever, moaning from the depths of his soul that he had never met with any woman so tantalizing in his life. At the same instant, Rosa found the letter and drew it out deftly. The question now was what to do with it.

She could not hide it in her bosom; at any second, that was in danger of becoming the unsafest place of all. She could not use her reticule because to open it she would need to remove her free hand from the sensitive ear. There was a pocket in her skirt, but Lord Pomeroy's hand roamed in its direction every so often, making discovery highly likely. "Bite me again," he whispered hoarsely, and she knew she had better settle on a hiding place without delay.

Just as she managed to slip the letter inside her shoe, his lordship's hand slipped along her arm. Worshipfully, he bent his head and kissed the inside of her elbow.

Pushing him roughly away, she rose with all the indignation of affronted maidenhood. "You go too far, sir!" she warned.

"The elbow is too far?" From the expression he wore, that had clearly not been his experience.

"A woman can tolerate some liberties and choose to ignore others, but that, sir, is beyond what any woman should be asked to endure."

"I swear, I won't go near your elbow again." Grasping her by the waist, he tried to pull her on top of him.

All at once, Rosa saw him ascend like an angel rising up in the air. Then, abruptly, he was deposited in a heap on the other side of the bench.

"If you are determined to offend this lady," said Viscount Sunley, "you may expect to take the consequences."

Sitting up and dusting off his pantaloons, Pomeroy said coldly, "I think I shall kill you."

"Name your time and place."

"That will not be necessary," Rosa interjected. "Cousin William, I thank you for your concern. I know it was meant for the best. However, your interference is not required."

"I think it is. I saw a struggle and heard an argument."

"You saw merely a tussle," Rosa lied.

Standing up, Pomeroy added, "I do not force myself on women. Generally, it is quite the opposite. Ask Miss Grahame if you doubt my word."

Rosa stamped her foot to claim their attention. "Lord Pomeroy, you will take back your threat to kill my cousin. I will not have any killing of any kind."

"You need not worry about me, my love. I am an excellent shot and have not missed yet."

"Lord Pomeroy, you will swear to me you will not call anyone out, for if you do, I shall show myself Lady Delphia's niece and never speak to you again."

Abashed, Pomeroy promised.

"And you, cousin, you will promise me not to be so quick to fight. It is very rash of you. You ought not to be so anxious to get yourself killed."

Looking at her hard, Sunley said, "I will promise on one condition—that you tell me you did not invite the addresses of this blackguard."

Rosa closed her eyes lest they well up under his penetrating regard.

When she did not reply, he turned on his heel and made for the Traitors' Gate.

◊ Sixteen ◊

Reassembled at the White Hart, the touring party tended to echo the sentiments of Lady Delphia, who announced that she was tired and famished to death. They demurred, however, when she declared that visiting historical sites was dreadfully provoking because the interesting adventures of people long dead always made life in the present seem dull.

"I should not like to have my head chopped off, no matter how interesting it might be," said Mr. Tripple.

To which Lord Pomeroy added with a nod at Rosa, "Perhaps our most interesting adventures are still to come."

Rosa sighed, saying, "Life in the present is quite interesting enough for me without having the block to worry about, too."

Miss Grahame could not see that time made much difference—past and present were equally tiresome—while her uncle thought it was far more comfortable to look back at the past from the safety of the modern age.

Viscount Sunley said, "The present is not dull, merely damnable. I should be grateful, in fact, for a little peaceful dullness."

And Mr. Bonwit observed that visiting historical sites would prove a great deal less provoking if people did not run off by themselves all the time, leaving one at loose ends among a lot of tedious old buildings and displays of outmoded fashions.

Immediately the party was invited to run off once more, this time to chambers upstairs where they might refresh themselves before supper was brought. All the travelers left the main room, except for Lady Delphia and Mr. Tripple. As soon as they were alone, her ladyship confided that Rosa had intentionally sought out Lord Pomeroy on the green before they had left the Tower.

"In the boat, he was more attentive to her than ever," said the old actor. He fairly smacked his lips in pleasure.

"I noticed it, too, and am perishing to know if she's come round yet. Ah, here's Sunley. Perhaps he can tell us something."

"Tell you what, aunt?"

"Whether Rosalind is engaged to Lord Pomeroy."

"If she is not," he said tersely, "I believe she will be soon." Before her ladyship could utter a cry of rapture, he interrupted her. "You must make my excuses to Miss Grahame, aunt. I am anxious about my father. He complained of dyspepsia before I left him this morning, and I think I shall take a hack to George Street at once and see if he has improved." He turned his back on her and immediately left the inn.

"Dyspepsia!" exclaimed her ladyship. "My brother has a stomach of iron. It is his cough that plagues him, the doctor says, not his innards. Sunley must have lost his senses, to accuse his father of dyspepsia."

Rosa, who shared a chamber with Miss Grahame, splashed water on her face and dried it with a scented cloth. Without remark, she permitted the young woman to study her every movement at the basin. When at last Miss Grahame demanded her letter, Rosa bent over, drew it from her shoe, and handed it to her. Miss Grahame looked disappointed, almost angry in fact, that Rosa had been successful in obtaining the missive. She would have left the room if Rosa had not stopped her.

"You have your letter now," she said. "I would like you to return the favor by explaining to my cousin William why he found me in company with Lord Pomeroy."

"William found you? I infer from your face that he came upon you as you were being your most persuasive."

"You will please tell him why I was forced to be persuasive. I do not want him to think I wished to be. He may draw the mistaken conclusion that I am engaged to Lord Pomeroy."

"How very awkward for you. Dennis thinks you are engaged to him, and so does William. I suppose you will have no choice but to engage yourself to the man and be done with it."

"I have already told you my intentions along that line. I will take the first opportunity to disabuse Lord Pomeroy. But you must explain to William about the letter."

"Ah, I do not see how I can do that."

Rosa regarded her in perplexity. "How very strange you are."

This caused Miss Grahame to laugh.

"In that case, I will take the letter back," Rosa said.

Miss Grahame tore the letter to shreds and sprinkled the pieces in the water basin. "You are welcome to it," she replied.

"It would cost you nothing to tell the truth. Yet you still refuse."

"But suppose William should become incensed on my behalf and call Dennis out? That is the very thing you wished to avoid."

Rosa blanched but persisted. "I will have to take the risk. I trust I can persuade him not to seek revenge in that way, or in any other way."

"And you are so very persuasive, are you not?"

"Allow me to persuade you to help me as I helped you."

"But you see I have no wish to help you. I have every wish of doing precisely the opposite, in fact."

"Why? Wouldn't I be more useful to you as an ally than as an enemy?"

"More than likely you would. But I much prefer seeing you as unhappy as I am." On this, Miss Grahame left to join the others downstairs.

Peering at herself in the mirror, Rosa saw that she was caught in a trap of her own making. Miss Grahame was right —right for all the wrong reasons, but right nevertheless. Viscount Sunley must not know the truth no matter how much she longed to be vindicated in his eyes. He must be allowed to think the worst of her. He must be allowed to think her engaged to that vile rake, think whatever he chose to think, so long as he did not think that he had cause to meet Pomeroy on some remote dueling ground at dawn.

The question was, could she play the self-sacrificing heroine? Could she continue to live in George Street, as Sunley had said she might, without blurting out the truth? Knowing that the truth would comfort him, Rosa doubted she could summon the strength to play the role. But knowing that the truth might also kill him, she determined to hold fast to her purpose.

Thus resolved, she collected herself as best she could and returned to the main room. There she saw everyone seated at the sumptuous table. The viscount was noticeably absent. Lady Delphia explained to her he had thought it best to leave, as he was sick to his stomach. Rosa thought she knew what it was that had made him ill and thus did not think it wise to comment.

The rest of the party was too busy addressing the supper to converse, but Miss Grahame was more animated than Rosa had ever seen her. Despite the rigors of the day, she appeared to experience a sudden surge of cheerful energy. Rosa speculated that the recent encounter in the upstairs chamber—an encounter which had ended in triumph for Miss Grahame and mortification for Rosa—had revived her spirits. So uncommonly lively was she, in fact, that Lord Pomeroy interrupted his attentions to Rosa long enough to ask the yellow-haired young woman, "What in thunder makes you so full of conversation? I declare, you go on and on like a poop-noddy," an epithet which effectively silenced Miss Grahame for the remainder of the outing.

Lord Divine greeted the weary travelers upon their return. Feeling well enough to sit downstairs with a shawl and a glass of ratafia, he asked Rosa and Lady Delphia for an account of the excursion. Lady Delphia supplied the details. Rosa simply waited for an opening and inquired after her cousin William's health. Was he feeling any better? she wanted to know.

His lordship appeared mystified. "Good Lord, is William ill?"

"I told Miss Grahame he was sick to his stomach and that is why he had taken himself off so unexpectedly," Lady Delphia explained. "I had to make some excuse for his rudeness. Perhaps he really is ill, to behave so outrageously. I have a good mind not to speak to the puppy ever again."

Lord Divine's eyebrows elevated. "He was perfectly healthy when he visited with me. Then he went into the library to review the case, and there he sits even now."

Rosa looked so serious at this that the old man took her hands in his and made various compliments on her beauty. He followed his with avowals of his intention to see her always content, and reminded her of the loyalty and devotion of her newfound family. This produced such a well of emotion in her that she was forced to retire to her bedchamber.

Lady Delphia contemplated the departing Rosa with a great beam of approval. As soon as the girl had gone, she informed her brother that despite the fact that it was a Frenchman who first said it, this was surely the best of all possible worlds!

To Lord Divine's surprised look, she replied that marriages were certainly made in heaven, and although she had made it a point to avoid one for herself these forty-five years, she thought that in certain circumstances marriage constituted a woman's salvation.

Lord Divine grew impatient, saying, "I wish, sister, you would stop talking in proverbs and say what you mean."

"'Pon my word, brother, you have no taste. Anything the least bit literary is certain to give you the fidgets."

"Who is getting married?"

"Rosalind. She is all but engaged to Lord Pomeroy."

With a great effort Lord Divine pushed himself out of his chair. His face red, he said, 'That is out of the question, Delphia."

"It is the most reasonable thing in all the world. It will solve our difficulties and pay our bills. I take it you oppose it on those very grounds. I ought to have known you would take the opposite view."

"I oppose it on any grounds."

"Is one permitted to know your reasons?"

"One is permitted to know this much—I have in mind a different husband for her, and as I am her guardian, I shall have it my way."

While his sister gaped, he walked slowly and painfully to the staircase.

Lady Delphia, who had never seen her brother so forceful, meditated on the list of matrimonial prospects he might have in mind for his niece. At last she concluded that he meant her to marry his old friend Mr. Grahame. As the difference

between Lord Pomeroy and Mr. Grahame was the difference
between twelve thousand a year and thirteen thousand, Lady
Delphia thought either husband would do, though she could
not help giving preference to the title.

Rosa no sooner changed into her nightdress and put her
head on the pillow than she fell asleep. In her dreams she
roamed a maze of endless stone corridors. Here and there
along the way she was bedeviled by headless women tugging
insistently at her skirts and masked executioners nibbling at
her neck.

She awoke and saw with relief that the maid had come in
while she slept and lit a candle. The taper had not yet burned
down very far, indicating that it was many hours yet until
morning. As she did not fancy another encounter with dream
ghosts, she searched for something to read. Unfortunately, the
only book that came to hand was *The Monk*, a tale so scarify-
ing that she doubted it would permit her to sleep ever again.
What she needed was a gentle soporific. Lord Divine had
recently favored her with a reading from Pope. Surely that
poet's rocking couplets and abstract philosphy would lull her
into the arms of Morpheus.

Candle in hand, she tiptoed through the hall and down the
staircase. Pushing open the door to the library, she was startled to see Sunley asleep in a chair. On the floor beside him
was a pile of papers in disarray. A lamp on the table sputtered
slightly beside a half-empty glass of wine. The viscount's
head rested back against the chair. With his cravat loosened
and an aged cat curled on his chest, he looked as though his
wish for peaceful dullness had been granted.

The noise of the opening door caused him to open his eyes.
When they met Rosa's, he smiled contentedly and closed
them again. Then he opened them wide, as though he was
really awake this time.

Rosa whispered a hasty apology and began to withdraw.

"Don't go," he said, sitting up. "Please come inside." He
dislodged the cat so that he might straighten his waistcoat.

"I did not know you were still here. I've come for the *Essay
on Man*. Lord Divine keeps it on that shelf." She pointed, but
he looked at her, not at the bookshelf.

His scrutiny, which took in the unpinned hair and the white nightdress, made her blush crimson. "Will you sit down?" he asked. "I want to ask you a question."

She closed the door and found a chair, wondering how on earth she would answer if he should tax her with difficult questions. Past experience had taught her that she could at times be a truly skilled actress. Somehow, though, whenever she was in company with the viscount, she forgot to act and always ended by playing herself. It was a deficiency of character which had brought her nothing but trouble and must be guarded against at all costs, lest it bring trouble on him as well.

"I am aware," he said, "of my aunt's plan for you. She wants you to marry Lord Pomeroy. Her reason is not to make you happy but to see the family regain some of its lost wealth, as it would have done if the inheritance claim had been successful. One way or another—either through marriage or the law—the Divines seem bent on using you to recoup their dwindling fortunes."

"You must not blame your aunt. I'm afraid it was Mr. Tripple who first thought of it. I told him I did not wish to marry anybody, but as usual, he did not care a groat for my wishes."

"It is not a question of blame, Rosa. It is a question of sacrificing you for the family's comfort. I blame myself for not telling the family the whole truth and sending you away when I should have. If I had, you would not be in the lion's den, preparing to be eaten alive."

"I'm glad you didn't send me away. As for the lion, perhaps he is really as tame as old puss there." She produced a sad smile.

The two of them studied the cat, who rolled on the floor in a sleepy ecstasy so that the viscount might rub her underbelly.

"Don't deceive yourself, Rosa. He is a dangerous fellow. And don't sacrifice yourself, either. We don't deserve it. We are not your real family, and even if we were, we would have no right to coerce you into marrying the likes of Pomeroy."

"Is Lord Pomeroy as good a shot as he is reputed to be?"

Surprised at the change of topic, Sunley looked at her. As her face failed to reveal the motive for the question, he replied, "Yes, he is."

"I am told he has killed two men in duels and wounded a third."

"There are two he is said to have killed, and I believe it. As for the wounding, I am certain he has wounded more than one. His temper is not only hot; it is vengeful as well."

"Is he as skilled with a rapier as he is with a pistol?"

At this question, Sunley's anger got the best of him. "Rosa, please do not ask me to document Pomeroy's prowess for you. If you wish to know more of his heroic exploits, you must apply to him. I have no doubt he will be glad to regale you with all the bloody tales you require."

Despite the tone of his voice, she could not forbear asking, "If you were to meet him, would you be killed?"

He rose from the chair and walked to a bookshelf. Losing the attention of the viscount a second time, puss marched to Rosa and demanded to be petted. From across the room Sunley said, "If you wish to know who is the better marksman, it is Pomeroy. He is the better swordsman, the better boxer, and without doubt the better courtier of women. You may join Miss Grahame and countless others in attesting to his excellent skill as a lover. Most important, he is richer by far than I can ever hope to be. There, I have confirmed for you all his most admirable qualities, and now you may be content."

"I am not content, and I do not admire Lord Pomeroy in the least."

"Then you are making up to him for the sake of the family, and I won't have it!"

Rosa wished she dared tell him how much she despised Lord Pomeroy. But she could not tell him now, and certainly not on impulse. Any revelations she made must be first given the most careful forethought; she must plan every word of her speech lest she say too much. She glanced at puss, who had had climbed upon her lap and settled in the crook of her arm for a nap. With a sigh of regret, Rosa gently lifted the cat to the floor and stood up. "I will just get my book and bid you good night, my lord."

"I have one more thing to say to you."

Rosa heard this with alarm. She did not know how much longer she could keep from spilling the whole truth and precipitating a duel, Sunley's death, and the end to all her hopes for happiness. She thought of Lady Jane Grey and shivered.

At the same time, she could not bring herself to deny the viscount a hearing, especially as it required her to stay near to him a little while longer. Therefore, she sat down again. Puss appraised her, trying to decide whether to attempt another nap.

"I want to thank you, Rosa," Sunley said formally.

Her face warming, Rosa shook her head. "I did not get you your bequests as I was supposed to have done. I merit no thanks."

Puss jumped onto her lap and settled down to lick her paws preparatory to sinking into sleep.

"I'm not talking about the bequests. I'm talking about Miss Grahame."

As Rosa shifted uncomfortably, old puss opened a warning eye and glared at her. "If I have done anything for Miss Grahame, it was because I thought you would wish it."

"I'm not talking about Miss Grahame. I'm talking about myself and Miss Grahame."

"Oh. Well, I've always known you are deeply attached to her."

"That is why I have to thank you. Not long ago, I was so deeply attached that I was in danger. I might well have become as foolish and obsessed as she is with Pomeroy. One thing saved me, however. I met you."

Rosa stood up. Evicted yet again, puss scolded her with an indignant mew and took herself off to a safely inanimate chair. With a raised hand, Rosa stopped him from speaking further. "No more, sir. Please do not say any more."

"I will finish what I started to say. Heaven knows it's difficult enough to say it, but I must tell you that knowing you has made me regain myself again. I have laughed again, smiled again, even spoken like a sensible man again from time to time. And it is because you made me laugh and smile and see the value in being sensible."

"You are forcing me to tell you what I swore I would not tell you."

Perplexed, he moved toward her. His nearness distressed her even more.

"I am not at liberty to explain, but I wish you to know that when you saw me on the green with Lord Pomeroy, we were not forming an engagement."

"I confess, I thought you were. If you say you were not, I will believe you."

Rosa nearly groaned at this forbearance. She turned her back to him so that she would not see his expression when she told him the truth. "I was picking his pocket," she said.

She waited. Considerable time went by and still she heard no sound, not even the sound of his breathing. It did not surprise her that he was momentarily stunned into silence. However, as the minutes continued to pass and he continued to say nothing, she grew a little impatient. She had given him the sort of news which ought to have produced something— outrage, disgust, even lofty contempt—but something more than silence. Piqued, she turned to face him and found him smiling.

"And did you get what you were after?" he inquired softly.

"Naturally. But I am awfully out of practice and felt that it was high time I found out how much I still remembered. Should it become necessary for me to quit George Street, despite your generous invitation to me to stay, I should need some means of earning my livelihood."

"And what did you discover?"

"I discovered that one's fingers quickly lose the requisite dexterity, unless they are kept nimble by frequent practice. Happily, I was very good at pickpocketing in the past and my fingers did not fail me."

"I am glad to hear it. If one goes in for any sort of avocation, one ought to be very good at it."

"I do not think I boast when I say I have never yet been caught."

"You know, it occurs to me that you might have Divine blood in you, after all."

"Do not tease me, sir."

"Very well, I won't tease you." Instead, he put his hands on her cheeks, tenderly lifted her face, and kissed her delicately on the mouth. Her arms went around him and clasped him to her so tightly that he was moved to enclose her in his arms and kiss her again, not at all delicately.

A quantity of time passed in this manner. Then, releasing her, Sunley smiled, noted again her nightdress and loose curls, and walked to the bookshelf. In a moment he found a leather-bound volume and brought it to her. "Here is your Mr. Pope. And so, good night."

"William," she said softly, taking the book from him. "There is so much I wish to tell you."

"It would be better if you took Mr. Pope upstairs now. And I would be obliged if you would do it quickly, before my envy of the fortunate fellow gets the better of me."

Kissing him lightly on the cheek, Rosa disappeared from the room. Sunley sat down in his chair, contemplating with contentment the revelations of the last half hour. Old puss, seeing her former nestling place restored, bounded over to the chair and jumped on the viscount's lap. He stroked her fur meditatively until he fell into the first restful sleep he had known in some time.

◊ Seventeen ◊

If Rosa expected the next day to bring a resumption of the previous night's tender dialogue, she was disappointed. The morrow—in the person of Nunn—brought her two notes on a salver, both of them containing bad news.

The first, and by far the worst, came from Sunley and announced his departure for the country. It vouchsafed no explanation for this sudden journey save a vague reference to business. It did not say when he intended to return. But it did say, "I will come back to you as soon as I can," which clearly meant that he had not regretted in the cool light of morning what he had said in the warm shade of night. That knowledge made it possible for Rosa to glide through the house, smiling merrily and greeting all who came her way with a fervent interest in their good health and happiness.

The other note came from Lord Pomeroy, who announced his intention to wait on Rosa that very day. He had something of a particular nature to ask her, the note said. No sooner did Lady Delphia hear of the intended visit than she instructed Rosa to wear her pink and blue muslin and to carry a fan in case the gentleman should become so ardent during the articulation of his particular question as to require a rap upon the hand.

Preoccupied with remembering Sunley's laugh, Sunley's smile, Sunley's delight in her career as pickpocket, Sunley's cat, Sunley's kiss, and Sunley's gallantry in sending her back to her bed, Rosa forgot to defy Lady Delphia's directives. She appeared in the sitting room in the exact dress her ladyship had recommended.

"I do not like this," said her ladyship to her brother in a confidential voice.

"It is a charming dress," Lord Divine replied. "I thought you expressly advised Rosalind to wear it."

"But why do you suppose she put it on?"

"Because it looks so well on her and shows her figure to advantage."

"Don't be an idiot, Grantley."

He shrugged helplessly. "How should I know why young ladies do what they do? Or old ones, either, for that matter."

This answer did not satisfy Lady Delphia in the least. Her anxiety continued to mount, especially as Rosa agreed with everything she said and did not even dispute with her when she pronounced *Daphnis and Chloë* far superior to any of the Italian operas.

When Mr. Tripple was admitted for his daily visit, her ladyship disclosed her uneasiness to him, and he had to agree that something was amiss. He had never known his Rosa to be so complaisant in her life. She smiled radiantly at Lady Delphia, let Lord Divine beat her unmercifully at loo, then playfully curled the old actor's beard round her finger. To his irritable, "What ails you, girl?" she answered with a mysterious smile and a wink.

This reply produced the profoundest gloom on Lady Delphia's face. She began to think Rosa's brain had been adversely affected by excessive exposure to history at the Tower.

Mr. Tripple had another idea. "Do you suppose she is in love?"

"I don't think so. From everything I have heard, love is not likely to make one agreeable."

"But look at the evidence, my lady. She enacts a tragic love scene with his lordship at the Tower, then deliberately seeks him out on the green. She permits his attentions throughout the journey home. The next day she receives a note announcing his visit—a visit whose purport is clearly to make a proposal of marriage—and she sings and dances as the hour draws near. What other conclusion can be drawn?"

"If you are correct, then we shall soon have an immense disaster on our hands. My obstinate brother says he will not permit Rosa to marry Lord Pomeroy. He has his heart set on Mr. Grahame."

"Well, if Mr. Grahame is rich enough, he is as good a husband for her as the other."

"But if she has her heart set on Pomeroy, what then?"

"Oh, I see," replied Mr. Tripple. "She may defy Lord Divine. In fact, if she loves Pomeroy, she is certain to defy him. Your brother in his turn would forbid her to marry Pomeroy. She in her turn would refuse to marry Grahame. In the end, she will have neither of them and then where shall we be?"

"Exactly. This is dreadful, Mr. Tripple, and it is all my brother's fault. He never used to know his own mind. I do not know what has got into him."

"I have a notion. We will enlist Viscount Sunley's help. He is a most sensible gentleman and will know what to do."

"My nevvew is nearly as impossible as his father. He is gone to the country. Heaven knows what he's doing there or when he will return."

"Then we must wait for him. Meanwhile, we will prevent Lord Pomeroy from making his proposal to Rosa today. No one must propose anything to anybody until his lordship returns."

"I suppose we must do as you say if we are to avoid a confrontation with my brother. But if he grows any more stubborn I shall be forced to stop speaking to him."

"My poor Rosa. How cruel it seems to keep her from

plighting her troth to her lover. I hope she will forgive us and understand that what we do, we do for the greater good."

Lord Pomeroy's behavior proved so egregious that it convinced Lady Delphia he suffered the most exquisite raptures of love. He regarded Rosa under heavy-lidded eyes, saying nothing to her once the initial cordialities had been dispensed. He addressed an inconsequential question to Mr. Tripple, then got up from his chair and walked to the window in the middle of the reply. He complained of unbearable heat in the room and, when the window was opened for him, complained twice as bitterly of a chilly draft. He paced in front of Rosa, stopping to scrutinize her every so often. His expression as he did so was so intensely burning that it persuaded her ladyship—if she needed persuading—that the gentleman would explode if he was not permitted to make his proposal soon.

Although her ladyship would have liked to oblige him, she remembered her late vow of prudence and held firm to her chair. She ignored his many hints that she and Tripple ought to leave the room, laughing at him archly.

Seeing that his hints failed to achieve their end, Lord Pomeroy sought to accompany Rosa to the music room to fetch the new song she had learned at Lady Sefton's behest. But Tripple intervened, volunteering to fetch it instead. Thwarted again, Lord Pomeroy made so bold as to request a moment alone with Lady Rosalind. Rosa, whose thoughts still dwelt on Sunley, made no objection, but Lady Delphia grew incensed.

"'Pon my word, sir, do you take me for some country clot? The moment I leave, you will be down on your knees to the poor girl, besieging her with pretty speeches. It would be most improper."

"I take my oath, I will not make love to Lady Rosalind."

"I don't believe you."

"I merely wish to speak with her about my letter." His voice had an edge. His fingers moved as though he wished to grasp something—anything—just so he might squeeze it within an inch of its life.

The reference to the letter jolted Rosa. Her merry smile vanished. She realized all at once how little forethought she had given to the consequences of picking his lordship's

pocket. Of course he had known instantly who had taken the
letter. Of course he was fiercely angry with her. She ought to
have known how it would be. She ought to have guessed from
the moment she'd allowed her hand to wander inside his coat
that he would know what became of the letter. Her excuse
must be blindness, blindness and stupidity. She'd grown blind
and stupid from worrying about Sunley. Watching Lord Pomeroy's twitching fingers move, she began to feel a little
frightened.

"Pah! That is merely another ruse to get rid of me," Lady
Delphia barked. "There is no letter, sir, except in your fancy."

Rosa had never been so grateful for her ladyship's obstin-
acy. The last thing she wanted now was a private interview
with Lord Pomeroy.

The door opened, Tripple came inside with her music, and
she ran to him and took his arm. As he handed her the music
sheet, he was surprised to see how very white she had grown
in his absence. The cause seemed to lie in the words Pomeroy
was addressing to Lady Delphia.

"I did have a letter, ma'am, I assure you, but it was stolen
from me—from my person."

Lady Delphia grew impatient. "You must take care not to
wander in certain sections of the town, sir. They are known to
be rife with thieves and pickpockets."

At the mention of these two species of Londoner, Tripple
looked at Rosa again. Her face now flamed with color.

"You may recall, ma'am, that yesterday I wandered in the
same sections of town as yourself. The letter was stolen from
me as we toured the Tower."

"Ridiculous," Lady Delphia told him. "There were few
tourists there besides ourselves. You must have dropped the
foolish thing. You must return to the Tower and search for it."

"Rosa," Tripple said sternly, "do you know anything about
a lost letter?"

Taking the music sheet from him, she crossed the room and
placed it on the harpsichord, where she immediately became
engrossed in perusing the music.

"I asked you a question," Tripple said in a voice that riveted
the attention of his listeners.

Smiling brilliantly, Rosa replied, "I know that a young lady wrote a letter and later regretted writing it. I understand that she wished to have it back."

Lady Delphia's brows shot up. "It was that kind of letter, was it?" She leveled a shocked look at Pomeroy.

Mr. Tripple breathed in relief. It seemed that there really was only a love letter at stake here, not crowns or pounds or guineas. He was sure his Rosa would not have picked a pocket unless there was profit in it. She had too much sense to jeopardize their shaky position by stealing a worthless piece of paper.

Lord Pomeroy addressed Rosa with barely concealed anger. "Will you help me regain my property?"

Keeping her voice steady, she replied, "I cannot."

"It will go very hard with the thief if you do not."

Mr. Tripple found his suspicions roused once more by this interchange. He asked his lordship point-blank, "Are you saying that Lady Rosalind has some knowledge of this thievery?"

"I am saying that Lady Rosalind knows what became of my letter."

Lady Delphia scowled disapprovingly at him. "Even if she does know, you ought not to say so, my lord. 'Pon my word, I thought you came to make love to Rosalind, not interrogate her like some barrister."

"If I had any idea of making love to her, ma'am, I have since learned to repent it. Nevertheless, I stick to my point. Lady Rosalind does know where I may find my letter."

"Good heavens, Rosalind. Tell his lordship what he wants to know. I vow, it is the most tiresome letter ever written."

"I will tell his lordship this much," Rosa said carefully. "The letter no longer exists. There is no purpose, therefore, in pursuing the matter."

Her ladyship could not help inquiring, "What on earth did it say?"

Tripple walked to Rosa. He opened one of the music sheets and invited her to sit at the instrument. Bending low and speaking so that only she could hear, he warned, "You know far too much about this letter. I can see that you do. You had best keep mum for now. Let nothing slip, I charge you."

Lord Pomeroy approached the harpsichord and studied Rosa.

She faced him boldly. Their eyes locked in silent struggle.

"Say nothing," Tripple whispered.

She ignored him, saying, "I saw the owner of the letter destroy it."

"*I* was the owner of that letter," Lord Pomeroy replied. "Those responsible for destroying it will answer to me."

"Was it a love letter? 'Pon my word, Rosalind, you have not been corresponding in secret, I hope."

Lord Pomeroy challenged Rosa as openly as he dared. "Lady Rosalind," he said, "I will stake my life there was a pickpocket in the case. Do you not agree?"

With a proud tilt of her chin, she replied, "I think it very likely. But it may be just as well the letter is gone. From what I am told, it would have been put to evil use."

Despairingly, Tripple asked the ceiling why any sensible pickpocket would risk so much for the sake of a deuced letter.

Lady Delphia rose from her chair to join the others at the instrument. Glaring first at Pomeroy, then at Rosa, she sniffed heavily. "You will put an end to any secret correspondence at once!" she commanded. "I will have your promise on that, Lord Pomeroy! No more communications of that sort shall pass between you and Lady Rosalind."

"I can safely promise you to have as little contact with her ladyship as it is possible for any human creature to have," he answered.

"I am relieved to hear it. And while we are in a promising mood, you will promise to form no secret engagements with her, either."

His eyes glittering, Lord Pomeroy gladly promised. As he bowed to take leave of Rosa, he vowed, "I will not forget you, my lady. You shall hear more of me in future." Nodding curtly to the others, he left the room.

Upon his exit, Tripple lamented, "I suppose we've lost him now, and all on account of that letter. Oh, Rosa, how could you be so foolish?"

"Nonsense, Mr. Tripple," said Lady Delphia, "I thought it most kind of his lordship to make it clear he will not forget Rosa. I was afraid he would give her up altogether when he saw he was not to be allowed to propose. It might be a very handy thing to have him loitering about, in case my brother should change his mind about Mr. Grahame."

At the mention of the name, Tripple shook a finger at Rosa. "Heed me well, my girl. When Mr. Grahame comes to you, you had better keep your fingers well in check!"

Rosa stared at him. "Mr. Grahame?"

"Yes. Lord Divine means you to marry him, and Lady Delphia and I mean you to accept him."

Lady Delphia sighed, "I suppose he will visit next, and when he does I hope he comes to the point quickly. But I insist, Rosalind, that you do not write him any letters. They are nothing but vexation."

Not knowing how to reply, Rosa wished that Sunley would return safely and speedily from the country.

Nearly a week passed without any sign that Lord Pomeroy meant to act on his threat against Rosa. Neither did any communication arrive from the viscount. In the uneventful days which followed, only one noteworthy event occurred. It took place during the last of a series of parties at the house of Lady Sefton. The young girls were asked to perform at the harp, pianoforte, or flute. Each girl's performance was greeted with polite applause and excessive praise. Lady Sefton particularly asked Rosa to play a Scottish air and beamed upon her as she played. In the middle of the song Lady Nitney and Countess Lieven rose from their seats and, holding their chins aloft, left the salon.

Although Rosa felt the slight, she managed to continue playing and singing to the end and to appear to have noticed nothing out of the way. In contrast, Lady Delphia sat as though she had been bludgeoned on the head. The instant the song was finished, she caused her carriage to be called and sent Rosa outside to wait for it. As she followed Rosa to the door, she confided to Lady Sefton, in a voice that penetrated to the farthest mouse hole in the house, that Lady Nitney and the countess were certainly the most flagrant old hens she had ever encountered and she would never again speak to such two ill-bred hawk faces as long as she continued to breathe the English air.

At supper, Lady Delphia indignantly related to her brother everything that had transpired. Still smarting from the slight,

Rosa awaited his verdict on the incident with some trepida-
tion. But Lord Divine was not disposed to feel the insult as his
sister and his cousin did. After all, he pointed out amiably, the
Divines would still do very well without the approbation of
two empty-headed women. The important thing was to enjoy
the dinner Nunn was setting before them—a baron of beef
with savory sauce. The two ladies permitted themselves to be
comforted and said no more on the subject.

Two days later, however, while he napped at his club, Lord
Divine wondered if the incident had, in fact, been less innocent than he had assumed. He was resting with his newspaper
over his face when he overheard a piece of gossip. The pur-
veyor of the gossip read a newspaper report regarding a young
man of the town—one whose reputation for taste in dress
would soon make him another Brummell (but one without
creditors hot on his heels, it was hoped). This arbiter of fashion had lately had his cravat crushed, so to speak, by a reputed heiress, an auburn-haired beauty who now looked to
make a match with the son of a marquess.

Even Lord Divine, who paid as little attention to the comings and goings of the ton as it was possible to pay, could not
mistake the references to Bonwit, Pomeroy, and Rosalind.
The listeners hooted at the report, and it wounded his lordship
to hear them laugh so. They waxed witty, making references
to Mr. Nitwit and predicting the burning of all his natty neck-
ties once he should take up permanent residence in the slough
of despond. As they left for the card room, one of them de-
vised a rhyme entitled "La Divine Rosaline," which the others
committed to memory and repeated over and over.

> If for a wife
> Thy heart doth pine,
> Make your bid to
> Rosaline.

> But beware,
> For, by your sword,
> She'll throw you over
> For a lord.

When the merrymakers were finally gone, his lordship threw off the newspaper from his face and sat up. Immediately he rushed to George Street. Finding everyone seated in the salon, he blurted out the tale of the report and the rhyme.

Rosa wondered where the *Clarion* could have heard such a rumor. Surely Mr. Bonwit would not have revealed to them details of a story which redounded so little to his credit. On the other hand, Mr. Bonwit was a rattle and could not always be depended on to know what did or did not redound to his credit.

Mr. Tripple suggested that perhaps an enemy of Rosa's had been the source, but Lord Divine declared it to be out of the question, as the girl could not possibly have an enemy in the world.

"'Oh God, that men should put an enemy in their mouths to steal away their brains'!" quoth Mr. Tripple. "Or to steal their letters, for that matter!" he added, examining Rosa closely. "If this is Pomeroy's work, he will regret it. I shall tell the viscount when he returns. He will know exactly what to do about the scoundrel. He will call him out, I daresay."

"No!" Rosa appealed to him. "Please say nothing of this to Viscount Sunley."

Frowning, Tripple shrugged. "He is not even here, and no one knows when he will return. There is no use in promising anything one way or t'other."

"Merciful heaven, what will Mr. Grahame think?" Lady Delphia asked in horror.

Lord Divine did not know why Mr. Grahame should think anything at all. "I expect he will be appalled, as we all are," he said.

Everyone in the room looked bleakly at Rosa, and she sank under their gazes. She knew not what to say, given the fact that the report was partly true—she had refused Bonwit, and more than once. But even if the scandal had been utterly false, she still had no idea what could be done about it.

In the midst of this general misery, Lady Delphia rose grandly from her chair to state, "It is ridiculous to think we cannot withstand a little foolish gossip. The Divines are an independent race. We care not for the opinion of the world."

Her audience was moved to admiration.

"Do you forget that a similar report was once spread abroad regarding myself and a young chandler?"

"I do remember, Delphia. I remember the poor fellow ended in the dock over your broken promises to him."

"Precisely. And what harm came to my reputation over it? None a-tall. As Mr. Tripple is so fond of quoting, 'He who steals my reputation steals nothing'"

Mr Tripple winced, then posed a question: "I do not mean to imply that your ladyship's allusion is not precisely accurate, but are you saying that such gossip can be ignored?"

"Exactly. In point of fact, I expect this little episode will enhance Rosalind's reputation very nicely. And if Mr. Grahame possesses any backbone a-tall, it will serve to intrigue him all the more."

The rest of the company paused to consider the matter in this interesting new light, while Lady Delphia looked down upon them as if from a pedestal.

In the midst of their meditation, Lady Sefton burst into the room on the heels of Nunn. "I must know if it is true!" she cried.

Lady Delphia remained calm. "'Pon my word, here's another one in an uproar over Mr. Bonwit's broken heart! I tell you all, it does not signify."

Lady Sefton stopped in her tracks. "Bother Mr. Bonwit!" she stormed. "I am speaking of Lord Pomeroy. It is all over London that Lady Rosalind picked his pocket."

The only sound following this announcement was the noise of Lady Delphia's crumpling in a heap on the carpet.

◊ Eighteen ◊

Sunley entered the salon to find his father and Mr. Tripple standing over a candle, attempting to burn a feather. His aunt lay sprawled on the carpet with her head in Rosa's lap. Although Rosa had her back to him, the Viscount could see that she waved a vinaigrette under her ladyship's nose.

Lady Sefton was the only one who saw him enter the room. Running to him, she implored, "Oh, tell me it is not true! She sings so beautifully, and everyone knows I have taken her under my wing. I shan't be able to show my face in London for years and years if it is true."

Rosa, who had turned around at these words, stood up quickly when she saw Sunley, permitting Lady Delphia's head to drop unceremoniously onto the carpet. The viscount walked to Rosa, took in her grave expression at once, and pressed her hand.

"Tell you what isn't true?" he asked Lady Sefton.

"That she picked Lord Pomeroy's pocket."

As his eyes met Rosa's, he could hardly keep from laughing. He remained composed, however, saying, "I am certain there is a good explanation for such an amazing story, but I must beg your indulgence, your ladyship. I have a matter of the utmost urgency to discuss with my family. As soon as we can revive my aunt, we must leave the house."

At that, everyone looked at poor Lady Delphia on the floor.

Lord Divine and Mr. Tripple blew out the feather and all the other items that they had inadvertently set afire. They then rushed forth to greet Sunley.

"Thank heaven," cried his father. His lordship attributed his son's timely return to providence, as was his wont. Inclining his head in his sister's direction and looking very glum, he observed, "I'm sure a burnt feather would revive her if only we could keep it from bursting into flame and burning up the household."

"I have news that will restore my aunt," said Sunley. He smiled warmly at Rosa. "I hope Lady Sefton will excuse us now."

Bursting with curiosity, Lady Sefton delayed her departure as long as she could, but as no excuse for staying came to hand, she took the hint and allowed Nunn to show her the way out.

Sunley knelt before his aunt and whispered in her ear, "Aunt Delphia, the nursemaid has been found."

Tripple and Lord Divine gasped, then exclaimed, then applauded.

Lady Delphia opened one eye.

"It is true, aunt. I managed to locate her in Surrey. She allowed me to bring her back to London."

Both eyes opened.

"She awaits us this very instant at the chambers of Messrs. Buffel and Buffel."

Lady Delphia sat bolt upright. "What are you gawking at?" she scolded her brother. "Come and help me up. We must lose no time in getting ourselves to Lincoln's Inn."

The solicitors' rooms radiated with the smiles of its inmates. Sir Virgil Thwaite, accompanied by Mr. Peter and Mr. Paul Buffel, rubbed his hands, swayed back and forth on his toes and heels, and smiled on the soon-to-be heiress. Lady Delphia, Lord Divine, and Mr. Tripple sat down in their chairs with consummate confidence, steadily beaming upon Rosa. Sunley sat next to her and smiled, too.

Of all the smiles in the chamber, none was greater than that of Sukey Dawes. At Rosa's entrance she looked up shyly and evidently saw a sight moving enough to make her weep for joy. "Why, she's a luvely thing, she is," Sukey declared, her voice half choking. She smiled beatifically with the others.

Rosa squirmed under these stares, wishing she could find a place to fix her eyes that did not confront her with another hopeful smile. As far as she was concerned, the discovery of the nursemaid boded nothing but disaster. She wished the others did not place so much importance on the woman's testimony. Surely they could see what she saw—that it would prove only one of two things—either that Viscount Sunley had succeeded in bribing the poor woman, or that the woman refused to be bribed and would demonstrate once and for all that Rosa was an impostor. She did not know which of the two she feared most.

"Yes, she is a luvely thing," Sukey said again. She seemed to derive courage from this declaration, for she did not lower her eyes to her hands again.

Hearing Sukey speak a second time, Lady Delphia turned loftily in her direction. "You have caused a vast deal of inconvenience, my good woman," she said.

Sukey turned slightly yellow and swallowed. "Yes, ma'am," she said. Her eyes rolled and she swayed a little.

"Running off like that after promising faithfully to swear that our Rosalind is who she is!"

The viscount walked to Sukey and caught her before she fell from her chair. After calling for a glass of wine and making her sip it, he said to his aunt, "I have promised there will be no recriminations. Mrs. Dawes has a great fear of her superiors, she says, and does not like to hear them talk to her in loud voices. I beg you, aunt, to say as little as possible to her."

"I don't know why she should be frightened of me. I am as mild as a lamb. But I'm sure it would be no punishment to me not to speak to her. There is nothing I should enjoy more."

"It was to avoid this sort of encounter that Mrs. Dawes ran away and hid. She was afraid of just such a confrontation."

Sir Virgil stepped forward and said expansively, "She has no cause to be afraid now. She has only to tell the truth."

Rosa coughed noisily at this.

"As to that," said the viscount, "I am not certain exactly what Mrs. Dawes has to say. She tells me now that she may not be able to swear to Rosalind's identity as she once thought. I hope we may persuade her otherwise."

All eyes looked at Sukey. Lady Delphia's glare so terrified her that she began to sway again. Finally Sunley prevailed upon the nursemaid to look at Rosa instead, which produced a blushing smile on the good woman's plump face.

"Ah, but she is a luvely thing."

"Now, Mrs. Dawes," said Sir Virgil, "can you identify this young woman as the daughter of Elizabeth Martin and John Divine, Earl of Beckwith?"

"I done a sinful thing, your worship," Sukey said. "I prays the young lady will not think too unkindly of me."

"I will not think unkindly of you," Rosa promised warmly, inspiring Sukey to wipe her eyes with a corner of her shawl.

The nursemaid drew her chair closer to Rosa's. "When as Viscount Sunley comes to me and says 'e wants me to take me hoath you be the infant grown up, I promises to swear because 'e is so kind a gentleman, not loud and angry like most of 'em be. But I 'aven't the right. Night comes hon night and I knows I 'aven't the right to swear. So I runs away."

"You must have been awfully frightened," Rosa said.

Sukey reached out her hand and Rosa took it. Her eyes brimming, the nursemaid continued, "Then his lordship finds me and says 'e still wants me to take me hoath. And still I am frightened and wants to run away again. But I 'aven't the right. Night comes hon night and I knows I 'aven't the right to run away. So I comes back with 'im."

Sir Virgil contained his impatience. "Mrs. Dawes, we do not understand your meaning. Could you be more explicit?"

"What is 'explicit'?" the bewildered woman whispered to Rosa.

"We should have got Lord Pomeroy while we had the chance," Lady Delphia said.

Rosa sighed. She knew she could still stop Sukey. At this moment there was still a chance of preventing the truth from coming out. In another moment, it would be too late. "'Explicit' means 'plain,' Mrs. Dawes."

"Yes, I see. Well, then, to be *explicit*, I comes back because I knows oo is and oo an't the infant grown up."

"Aha!" said Sir Virgil. "Now at last we are getting somewhere."

Mr. Paul Buffel inquired gently, "Is this young lady sitting before you the daughter of Beckwith and his bride?"

All leaned forward as Sukey leaned forward to inspect Rosa. Finally she sat back and said, "I don't know."

Amid the ensuing gloom, Sunley stepped near her to ask,

"Mrs. Dawes, you say you know who is and who isn't the infant grown up. How do you know?"

Sukey looked up at him shyly. "There be a port-wine stain."

All her listeners stared at one another in bafflement.

"A port-wine stain," Sunley repeated. "What is that, Mrs. Dawes?"

"Behind the baby's ears. Such sweet tiny ears they wuz, too."

"The woman tipples," said Lady Delphia. "Mark my words."

"I does not!" Sukey defended herself. "Hit just don't seem right to make the young lady show us 'er ears. Hit just in't dignified, she bein' such a luvely thing and all."

"Mr. Tripple," Sunley asked, "does Lady Rosalind have any unusual markings behind her ears?"

"Stap me if I know. I never noticed a one."

All sighed and stared at Rosa, looking pained.

One after the other, she returned their looks. Then, knowing that she would undo the fondest hopes of everyone she cared most about, she unpinned her hair. The curls fell about her shoulders as she shook them out and put the pins in her lap. She then bent her head low and pulled up the auburn locks until they cascaded over her brow. Everyone gathered round to examine her behind the ears.

For some time there was no sound. Then Sukey Dawes began to sniffle. Mr. Tripple murmured, 'Time's glory is to unmask falsehood and bring truth to light.' Lady Delphia declared she didn't see that a pair of ears was worth making such a fuss about. When he was able to tear his eyes from the sight of Rosa's bare neck, Sunley walked to the window for a breath of air. Mr. Peter Buffel removed his spectacles and wiped the dust from them with a piece of linen. Putting the spectacles on again, he closely inspected the ears once more, saying, "Did the woman say *port*? I see no port-wine stain there. Looks more like Burgundy, if you ask me." He wiped his hands as though they were dusty.

Lord Divine entreated Rosa to lift her head up. As she did so, she looked at Sunley. He smiled at her and said, "You have the marks. It seems we've been telling the truth all along!"

Rosa stood up and put her hands to her cheeks. The emotions she felt astonished her. A moment ago she would have sworn she had long since given up wondering who her real parents were, long since stopped longing for them, long since stopped wishing to find them and to live with them. But now she could hear her pulse pounding and feel the heat on her face, and she knew that she had never for a moment stopped wondering, longing, and wishing.

That she might in reality be Beckwith's daughter had never entered her mind. Not seriously. Glimmers of hope had penetrated her determined stoicism, telling her that, after all, she did bear the name, that Tripple had found her by the workhouse where Elizabeth Martin had died, and that she had at one time worn a locket that might have been inscribed with a *B*. But she had always dismissed these circumstances as coincidence, or as providence, as Lord Divine like to say. It was better to deny hope entirely at the beginning than to nurture it and later see it utterly withered in the end. And so she had not allowed herself to hope.

Abiding by this philosophy, she had gotten along very well. Now, however, the greatest wish of her heart had been answered, and she wondered how she had survived so long in uncertainty.

"The news should not surprise me, of all people," said the viscount. "I always said you exhibited the most notable traits of the family. My compliments, cousin." He kissed her hand.

"Behave yourself, Sunley," said Lady Delphia. "There is the matter of the bequests to settle. Leave our cousin's hand in peace."

Kissing it one more time, Sunley returned the hand to its owner. His smile was alight with irony and Rosa smiled back.

"As to the bequests . . ." Sir Virgil began.

"You say there are bequests in the case?" asked Mr. Peter Buffel.

"As I recall," Sir Virgil went on, "there is the matter of forty thousand pounds in capital and shares to Lord Grantley Divine, thirty to Lady Delphia and Viscount Sunley. Then there is, of course, the young lady's inheritance."

"We should like to have it right away, if you please," Lady Delphia said.

"We shall do our best to get the funds released. As for the inheritance, it is to stand under Lord Divine's trusteeship until such time as the young lady marries."

"I shall be glad to advise my brother in its administration. I am known to have an excellent head for matters of money."

"For spending it, I believe you mean, sister!"

"I warrant I manage better than you do, brother. Unlike yourself, I have not lost my house in town for want of funds to keep it."

Sukey Dawes, who had remained perfectly quiet during this interchange, now commanded everyone's attention by shrieking, "No! You 'aven't the right."

"I thought you said she was too frightened to speak, Sunley," said her ladyship.

"It's the money they're after!" Sukey cried.

"Please, do not alarm yourself, Mrs. Dawes," Rosa said soothingly.

"And you such a luvely thing, too," sobbed the nursemaid.

Rosa moved to comfort her and soon found the distraught woman weeping on her bosom. "'Tis a pity, it is," she mourned.

"Do you care for something to drink, a bit of wine perhaps?" Rosa asked solicitously.

"Wine?" Sukey cried in anguish. "Did you say port wine?"

"I do not know what sort of wine Mr. Buffel keeps."

"I do not need any wine!" Sukey cried. She rose from her chair, her red face storming defiantly. All at once she hardly seemed like the frightened creature who had greeted Rosa upon her entrance.

The others looked at her as though she were a lunatic.

"I cannot testify," Sukey said. "I can never go into court and swear before God and judge."

"But a moment ago you positively identified the young lady," Sir Virgil protested.

"You haven't changed your mind again, Mrs. Dawes?" Lord Divine asked.

"I cannot say as she is Beckwith's daughter! I 'aven't the right. Night comes hon night and I know I 'aven't the right."

"But the port-wine stains? What about the port-wine stains?" asked Mr. Paul.

"There be port-wine stains all right, but they ben't Beck-with's port-wine stains."

"Whose are they?" cried Mr. Tripple.

"They be my baby's port-wine stains. My baby's!"

No one spoke. Sukey looked down at her shoes, then shyly at Rosa. She looked as though she expected to be thrashed.

Rosa had the presence of mind to ask, "Do you mean I am not Elizabeth Martin's daughter, but yours?"

Sukey bowed her head.

"Certainly she tipples," Lady Delphia said. "It's the only explanation."

Sunley took Rosa's hand and pressed it reassuringly. Then he turned to the nursemaid. "Sukey, are you telling the truth this time?"

"She be my baby with the port-wine stains. Hit was the hother baby as died."

Rosa looked at Sukey Dawes, trying to see some likeness between herself and the frightened woman. "Why did you lie?" she asked in an unsteady voice.

"I wanted me baby to 'ave a good life, not a beggar's life."

Rosa looked at the others. Their faces were drawn in horror.

"And you did not 'ave a beggar's life, did you?"

"No, Mrs. Dawes."

"I be your mother now and so you must call me."

Rosa did not answer. She thought the woman was kind enough, and she pitied her greatly, but she could not bring herself to call her mother.

"My luvely child. Now I sees you and I sees these leeches sucking at your life's blood, I 'aven't the right to keep mum. Hit's time as you comes home with your mother now."

Rosa looked about her helplessly.

The viscount said, "Surely, Sir Virgil, there is some way to prevent this action."

Sir Virgil looked stupefied.

"Surely the law will not tear Lady Rosalind from the house where she is comfortable and from the family she has known these past months. We will not let the law act so cruelly and so precipitously."

"She bees my daughter, sir, even though you are kind to me

and speaks in a pleasant voice. I cannot leave 'er to stay with you as I 'aven't the right. I must hown her now, as hit be right for me to do."

Rosa stared at the woman. She could hardly absorb what had happened. Events had fallen about her like dominoes. She was not an orphan but Beckwith's daughter—more than she had ever dared to dream. She was not Beckwith's daughter but a nursemaid's—worse than she had ever allowed herself to fear. That she could be raised so high only to be brought so low in the work of a moment—it took her breath away. All along she had told herself that Sukey Dawes's discovery meant disaster. But she had not imagined disaster could take the shape of such an odd, round, frightened, pathetic creature —one, moreover, who claimed to be her mother.

◊ **Nineteen** ◊

"I don't believe it. Not for a second," Lady Delphia said.

She sank into the sofa cushions and gazed moodily around the sitting room. The wainscoting stood in need of repair. New furnishings should have replaced the shabby chairs and settees years ago. A worn path in the carpet led from the door to where she presently sat. Taken all in all, it was a shameful room, and now that the means of improving it had once more been plucked from her grasp, she peered into the future only to see it furnished with more of the same. "That unspeakable woman. Do not ask me to be in the same room with her ever again, Grantley. I do not wish to speak to her."

"I wish I had never set eyes on her at all," said Lord Divine with a sorrowful sigh. He appeared pale and aged. Rosa suspected that he was feeling genuinely ill.

"I wish I had not pawned that locket," Tripple said. He seemed to Rosa very weary. The fire of energy that customarily animated him had been almost completely damped, leaving only the merest spark.

"I wish I had never found Sukey Dawes," Sunley said warmly. "She wanted to be lost. Why did I not let her stay lost?"

Rosa watched him as he leaned against the mantelpiece, one hand raking his hair. She wanted to say something to soothe him but was too grieved by the sight of his distress to speak.

The sight of them together—her family, so to speak—moved her deeply: Lady Delphia, looking like a general who had lost the most important campaign of the war; Tripple, looking as though he sat for a portrait of Heartache; Lord Divine, looking bewildered and hurt; and Viscount Sunley, looking furious and handsome and reminding her of the smiling gentleman she had met in the theater alleyway. She longed to find a way to give them all ease.

Lady Delphia wrung her hands. "I suppose Mr. Grahame will lose interest now. He may have made his money in trade, but he will think himself much above the daughter of a nursemaid."

This allusion to his friend offended Lord Divine. "I assure you, sister, Mr. Grahame will always be loyal. He is one friend who is not likely to prove fickle."

Lady Delphia revived a little. "I am very glad to hear it, brother. If, as you say, he will still wish to marry Rosalind, it will perfectly answer everything. Rosalind will not have to go and live with that creature, who, I am convinced, tipples the gin from morning until night. And each of us may have a little money to pay our bills. I am glad Mr. Grahame will not fail us. I always liked him excessively."

Lord Divine, who had stared at her throughout this entire speech, now cried out, "Do you mean Mr. Grahame wishes to marry Rosalind? Why did he never tell me this? Oh, it is the worst turn of all. I shall have to speak to him, I'm afraid."

"Are you raving, brother? I thought you were forwarding the match."

"I forward no matches. I may entertain certain matrimonial hopes for Rosalind; however, I keep them private and do not interfere."

Mr. Tripple interjected here, "Then if you never meant her to marry Mr. Grahame, she might have had Pomeroy! Good God, what fools we mortals have been!"

"I should not have permitted her to marry Pomeroy," said his lordship. "I had hoped to keep her nearer the family than that." He threw a glance in Sunley's direction and sighed. The viscount, preoccupied with thoughts of Sukey Dawes, did not heed the exchange.

Seeing them bicker and worry, Rosa could hardly contain her emotions. She blamed herself for letting events come to such a pass as this. Why had she not left George Street as soon as Viscount Sunley said she must go? Why had she waited for him to set the time and manner of her departure? She ought not to have spoken to Tripple and allowed him to concoct his ridiculous scheme to marry her off, a scheme which had failed anyway. She ought not to have gone to the Tower, or tangled with Lord Pomeroy, or fallen in love. In short, she ought never to have been born.

If she could not feel hopeful, however, she could act as though she did. She had not been separated from her former vocation so long that she'd forgotten how to simulate whatever attitude the situation required. Therefore, she rose from the sofa and said with spirit, "I must ask you all to stop looking so desolate. It is no great tragedy."

"Ah, my girl," Tripple moaned, "you never did have any idea of tragedy. You are a comedienne by training and inclination."

"Well, I do not play the fool, for all my comical flair, and I have made up my mind. I shall go and stay with Mrs. Dawes for a time until she wearies of me and decides she is not my mother after all. No doubt she will change her mind. She seems to change her mind from day to day and from minute to minute. I see no reason why she should break a habit which evidently gives her so much pleasure." Here Rosa produced a determined smile.

Sunley folded his arms and regarded her. "If you don't wish us to look desolate, then you must not talk of going away."

It was impossible to keep to her purpose while looking at him, so she directed her glance at Mr. Tripple. "It isn't as though I should be gone forever. Besides, have you thought what might happen if I do not go to her?"

Lady Delphia nodded wearily. "It is true. The woman will go to the law over it, I've no doubt. People of that sort go to the law on any pretext, however meager."

Lord Divine sighed in resignation. "I suppose it would not be the first scandal the family has had to endure, Delphia. You said as much yourself."

"There will be no scandal and no word of any kind spoken in a court of law," Rosa said. "I will not see the family treated so. I will go to Mrs. Dawes of my own free will, and when she has had enough of me, I shall return."

Sunley walked to her. "Rosa, I beg you not to do anything hasty. We cannot count on her ever having enough of you. She may want you with her for the rest of her life. No one in this room would blame her if she did. Give me time to think, to find a way out of this."

She avoided his eyes. "Very well. I will give you time. I will give you a week. If you have not thought of anything by then, I shall go to Mrs. Dawes." Then, rather than face the stricken looks which greeted this announcement, she made for the door. As she walked slowly up the grand staircase, it occurred to her that now she really understood what it must have been like to be Anne Boleyn marching to the chopping block.

In the course of the next week, Rosa received daily missives from Mrs. Dawes. These notes were dictated by the nursemaid, who could not write, to a clerk employed by Buffel & Buffel, and they repeated what Rosa had heard at the law chambers, namely, that the woman had seen what a "luvely" girl Rosa had grown up to be, that she yearned to have her come to live with her so that she might care for her again, and that she wished nothing more than to save her from the schemes of those who were out to use her for their own avaricious ends. Appended to each note was a plea for forgiveness; she hoped, the nursemaid wrote, that Rosa would endeavor to forget that she had been abandoned at an early age and would now embrace poor Sukey Dawes as her mother.

Although the notes nearly overset Rosa each time one arrived, she maintained enough self-command to answer in proper form. Lady Delphia peered over her shoulder as she sat at the writing desk, advising her as she wrote.

"I do not see why you insist on replying at all," her ladyship complained. "The woman deserves no such politeness from you, nor from anybody else."

"She is my mother, your ladyship. Therefore, she deserves every politeness."

"Pah! Next you will ask me to believe that the Whigs will say something intelligible before the next election. Your mother, indeed!"

Despite her ladyship's scorn, Rosa continued to answer the notes. The one thing she did not do was address the nursemaid as mother.

Lady Delphia's attention was soon drawn away from Rosa's notes by a very peculiar circumstance, one which could not be ignored after the passage of some days, to wit, that no visitors—not a single one—called in George Street. Every day closed without a tattoo on the door knocker or a card sent into her ladyship's sitting room. Whenever she inspected Nunn's salver, she invariably found it bare. Scowling prodigiously, she wondered aloud at dinner why her acquaintances had suddenly conspired to neglect her so abominably.

To satisfy herself on that head, she sallied forth one afternoon to visit Lady Jersey. As Rosa declined to accompany her, she went alone, and no sooner had she left than she was forced to return. Lady Jersey was not at home, and neither were various other ladies of her extensive acquaintance. Only Lady Sefton would receive her, and that brief visit was allowed only upon condition that Delphia would keep Rosa away until this matter of the stolen letter was settled. After all, Lady Sefton had sponsored the girl. Any scandal attaching to her protégée reflected badly on herself. Surely Delphia had too much regard for the Sefton family name, not to mention the Divine family name, to permit one silly girl to drag them all through the mire, regardless of how prettily she sang.

Incensed beyond speaking, Lady Delphia forgot to vow never to speak to Lady Sefton again. She returned home, pled the headache, and for the next three days reclined on a divan with a cool cloth soothing her forehead.

For as long as he could, Lord Divine kept Sunley from

Waiter's. His object was to prevent him from hearing the gossip about Rosa, which now held all of London spellbound. No other subject could be found on noble lips. No other subject could arouse such savored whisperings and derisive snickers. Should Sunley be exposed to the tittle-tattle, his father knew, he might not be able to contain himself. There was no one so rash, so hot-tempered, so ready to whip out his sword in defense of a woman's honor, as a young man head over ears in love with her.

Managing to elude his father one day, the viscount did stroll into one of the parlors at Waiter's and found himself a quiet corner chair facing a window. He entertained himself for half an hour by reading a pamphlet on the Corn Laws, when a shout of voices interrupted him. As he was on the point of making his presence known, the intruders surprised him into silence with a reference to Rosa. Above the sniggering, Sunley discerned references to Pomeroy and a letter. The former reference he ascribed to the pickpocketing gossip, of which he had taken little notice except to laugh. The reference to the letter, however, puzzled him.

In another moment, anger was added to puzzlement, for the wag who had composed the rhyme about Rosa and Bonwit now spewed forth the results of his latest courtship with the muse:

> La Divine
> Rosaline—
> The Queen of Coquetry—
> Will steal your heart
> (And letters too!)
> With sly pickpocketry.

Stepping forward from the shadow of the corner, Sunley quickly snatched the poem from the author's hand and crushed it in his fist. Contemptuously looking from one abashed face to the next, he let the paper fall to the floor. "I had thought that Waiter's was a gentleman's club," he remarked on his way out the door.

"You said nothing about a letter," Sunley said to Rosa.

He had sent Nunn to fetch her to the library, where she sat rigidly, trying not to recollect their last tender meeting there.

"Rosa, you led me to believe that you picked his pocket for the sport of it, to keep in practice, you said. That was not the truth, was it?"

When she looked up, she saw a light of anger in his eye. It stopped her from saying what had nearly spilled from her lips. It reminded her sharply of her reason for stealing the letter in the first place.

"You must promise not to be angry," she said.

He shook his head. "I make no promises."

Silently she turned her head away.

All at once she felt herself seized by the shoulders and raised to her feet. She was aware of his nearness, aware of his determination. "I will know about the letter," he said. "If you do not tell me, the gossips will. But you must know that I prefer to hear it from you."

Rosa was glad that he held her firm, for she felt her knees begin to give way. There was no means of keeping Sunley safe from Pomeroy, she saw. One way or the other, he would find out the whole, call the scoundrel out, and be killed. Nothing she concealed now would save him. And nothing she told him now would save him, either. She was completely helpless.

"Oh, William," she said in a near whisper, "I have done nothing but harm to all of you. I meant to do exactly the opposite." Here she paused and smiled tearfully at the irony.

"I expect there is some awful secret about this letter of yours. Was it a love letter?"

She drew a tired breath. "You must ask Miss Grahame about the letter."

"Miss Grahame? What the devil has she got to do with it?"

"Only she can tell you that."

"Then there really was a letter! You really did steal it, and you lied to me. You wanted me to think you had picked Lord Pomeroy's pocket as part of a mischievous escapade. You did not want me to know the real reason, that you had written him a love letter and wanted it back. And so you lied. Tell me this, if you would. What else about that day was a lie?"

She paled. "Nothing!"

"A very convincing denial. Is it, too, a lie? Was that night a lie as well?"

She bowed her head until she had calmed herself enough to speak. "You know very well what my true feelings are."

"Do I indeed? What do I know about the true feelings of an actress? I am no better than the rest of your audience. I believe what it suits you to make me believe."

"William, if you do not believe me, no one will."

"But I am the last one to ask for trust, my dear Rosa. I know what the Divines are made of, and honesty plays no large part in it, no part at all, in fact. I told you we were all liars and thieves, and you have been so complaisant as to bear witness to my assertion."

Rosa's eyes narrowed. Now she was angry too. "But I am not a Divine," she retorted. "I am the daughter of a nursemaid!" And, hoping that would prove her veracity once and for all, she returned his infuriated look full in the face.

◊ Twenty ◊

"Suzanne," the viscount said when Crouch had left them alone, "there is something you must do."

She gazed at him under her lashes with a thin smile. "You did not used to give me orders, William. You used to behave like a friend and a gentleman."

"There was a time, you know, when that sort of reprimand would have distracted me from my purpose. It doesn't any longer. You must tell me about this letter of Pomeroy's."

Miss Grahame turned ashen. "She had no right to tell you. It was to be a secret. She has betrayed me. I knew she would."

"She has told me nothing. That is why I am here, to get the truth from you."

She directed a sullen glance at her fingernails. "I have a

dreadful cough. I cannot possibly entertain any visitors this day. You will excuse me, I know." She would have left the parlor, but his firm grip on her arm detained her.

"I will not bother to appeal to your sense of honor, Suzanne. You have finally persuaded me that such a thing does not exist. And I will not bother to appeal to your sense of fairness, or of decency, or even to your good sense. You will only sneer at such appeals. I will therefore save my breath and tell you this. If you do not tell me everything, I will speak to your uncle, and in such a way as to convince him you do not belong in London, not for another ten years at the very least. Imagine, Suzanne, ten years without setting eyes on your precious Pomeroy."

The beginning of this speech amused Miss Grahame. She had lately heard a similar threat and, thanks to Rosa, had managed to get round it. As Sunley continued, however, her expression grew increasingly bitter. At the final sentence, tears began to stream down her cheeks. "You have deserted me," she said hoarsely. "I knew it would come."

Sunley took her by the hand and led her to the sofa, where they sat. "My dear Suzanne," he said softly, "you will tell me everything."

She lifted her brimming eyes to him. "I cannot. I am too ashamed."

He patted her hand. "That is a promising sign, I think. Telling the truth will do you a world of good."

She snatched her hand away. "You have changed, William. I used to love you once. I believe I quite hate you now."

Smiling a little, he took her hand back in his. "I am very obstinate, I own. It is in the blood of the Divines, and I am powerless against it. How fortunate that you did not accept my proposals of marriage and bind yourself for life to such a difficult fellow."

Although it required a vast deal of prying and urging from the viscount, Miss Grahame did at last confess that it was she who had written the letter to Pomeroy.

"But why did Rosa agree to get it from him?"

Blushing, Miss Grahame said, "She feared you would call him out over it."

Still, he looked mystified. "Why should she think so?"

"Because you do have flashes of anger, William. You know you do. And in such moments, you are fully capable of anything."

"Yes, but I hope I am not such an ass as to call out a man who would surely kill me. What caused her to think I would?"

Turning quite pink now, she answered, "I told her you would. I told her you would demand the letter from Pomeroy and be shot for your trouble."

Because this reply did much to reassure Sunley, he did not scold Miss Grahame as much as she feared he would. Indeed, he immediately prepared to leave, saying he was anxious to return to Hanover Square. Before he left, he promised to come to her again the next day. He meant, he said, to bring Lady Sefton with him so that she might hear the entire story from Miss Grahame's own lips. Once Lady Sefton knew the truth, she would have it in her power to set the gossips' wagging tongues to rest.

To Sunley's disappointment, he was unable to see Rosa, who had taken it upon herself to pay a visit to Mrs. Dawes at the nursemaid's humble lodgings. As soon as she returned to George Street, she went directly to her bedchamber. The note he sent up to her room was returned unopened.

The following morning, he sent Rosa another note and received the following answer:

> My lord,
>
> You were once so good as to thank me. It is now my turn to thank you. When you brought me to George Street, you introduced me to more sweetness and gentleness than I imagined existed. I am thankful to you and to Lord Divine and Lady Delphia, too, and I feel toward them as much as any real cousin could—more, to say the truth.
>
> In addition to my obligations to you and your family, I have an obligation to Mrs. Dawes. The week I promised you is now past, and I must and shall go. Do not think, however, that

my leaving is a sorrowful event. To me it
appears a blessing, for my continued presence
brings those I love most in the world nothing
but mortification and unjust scorn.

I must now ask you to add one more kindness
to the many you have already done me, and
that is to make no difficulty over my departure,
to say nothing whatever of a particular or
sentimental nature, and to treat me as you
would any friend who departs on a necessary
journey.

I am, with sincerest wishes for your good
health and happiness,

Rosalind Divine

He would have responded on the spot, pounding on Rosa's
door and shouting through it if it came to that, but he was
promised to Lady Sefton. He set off for Bloomsbury Square,
determined to set the letter nonsense to rights. That done, he
would deal with Rosa, and before he was finished, she would
know that he could no more refrain from saying something of
a particular and sentimental nature than he could let her disappear from his life.

Miss Grahame had by this time reconciled herself to the
duty she must perform. She invited Lady Sefton to sit opposite her while the viscount stood behind her and a little apart.
Lady Sefton, whose rabid curiosity had led her to accept Sunley's invitation, now glanced from the gentleman's serious
countenance to the lady's sallow one in the hopes of detecting
some intrigue.

Miss Grahame came to the point directly. "I understand
your ladyship has questions regarding Lady Rosalind and
Lord Pomeroy. I believe I can satisfy you there."

Lady Sefton prepared herself for a juicy tale.

"I asked Lady Rosalind to obtain a letter of mine from his
lordship. I very much regretted ever sending it, but he refused
to return it to me."

"And so Lady Rosalind stole it for you?"

"She put herself at risk on my account, yes."

"What a brave thing for her to do. And she sings like an angel, too."

"It is wrong for Lord Pomeroy to set it about that Lady Rosalind is a thief. I hope you will do what you can to scotch the rumor."

"I am afraid I cannot help you there, Miss Grahame."

"But I have just explained everything."

"Yes, and even if I believed you, it would do no good. Because, you see, Lady Rosalind did steal the letter. Her motives may have been the noblest, but that does not change the fact of what she did."

Miss Grahame looked at Sunley. Then she burst out laughing. Lady Sefton peered at her through her glass and asked her if she was feeling feverish. Wildly, the young woman gestured. At last she rose to her feet and began to weep. "You see," she said, "whichever way I go, I cannot do any good, not even by telling the truth!" She ran from the room, leaving Sunley to make her excuses to the visitor.

Lady Sefton looked at him expectantly. She had heard he nourished a tendre toward Miss Grahame and now hoped to glean the evidence of it.

"Miss Grahame told the truth," he said.

"I am sure you think she did. You are on terms of intimacy with her, and therefore feel obliged to believe her."

"You are a good-hearted and fair-minded woman, Lady Sefton. I know you will do what you can to quash these rumors."

"You and Miss Grahame put me in mind of myself and a young soldier I once knew. He was as devoted to me as you are to her."

"It would be wrong if Rosa should suffer because Lord Pomeroy spreads lies about her."

"But, you see, it is not a lie. It is the truth. And were it the falsest of lies, I should still not be able to undo the damage that has been done. The ton love a rumor and care not whether it has any foundation in fact. Retraction is useless, I'm afraid."

Sunley frowned a little; then, concluding that the situation was not to be resolved as he had hoped, he offered to escort her ladyship to her carriage. After seeing her off, he attempted to invent some cheerful word to say to Rosa and his family upon his return. He settled at last on the idea that the family fortunes could do nothing but improve hereafter. After all, they could not possibly get any worse.

Unfortunately, there was no opportunity to deliver this word of cheer. A commotion greeted the viscount when he entered George Street, one of such proportions that it drove his message completely from his head. It took some time to discover the cause of the disruption.

Lady Delphia was in a towering snit, threatening to cease speaking to everyone who came within earshot. "How could Rosa ever have thought of marrying such a scoundrel as Pomeroy?" she lamented. "I will not call him a gentleman, for he is no such thing!"

Sunley entreated his aunt to calm herself. When he at last managed to quiet her, he turned his attention to the others. Between his father and Mr. Tripple, both of whom looked perfectly funereal, stood a rotund fellow sporting an air of importance.

"Where is Rosa?" asked the viscount.

"In her room, gathering her things," Lady Delphia replied. "And what she saw to love in Lord Pomeroy I shall never know."

"Who is that?" Sunley inquired, looking at the stranger.

"You might well ask!" said his aunt darkly. But she did not elucidate, and so the man was forced to step forward and explain his presence himself.

"Wally's the name, sir. Constable Simon Wally, at your service. I come on an errand which is regrettable in the extreme, but which it is my sworn duty as to carry out."

Sunley looked from his father to Mr. Tripple, neither of whom would meet his eye or utter a syllable.

"I come for Lady Rosalind Divine," said the constable apologetically. "Her ladyship has been so good as to say she will not make a fuss but will come along straightaway."

"What for? Where are you taking her?"

"As to your first question, sir, as to what for—I have a writ against her and am required to arrest her on a charge of pickpocketing. I believe that's the long and the short of it, sir, but if you've a mind to see the legal lingo of it, here it is." Mr.

Wally handed Sunley a paper, which he read without comprehending. "As to the where—my orders is to take her to the prison."

"I am certain you act with the best of intentions, Mr. Wally, but you are not taking Lady Rosalind to prison."

"Her ladyship asked if she might go to the Tower, as she would rather fancy staying there a bit, but it isn't used in that way much these days, more's the pity."

Sunley turned on his heel. Taking the stairs two at a time, he knocked at Rosa's door. As soon as she opened it, he reached for her. She held him away. "I am expected below," she said softly.

"You are not to move from this house."

"You Divines must learn that you cannot always have things your own way."

"It will take more than the likes of Pomeroy to teach me a lesson like that." He pulled her to him and kissed her hard.

Rosa did not respond, but the effort to hold back cost her the better part of her composure. She summoned every acting skill she had ever acquired to keep from throwing her arms around his neck.

Feeling her still lips under his, he let her go.

"I ought not to have accused you," he said. "I had no right to doubt you. It was stupidity and jealousy, and I am very sorry."

"I know you are sorry, and I've forgotten it already. But you see, it is too late. The truth, whatever it is, does not matter."

"It does matter. Do you expect me to stand by and watch you march off to prison?"

"If you would do something for me, then let me alone."

"That's the one thing I cannot do."

"In that case, you will increase my pain beyond bearing."

He regarded her, hoping that when her eyes met his, she would melt. But she held firm.

"I will return as soon as I can," he said at last and left her. A moment later, she heard him quit the house.

It was several hours before he came back, during which time Lord Divine continually implored Mr. Wally to wait just a moment longer for Viscount Sunley. He came in to find Rosa alone with the constable. Lady Delphia had gone to bed, predicting she would never rise from it again. Lord Divine had retired as well, having suffered a relapse of his former indisposition. Mr. Tripple had gone back to his lodgings and would look in on them all in the morning. Mr. Wally was regaling his prisoner with stories of crazed murderers and the heroic constables who had apprehended them.

Sunley had little of a comforting nature to report. He had not succeeded in getting the charge against Rosa dropped. Pomeroy was adamant. He would see Lady Rosalind tried and convicted, if it took him his entire life to do it. The judge had seen no way out of the charge if his lordship insisted on pressing it. Only Sir Virgil Thwaite had been able to help, and even he had not accomplished very much.

He had succeeded in obtaining permission for Lady Rosalind to await trial at the home of Mr. Peter Buffel. Sir Virgil had vouched for the integrity of both the lawyer and the prisoner. He would see to it that Lady Rosalind remained in Mr. Buffel's custody and did not violate the terms of her confinement. He himself would accompany the lady before the bench on the appointed day, and would lend his learned assistance to her defense.

Rosa heard these words as though she had already been pronounced guilty and had only to hear her sentence. She watched numbly as the viscount picked up her carpetbag and took her by the elbow to lead her to the door. She hardly noticed Mr. Wally following discreetly behind them.

In silence, they drove to Kensington in Sunley's coach, followed by Mr. Wally in a conveyance furnished by Bow Street. At Mr. Buffel's neat, narrow house, the carriages stopped, the riders alighted, and the three of them approached the door. Mr. Buffel himself answered their knock.

"Here is Lady Rosalind," Sunley said. He attempted to press her hand, but she drew it away.

"Lady Rosalind, you say?"

"Yes. You agreed she would stay with you until the trial."

"I agreed to that, did I? Well, I shall certainly have to tell Mrs. Buffel."

He disappeared, leaving the three to stare at an open door.

Mr. Wally delicately withdrew to the street again, so that the lady and gentleman might have a word or two of leave-taking in private. He tried not to look at them but could not help noticing that although they did not exchange a word, the gentleman managed to make himself ardently expressive. He failed to penetrate the lady's silence, however, and soon a large woman dressed all in black filled the doorway.

She looked Rosa up and down, scowled, and said, "So it's the quality as is come to honor us with a visit. There is only tea and a biscuit in the morning, so don't you be expecting more."

As that appeared to be all the invitation Rosa would hear, she went inside, looking neither to the right nor left, and heard the door close soundly behind her.

◊ Twenty-one ◊

To Mrs. Warrinda Buffel, the beau monde represented corruption, selfishness, ostentation, affectation, and excess. As the representative of the beau monde, Rosa appeared to her the very incarnation of everything that was wrong with England. Thus it was that Rosa found herself scowled at, sneered at, and snapped at from the moment she entered the lawyer's portal.

Unlike the rooms at Lincoln's Inn, the Buffel household was free of dust, books, and Mr. Buffel. Mrs. Buffel chased after dirt as though it were a minion of the devil himself. She expostulated whole mornings to Rosa on the evil of mud tracked in at the door and of grime left on clean surfaces by soiled fingers. In all matters pertaining to the maintenance of a sparkling household, Mrs. Buffel saw symbols of the human condition and its tireless struggle against moral decay.

Apart from dirt, Mrs. Buffel knew of no greater corrupting force in the universe than books. If not for books, she informed Rosa, the world might still revel in its early pristine state. If not for books, the beau monde would never know what sins were available for the committing. Without books to guide them in their gross extravagances, the aristocracy of Britain would now stand proudly alongside the upright men and women of bygone days.

In Rosa's view, the absence of dust and books accounted for the absence of the lord of the house. He put in a single appearance each day, late in the afternoon, to sit down with the two women for an unvarying and spartan dinner—beef, potatoes, and greens mercilessly boiled a full day. At all times he confined himself to two snatches of conversation, to wit: "Did I say that, my dear?" and "Did you say that, my dear?" He never interrupted his wife's harangues against Rosa and the rest of the quality, on whom his livelihood depended. Nor did he blink whenever she saw fit to instruct Rosa in the meaning of the eighth commandment.

During one of Mrs. Buffel's most virulent attacks on the indiscretions of the nobility, Rosa was moved to protest. "I am not a noble lady!" she said.

Mrs. Buffel turned to her husband. "I thought she was an earl's daughter."

"Did I say that, my dear?"

"It is not true," Rosa said. "I am a nursemaid's daughter."

"She says she is a nursemaid's daughter."

"Does she, my dear?"

"I believe she must be telling the truth. I see no reason why she should lie about it. Were she one of the quality, she would insist on being an earl's daughter. The daughter of a nurse-maid would exhibit no such propensity to vanity."

"Had I not been brought here," Rosa pointed out, "I should be living with my mother even now."

"I told Mr. Buffel as soon as you came in the door that from the look of you, you might not have been wholly infected by the noxious influence of your surroundings and there might possibly be some detectable good in you."

"Did you say that, my dear?"

"You know very well I did, and please hold your spoon properly. All the custard is dropping onto your lap."

Having exhausted his fund of conversation, Mr. Buffel employed his napkin to wipe his lap, his mouth, his chin, his fingers, and his knees. When he had done, he rose and bowed his way out of the room to return, as Rosa imagined, to the comfort of his dusty chambers.

Thenceforth Mrs. Buffel addressed Rosa very differently. "So, a nursemaid was your mother," she said. "Now, that is a useful occupation. You are very welcome in my home, dear."

She was not so forbearing, however, when Viscount Sunley visited, for she no sooner heard the title prefixed to his name than she planted herself between them on the hard sofa and glowered straight ahead.

Sunley was silent for some time in the hope that the formidable lady would grow bored and take herself off. When it proved impossible to bore her, he said to Rosa, "I came expressly to ask if there is anything I can do to help you."

"Miss Divine is well cared for here, sir," declared the lady of the house.

An uncomfortable silence followed.

"I am going away," he said.

The only reply Rosa could manage in Mrs. Buffel's presence was, "I wish you a safe journey."

"I am hoping to find something that will help the case."

Rosa shook her head. "I do not know which case you hope to help, nor what can possibly be done to help either of them now."

"Confession and repentance," stated Mrs. Buffel. "They are the twin blessings which help even the most hopeless of cases."

"Thank you, Mrs. Buffel," said the viscount. "I shall remember that, along with your kind hospitality to my cousin."

"She is not your cousin. She has told me the entire truth of her birth."

"And what truth is that?"

"Why, that she is a nursemaid's daughter."

Sunley looked at Rosa over the head of his hostess. Feeling his eyes on her, Rosa said, "Yes, my lord, I told Mrs. Buffel that Sukey Dawes is my mother."

With all his heart, he wished Mrs. Buffel would disappear. "We do not know that for certain," he said.

"I am certain I am not Beckwith's daughter. That was

merely a dream. The reality is as different as it can possibly be."

"For which we must be very thankful," said Mrs. Buffel.

Sunley declined to debate family matters in the presence of a stranger. Rising, he began to take his leave. He quickly saw that he was not to be allowed to say his good-byes in private. He therefore took Rosa's hand, and, under the disapproving nose of Mrs. Buffel, put his lips to her palm. Commending her to the care of Mrs. Buffel, he gave one parting look and left.

Rosa put the hand he had kissed to her cheek and kept it there throughout most of the day. She had much to do to understand her own mind, for as soon as he left, she knew she did not want him to go; as soon as she told herself that he must not be allowed to visit her again, she wished immediately to see him again; as soon as she declared that he was better off getting as far from her as his journey could take him, she wished he would change his mind and come back.

Tripple, who visited Rosa some days later, fared better at Mrs. Buffel's hands than Sunley had. Hearing that the gentleman merely called himself a mister, the good woman delicately left him in private with the prisoner, although the door remained open.

"I hear the trial is to be next week," Tripple told her.

"I do not understand why Lord Pomeroy persists. I should think he would have abandoned the case by now. Surely it cannot increase his standing in the world to bring a female to court over a matter of a letter. It makes him out a coward and the very opposite of a gentleman."

"Very true, but put no faith in your excellent logic to change Pomeroy's mind, my girl. Do as I do and rely on more practical resources."

"What resources could I possibly have?"

"You have me, and I have a plan," Tripple said quietly.

"Dear Tripple, I hope it does not depend on marrying the sons of marquesses."

"That was a very excellent plan, in the main. It is not my fault it went awry. But this new plan of mine is much simpler. It merely requires me to effect your escape."

"You would have me run from this house?"

"It is not such a fine house that you have grown attached to it, I trust. So polished and bare a house it is, too. Does no one actually live in it?"

"Mrs. Buffel has no children. She says that children muss a house. She grows peevish when her house is mussed."

"All the more reason for you to run from here and come with me to Ireland. There are one or two very good companies there."

"I will not escape, Tripple."

"You are the most obstinate girl. Did I not tell you to go to George Street with his lordship and Viscount Sunley? And was I not right to insist on it when you held back? Well, this, too, is a sensible plan. I should like to hear one argument against it."

"I do not propose to spend the rest of my life running from the law. Nor do I propose to jeopardize your future by shackling you with a fugitive. Sir Virgil vouches for me and I am obliged to repay his trust. Mr. and Mrs. Buffel promised to keep me in their custody, and it would go very hard with them if I were to violate the terms of my sojourn here. And furthermore, I do not wish to escape."

"I asked for one reason, Rosa. That was half a dozen at least."

Mrs. Buffel poked her head in to offer some refreshment, which was gladly accepted. The good woman cordially agreed to join them and in the course of conversation happened to ask Mr. Tripple his occupation.

"I am a humble actor," he replied.

Mrs. Buffel stood up abruptly, upsetting a plain hard cake. She bent to retrieve the crumbs, and when she was satisfied that they had all been captured, she rose and faced the gentleman. "I must ask you to leave my house," she said.

Quickly swallowing his last bite of cake, Mr. Tripple moved to comply. "I am sorry if you have seen one of my performances and disliked it. I am well aware the public is also a critic, but I feel it deeply whenever one of my portrayals is so realistic as to offend."

"I have never seen a performance of yours or anyone else's. Nor do I mean to."

"My dear lady, you cannot dismiss me from your house without giving me an audition."

Before Mrs. Buffel could object, he launched into Polonius's advice to his son. "'Give every man thy ear, but few thy voice,'" he declaimed, and Mrs. Buffel had to allow that those were the very words she lived by from day to day. "'The apparel oft proclaims the man,'" he quoted, which Mrs. Buffel thought an amazing piece of wisdom, worthy of a sermon, in fact. "'Neither a borrower nor a lender be,'" he intoned, to which Mrs. Buffel replied, "I have been telling Mr. Buffel that for ages."

At the conclusion of the speech, Mrs. Buffel grew very quiet. An expression of abysmal woe suffused her face. When Rosa and Tripple voiced their concern, she confessed that she had begun to doubt an opinion she had always held as inviolate. "Perhaps," she said, "perhaps I have been mistaken in my idea of actors."

Mr. Tripple assured her she had been; actors, he proclaimed, were the finest fellows in all the world. Rosa joined her voice with his in saying that one might associate with actors without irreparable damage to one's character.

This produced a shower of tears from Mrs. Buffel, who sobbed that, having been mistaken in this, she might come to discover she had been mistaken in other things, and that if she had been mistaken in other things, she might be mistaken in everything, and that if she had been mistaken in everything, her entire life was a sham.

At this dire view of the matter, Mr. Tripple changed his tune. "If you put it that way, dear lady, then you are not mistaken. Actors are not proper company for a woman of your stamp, and you have every reason to boot me from your doorstep."

Relieved, Mrs. Buffel ordered him to leave at once. He bade Rosa good-bye, saying he could not bear to see anyone, not even Mrs. Buffel, think her entire life a sham. That good woman spent the remainder of the day in as cheerful a condition as Rosa had ever seen her.

The good woman was still cheerful a week later when Lord Divine called; so much so, in fact, that she employed her fullest energies to be rude to him. She would have stayed to prevent any private conversation had not a maid informed her of a hideous accident; a pot had spilled in the kitchen, staining the floor. Mrs. Buffel ran off to supervise the cleaning, leaving Rosa to inquire closely into the state of his lordship's health.

Even before he answered, she could see that he was not well. The indisposition which had afflicted him earlier in the month had returned with greater virulence than before. His eyes were rheumy; his voice cracked; his brow perspired with fever. The old gentleman looked as though he needed to take to his bed immediately and stay there, and so Rosa told him.

"I am afraid I shall have to do as you say, Rosalind, for I do not know how much longer I can stay on my feet. But I did not wish you to think the family had deserted you in your hour of tribulation."

"I should never be so ungrateful as to think that."

"Oh, but you would be perfectly justified in thinking that —with William gone off so suddenly. And then, of course, there is my sister."

"I hope her ladyship is well. Please extend my warmest greetings to her."

"Ah, I cannot, my dear girl. I cannot bring any messages of any kind from you."

"Is Lady Delphia ill?" In her alarm, Rosa stood up from her chair and ran to sit next to his lordship.

Miserably he shook his head. "She is not ill," he said.

"What is it? What has happened?"

He gazed at her with the most sorrowful countenance she had ever seen. "She is not speaking to you."

Rosa attempted to smile. It was, after all, amusing. And she was not a bit surprised. Having seen her ladyship's manner toward the rest of the world, she had never deceived herself that she would meet with better treatment. It was only a matter of time, she had always told herself, before Lady Delphia turned her back on her, too, cut her, snubbed her, and froze her with icy silence.

Now the time had come, the time she had expected. The odd thing was that it hurt. Knowing it would come did not prevent it from stinging. Unaccountably, it stung more than all the indignities, insults, and injustices that had overtaken her in the past weeks.

Rosa walked to the window to gaze outside at the heavy rainfall. For some time, she watched the droplets make paths along the panes. She leaned her head against the window so that her tears mirrored the streaks on the glass. When she had collected herself, she returned to her visitor.

"I ask you again to take my greetings to her ladyship, my lord. She may choose to be angry with me, but that confers no obligation on me to be angry with her."

Lord Divine gave her hand a tender squeeze. "My dear child," he said. "Beckwith would have adored you."

"Do you think he would have adored a nursemaid's daughter?"

Sighing, his lordship confessed he had forgot all about Sukey Dawes. He could not believe the woman's claim to be her nearest relation, he said, but he was sure she was an honest, good-hearted woman in her way. "Well," he concluded with as bright a smile as he could muster, "your being a prisoner has this advantage—you do not have to go and live with her and call her mother." Then he had a sneezing fit, followed by a coughing attack, and Rosa was compelled to send him home.

The day before the trial, Rosa received a visit from Mr. Grahame. Seeing that the gentleman was agitated, she tried to assure him she was being extremely well looked after. Mrs. Buffel, she said, fed her wholesome victuals and permitted her to entertain visitors. Moreover, the woman certainly kept a clean house. None of these assurances, however, appeared to console him.

He could not say more than half a sentence before rising from his chair and walking to one of the tables, where Mrs. Buffel kept a number of well-dusted items of an inspirational nature—a collection of alabaster cherubim, a number of embroidered homilies, and, propped on a stand, a drawing of Judith holding the bleeding head of Holofernes. Prolonged admiration of these ornaments did not appear to console the gentleman one jot.

"What is it, Mr. Grahame? I have never seen you like this."

"I hardly know what to say to you, Lady Rosalind. My niece has told me everything, and I can hardly face you."

"We have always been friends, sir, regardless of your niece. I should like us to continue friends."

"I have begged her to go to the court and tell the whole, but to no avail. She gives herself up for dead now and will not move from her divan."

"It is just as well. Her going to the court would serve no purpose."

"Suzanne might testify to your motives for taking the letter. She could show that there were circumstances which forced you to act as you did. The court must rule that, as you did not steal out of malice or desire for profit, it cannot properly be called stealing."

As he spoke, the passion in his voice resounded in Rosa's ears. She was surprised, surprised and touched. Mr. Grahame had always appeared the very model of reason. His customary tone was detached, cynical, avuncular. Never before had he permitted her such an intimate glimpse into his emotions.

"I am glad Miss Grahame is not to testify," she replied. "It would merely make public the very facts we were attempting to conceal."

"I don't care about that. I would like her to do what is right."

"You are very kind, Mr. Grahame."

"I am also very angry, Lady Rosalind."

"I can see that."

"No, I don't think you can. Angry as I am at my niece, I am even angrier at Sunley and Lady Delphia. They have turned their backs on you."

Rosa felt the warmth rush to her cheeks. "They have done no such thing," she murmured.

"I do not censure Lord Divine. Were he not so ill, I know he would be here with you in this dark hour. But his sister is not so loyal. She hasn't a single notion of loyalty in her heart, if she has a heart. Her single loyalty is to her own exalted position."

"If you knew how this sort of talk wounds me, sir, you would stop it at once."

"Sunley left London almost the very day you took up residence in this house. The whole world knows he has gone. The whole world whispers about it, too. And no one expects him to come back."

"I expect him to come back."

"You have heard from him, then?"

Rosa lowered her eyes and admitted that she had not.

"Then what you mean is that you hope he will come back."

"Yes, I hope it. I hope it every second."

He put his hands behind his back. "Hear me out, Lady Rosalind. I have a speech to make to you, and then I shall not trouble you further with my presence."

"Your presence does not trouble me."

"I hope it does not, because the aim of my speech is to ask you to be my wife. Even if you must spend a month or two in prison, I wish to marry you. There, I've said it."

As no answer appeared quite adequate, Rosa did not speak for some time. When she finally found words, she expressed her gratitude for his kindness and loyalty.

Impatiently he stopped her. "I do not want to be thanked. I want to know what you think of my offer."

"I think I feel very silly."

"Oh, dear. That is the last thing I expected."

"I do not mean to suggest that your offer is silly. It is the most generous gesture you could have made. But I have been frequently proposed to of late, and I cannot see how I am worthy of so many declarations from so many gentlemen. You see, I am not the daughter of an earl, but of a nursemaid, and nothing more."

"You are wrong. You are much more than that."

"True. I am also a pickpocket."

"Never! I refuse to hear you say so. You are an intelligent, brave, and adorable woman. You are everything that is fine. Your character is not only admirable, but lively and interesting as well. And I know you can never have picked a pocket or done anything dishonest in your life!"

Rosa was forced to smile at him. "After hearing such praise of my honesty, I certainly cannot accept you, Mr. Grahame."

"I am genuinely fond of you, Rosalind. I think we would do very well together, and my niece would benefit greatly from having you as her aunt. Are you very sure you will not have me?"

"Very sure, sir. If I ever do marry, it shall be to a man who knows exactly who and what I am and does not deny my faults or exaggerate my virtues. And as I do not know who or what I am myself, it appears highly unlikely that I shall ever marry at all."

◊ **Twenty-two** ◊

The day of the trial broke gray with fog. Mrs. Buffel sincerely prayed, as Constable Wally handed Rosa into the carriage, that the coachman would not drive his horses off a bridge or, worse, into a pothole. On that prayer, she bade Rosa good-bye, buffed the brass door knocker with the corner of her pinafore, and disappeared into the house.

Although the fog prevented Rosa from seeing very much of what lay along the route, she peered out the window expectantly. Soon she saw the spires of Westminster poking through the mist. But when she put her head out the window to have a better look, she smelled a smell so foul that she was compelled to hold her breath.

They alighted before a daunting edifice encased in the fog. Their progress to the door was impeded by a procession of clerks strewing posies, petals, and herbs in their path. Sweet fragrances began to mingle with the odors of sickness and ordure, so that Rosa could still not inhale without serious risk to her equilibrium.

"It's best to put a kerchief to your nose," advised the constable. "The smell of Newgate fairly penetrates the Old Bailey, and you will not be wanting to catch the jail fever."

Taking this excellent advice, Rosa covered her face with her linen and followed the constable into the building. She fully expected to see the court loom into view, but instead the constable led her down a dingy corridor to a small chamber.

Inside sat Lord Pomeroy, who glanced up as Rosa came in and then looked coldly at Sir Virgil Thwaite, who stood majestically by a table. The only other person present was Mr. Peter Buffel, who dusted off a chair for the young woman and begged her to sit. The constable, having done his duty, quietly withdrew and placed himself outside the door.

"My dear Lady Rosalind," Sir Virgil greeted her cordially.

Hearing herself addressed as Lady Rosalind, Rosa began to wonder how she would endure all the other mortifications to come.

"Lady Rosalind," Sir Virgil went on, "it is with great pleasure I am able to tell you of the postponement of your trial for half an hour."

He paused, expecting Rosa to smile, or at least look relieved. As her face remained impassive, he had no choice but to continue.

"Milord has granted me the opportunity to try to settle this matter of the letter in the privacy of these ancient and revered walls."

All looked at the walls, which ran with leaking drops of water and smelled only a little less revolting than the entrance.

"My purpose is to try to avoid the rancor and expense which necessarily attend upon a court proceeding."

"I am grateful that Lord Pomeroy has thought better of the action," Rosa said quietly.

"I have thought better of nothing!" his lordship stated.

"It is the Crown which hopes to settle this case," Sir Virgil explained. "Having read the evidence, the worthy prosecutor has concluded that all parties concerned might be wise to submit to an intermediate proceeding. If it is not satisfactory, then, of course, we shall go before the bench."

"As far as I am concerned," stated Pomeroy, "this proceeding is a failure, regardless of anything anyone may have to say. There is only one outcome that will satisfy me, and that is to see this thieving female found guilty by a jury and sent to Clink."

"As far as I am concerned," stated Rosa, "it does not matter whether the trial is held here or in the court. It is all one."

"But it must matter to you, Lady Rosalind. You must realize that hideous consequences may befall you as a result of a trial. The extreme penalty for pickpocketing is death."

Rosa caught her breath. Pomeroy laughed.

"Naturally," Sir Virgil went on, "juries are reluctant to recommend such a penalty. Indeed, because the penalty is so heavy, juries are reluctant to convict accused pickpockets at all, especially when they are young and pretty and well-behaved. Which is why the Crown sees the wisdom of settling this affair without recourse to the court. One can only hope that Lord Pomeroy will be brought to see the wisdom of it, too."

"It is very kind of you to take an interest in my case, Sir Virgil," said Rosa.

Brushing away this praise, Sir Virgil assured her he would always take a great interest in the affairs of such an old and respected family as the Divines.

"Is there no one else here?" she asked. She hoped to see a kind, or even just a familiar, face. Mr. Buffel was benevolent enough, but he spent his time looking for lost papers and brushing dusty surfaces with his fingers. Sir Virgil was far too grand and learned to seem quite friendly, and Pomeroy made no effort to conceal his desire for revenge.

"Mrs. Dawes has asked if she might be permitted to sit with you. I have told her I would ask you."

"Is there no one else?"

"Mr. Tripple is come, too."

"And is that all?"

"Yes."

"Then please ask them to come in."

Mr. Buffel leaped to the door to fetch the nursemaid and the actor. Solemnly, they entered the room and stood next to Rosa. She smiled a little at them both, causing them to join one another in a round of noisy sniffling.

"Well, then, I suppose we may proceed," said Sir Virgil. "I put it to you, Lord Pomeroy, that there is still time to drop the charge against this lady, that there is time to save your reputation as well as hers by preventing a public display of the differences between you, that there is time to settle accounts and make amends for any losses you may have incurred, which, by the by, would not be the case should we go to trial.

Even if her ladyship is convicted and sentenced, there would be no restitution forthcoming."

"I cannot make restitution to his lordship in any case," said Rosa. "I do not have anything, not a farthing."

"Lady Rosalind, I beg you will let me proceed without interruption."

"She is right," said Lord Pomeroy. "She cannot make amends. We are talking about a priceless letter upon which no monetary value can be set."

"Lord Pomeroy, do you seriously intend to put a woman of Lady Rosalind's quality and character in the dock and see her sent to prison, or else hanged?"

Lord Pomeroy looked squarely at Rosa for the first time. "If I have a choice," he said, "I should prefer to see her hanged. Prison will do as well, however."

With great sadness, Sir Virgil bowed his head and extended his hand to assist Rosa from her chair. "Sir Virgil," she said, causing him to stop a moment, "I must ask you to do one thing for me."

"Certainly."

"Never again call me Lady Rosalind."

The court was small and narrow. Its ceiling, sustained by numerous columns, seemed to reach to the sky. It was relentlessly gloomy, from the dark wainscoting of its walls to the benches black with age-old grime, from the black-robed officials of the court to the jury box filled with severe-looking men with black whiskers. The judge's white wig was the only spot of brightness in the hall.

Seated in the prisoner's box, Rosa saw Mrs. Dawes and Mr. Tripple take their seats. She scanned the rest of the gallery, which was filled to brimming with curiosity-seekers, but saw not another face she knew. She turned about again and saw Mr. Bonwit, of all people, enter the witness-box.

The Crown, in the person of Sir Solomon Levi, took one glance at the exquisite Mr. Bonwit and rolled his eyes to heaven. Calling upon his ancestors to tell him why he had been chosen for this ordeal, he looked at Lord Pomeroy and groaned. "My dear sir, let us have done with this nasty business. Let us not make laughingstocks of ourselves by questioning this fellow."

When Pomeroy remained adamant, Sir Solomon was forced to proceed. His shoulders hunched, his sighs reaching to the top of the ceiling, he put his hands on his hips and glared at the witness.

Mr. Bonwit appeared extremely ill at ease. He took umbrage at Sir Solomon's scrutiny of his cravat. For a moment, his eyes met Rosa's, but he immediately looked away.

"You have sworn to tell the truth, Mr. Bonwit."

"Yes, my lord."

"I presume you know what that means."

"Well, not precisely."

"It means that if you look me in the eye and tell me a lie I shall lock you up for perjury and no one will ever hear from you again. Is that clear enough?"

Mr. Bonwit gulped, which Sir Solomon took as sufficient indication that he now understood.

"Will you please tell us what you can about this matter of Lord Pomeroy's letter?"

Mr. Bonwit took a breath. "I met Lady Rosalind Divine at Almack's, where she singled me out for favor from among the many other gentlemen who sought the honor of dancing with her. Shortly after that, we formed an engagement, which she chose to ignore when it appeared she might make a match with his lordship there."

"She never engaged herself to 'im!" Sukey Dawes cried out. "Anyone with eyes would see that!"

The judge, who had been napping on his hand, now wakened with a start at Mrs. Dawes's outburst. He looked at her and yawned, and as the enormity of what she had done dawned upon her, the horrified nursemaid sank back into her seat.

Sir Solomon studied the tulip from his coiffed head to his dainty foot and sighed heavily. "I collect you think Lady Rosalind is guilty of, shall we say, a breach of promise to you."

"Guilty as sin! For weeks she has seduced me into thinking she meant to marry me. I honestly believed she liked me, the more fool I! Then, to read in the *Clarion* that she's set her cap for Pomeroy—it mortifies a fellow to look his friends in the eye."

The judge's eyelids fell to half-mast.

The crowd in the gallery murmured that ladies were known to be fickle and it was a wonder that gentlemen were willing to marry at all, given what it was they had to bind themselves to for the rest of their lives and the one to come.

The judge woke long enough to bring the public to order and assume a listening posture.

With infinite patience, Sir Solomon said, "May I point out, Mr. Bonwit, that you have said nothing pertaining to the letter."

"I never heard of any letter."

"Then you did not see Lady Rosalind take a letter?"

"No."

"Nor did she tell you she took one from his lordship?"

"Certainly not. Why would she? If I took a letter—which I can't fancy myself doing for love or money—I shouldn't tell the world about it."

"Mr. Bonwit, you are a more sensible fellow than you look."

The gentleman nodded, acknowledging at the compliment.

Sir Solomon bowed in response to the gentleman's nod. "May I be permitted one last question, sir?"

Bowing again, Mr. Bonwit invited him to question away.

"What the deuce are you doing here?"

The gentleman deflated. "I do not know precisely. Pomeroy said I could testify to the lady's character, and so I have."

"It is commendable of you to come forward to give testimony. You have no idea how many hang back for fear of looking like an ass in the witness-box. You evidently have no such fear, sir?"

"I thought it my duty to tell what I know."

"But you know nothing of the letter?"

"Nothing."

Sir Solomon thanked him and invited him to leave the box. He would have called upon his revered ancestors to preserve him from dutiful witnesses had not the judge summoned his attention.

"Did I miss the Crown's testimony?" the judge asked. "I am afraid I dozed off for a bit and did not catch all the questioning."

"I have just concluded this portion of the Crown's testimony," replied Sir Solomon.

"With testimony like that, we shall not need to hear a defense."

"Perhaps milord will like the next witness better."

The next witness proved to be a stranger to Rosa. Introduced as the owner of a company of traveling players, he claimed he had met Mr. Tripple and Rosa seven years before when they toured the west country with his original dramatization of the Book of Deuteronomy. He related that before one of the performances, Rosa Divine, as the actress was then known, had picked a gentleman's pocket.

"She never picked no pocket!" Sukey cried out.

"Who is that woman?" the judge inquired.

"I am the child's mother, and a luvely girl she is too."

"I thought Lady Beckwith was dead," the judge said.

Sir Virgil interjected here, "Her ladyship is dead, milord. I am afraid the inheritance case is a muddle and ought not to enter into this proceeding at all."

"I shall be very happy to exclude anything you like from this proceeding, sir, just so we get on with it. You may proceed, Sir Solomon."

"Did you see Rosa Divine pick the pocket in question?" Sir Solomon asked the witness.

"No."

"Did she confess to you that she picked it?"

"No."

"How do you know she picked it?"

"It was said that she picked it."

Sir Solomon threw his head back, nearly losing his wig, and raised his arms to the frescoed ceiling. "Is this court to be insulted with vile rumors in lieu of facts? Do none of the Crown's witnesses have a shred of proof to offer against this gentle lady?"

The question so stunned the assemblage that no sound could be heard in the court.

Sir Virgil beckoned nervously to his esteemed colleague. When he came close enough, he whispered to him, "Sir Solomon, you represent the Crown. This gentleman is your own witness."

"Lord help me," the prosecutor replied with a sigh. "I do not fancy prosecution. I dislike disputes altogether."

"Perhaps this one will be over soon," suggested Sir Virgil.

Wiping his weary eyes with the sleeve of his robe, Sir Solomon called his final witness—Lord Pomeroy. His lordship walked to the box with graceful bearing, causing the listeners in the courtroom to crane their heads for a better view. Pomeroy slowly and smoothly related the story of the stolen letter in accurate detail. He explained the nature of the letter without naming its writer. He described Rosa's several attempts to persuade him to give it to her. He drew a vivid picture of the postures he and Lady Rosalind had assumed which permitted her to slip her hand into his coat. He even described the bite she had given him on the lip, at the mention of which, every male in the room stared at her and swallowed.

"Amazing," said Sir Solomon. "And you wish to hang the lady instead of marrying her? It is the decline of the empire in a nutshell."

Lord Pomeroy grew angry. "You ought to be proving her guilty, sir, not taking her part!"

Woefully, Sir Solomon shook his head. "Why me?" he asked.

As neither providence nor his ancestors vouchsafed an answer, Lord Pomeroy performed that duty. "Because you represent the Crown, sir!"

"Ah, yes," said the prosecutor with a teary look at Rosa. "So I do."

"I believe you have another question for me."

"Oh, very well. Lord Pomeroy, what other witnesses can attest to this thievery?"

"None."

"Do you mean to say it is your word against that of the Earl of Beckwith's daughter?"

"She cannot prove she is his daughter."

Here the judge called Sir Solomon to the bench. He leaned over to say, "I thought she was that dreadful shrieking woman's daughter."

"There are conflicting claims, I understand."

"Let us stay clear of conflicting claims, or we shall never see the end of this tiresome case."

Acquiescing, Sir Solomon said to Lord Pomeroy, "The case would go better for you, sir, if you could produce a credible witness."

"Miss Suzanne Grahame," Pomeroy said. "She wrote the letter and persuaded that lady to steal it for her. Bring her in as a witness."

As one voice, the gallery gasped. Whispers could be heard to the effect that Lord Pomeroy was certainly no gentleman to have named the lady.

Sir Virgil rose from his chair and conferred with his colleague. "I have sent Mr. Peter Buffel to fetch the lady, but I do not expect to see her here. She maintains steadfastly that she knows nothing of the matter, although her uncle takes his oath she does."

Sir Solomon shook his head. "I detest it when ladies and gentlemen do not get on well together and try to tear each other's throats out. It is most distressing."

Sir Virgil nodded and sat down. Sir Solomon continued his examination. "Lord Pomeroy, Miss Grahame has not come forward to testify. If you have no more evidence than your own say-so, I am afraid I must ask milord to dismiss this action."

"I know of only one more witness," said Lord Pomeroy.

"I was afraid of that."

"She will tell you the entire truth."

"Is she in these chambers?"

"She is."

"If you tell us her name, we shall call her to the box."

"Rosalind Divine."

◊ Twenty-three ◊

Rosa waited patiently in the box as the onlookers murmured commendations on her beauty. Several of them suggested that she might appear to greater advantage if she smiled. Ladies who gave themselves airs and were above being pleased had never a hope of catching a husband. With that grave look she wore, it was no wonder Lord Pomeroy had thought better of marrying her.

"Lady Rosalind," said Sir Solomon with heartfelt sympathy, "I shall have to ask you a number of questions."

"I am not Lady Rosalind. I am that lady's daughter."

"There, you see!" cried Sukey.

Mr. Tripple stood up. "I can keep still no longer." Pointing at Sukey, he cried, "That female is a liar!"

"You there," barked the judge.

Tripple looked around to be sure it was he who was being addressed. "I, sir?"

"Yes, you, sir. Sit down and keep quiet!"

Tripple did as he was bid, leaving Sir Solomon at liberty to ask Rosa, "What shall I call you, then?"

"Rosa Divine. It is my stage name and I am used to it."

"Well, then, Miss Rosa Divine, why do you suppose this gentleman—Lord Pomeroy—thinks you picked his pocket?"

"Because I did."

Sir Virgil shot out of his chair. Sir Solomon sank into his. Both attorneys trembled to hear the judge's words.

"Did you not rehearse your client, Sir Virgil?"

"I never thought for a moment she might have done it."

"Nonsense!" said Sir Solomon. "She could not have done it. Why, you have only to look at her to know she never picked a pocket in her life."

The gentlemen looked at Rosa, who stood patiently in the witness-box. Her auburn hair was curled exquisitely about her ears and piled high on her head. Her graceful neck, framed with a pretty lace, gleamed charmingly in the dim light. Although she was the defendant and might be thought to suffer violent attacks of nerves, she appeared as tranquil as the full moon sailing across the clear ocean. The gentlemen sighed. The judge scratched his head under his wig and said, "Well, whether she picked it or not, she has confessed. I suppose, therefore, we may call an end to this trial now."

Sir Solomon begged another moment to question the witness, which the judge granted.

"Why," said the prosecutor to Rosa, "did you pick his lordship's pocket?"

"I cannot tell you that."

"Was it as Lord Pomeroy says, on account of Miss Grahame?"

"Lord Pomeroy may not choose to behave as a gentleman should, but I do not choose to emulate him."

The courtroom broke into thunderous applause. A gentleman in the rear of the gallery shouted that the lady ought to be knighted for gallantry. He was summarily silenced by a female who knighted him with her parasol and threatened him with worse if he continued to speak out in defense of villainy.

Sir Solomon turned to Sir Virgil. "I cannot get her to say a word in her own defense," he lamented.

"Perhaps I ought to try," suggested the solicitor general.

Bowing, the attorney for the Crown sat down and permitted the defense to have a word.

"Now, my dear," began Sir Virgil, "you are understandably wrought up over all this muddle. But I am sure if you think about it—think about the consequences of your silence—you will realize that it is best to tell the truth. The court may be leniently disposed toward you if it understands any circumstances extenuating the commission of the act you have confessed to."

"I will cooperate as best I may, sir. You have been so very kind to me. Perhaps it would not betray any confidences to admit to you that I did what I did to help a friend."

"Aha!" cried Sir Solomon. "There you have it. I knew it must be something like that."

"Who is that friend?" asked Sir Virgil.

William Divine, Viscount Sunley."

Everyone in the court inhaled with a single breath.

"Your cousin?"

"He is not my cousin, sir. I only pretended to be his cousin."

"What do you mean you pretended?"

"I impersonated Lady Rosalind Divine in order to get the inheritance."

The judge paused in midyawn to consider this new admission, while the onlookers debated whether it was ever wise to trust a pretty face.

Shaken, Sir Virgil asked, "Are you confessing to fraud now, my dear?"

"I suppose I am."

A beaten man, Sir Virgil grasped for his chair. Rosa turned to the judge and begged him to cause a glass of wine to be fetched for the lawyer, which the judge promptly did.

Seeing his colleague drooling wine on his robes, Sir Solomon rose.

"Miss Rosa Divine," he said, pained, "have you any other crimes to confess to this court?"

"I think I've told you everything."

"Not everything!" Tripple shouted. He stood up and pounded his fist on the railing. "'Doubt truth to be a liar!'"

As every eye in the court was on him now, he struck a declamatory pose, with one hand over his heart and the other raised in the air with pointed forefinger. "I have evidence to offer!" he declared.

Sir Solomon raised a questioning look to the judge.

"I don't suppose it can harm her case any," the judge remarked. "It's as bad as it can possibly be."

With that, Mr. Tripple walked forward and stood in the witness-box. Considerable time had passed since Mr. Tripple had played for an audience. He appraised the house with shrewd eyes, estimating that nobody appeared to be armed with cabbages, eggs, or overripe apples. In fact, it was unlikely anyone would impair the dignity of the court by throwing anything at all. He therefore pulled his shoulders back with confidence, and, pausing just long enough to allow Sir Solomon to phrase an opening question, he launched into his soliloquy.

In a voice which boomed and echoed through the chamber, he absolved Rosa totally and absolutely of any and all wrong-doing whatsoever. "If crimes have been committed, your worships, I am the one responsible."

When the Crown's attorney inquired how so, he smacked his lips and elucidated.

First of all, he said, he wished them all to know that he was Rosalind's father.

As soon as the gasps of horror subsided, he took the first opportunity to deny that he had ever had anything to do of a connubial nature or any other nature with Mrs. Sukey Dawes. Indeed, until a few weeks ago, he had never so much as laid eyes on that irrational female. If she was claiming to be Rosa's mother, she was lying in her teeth, and he knew it for a fact because he was the girl's true and only father.

Rosa stood up when she heard this declaration but sat down again immediately when she heard Sir Virgil whimper. Was Tripple telling the truth? she wondered. She had always thought he would end by owning her. Was this the truth at last? Or was he shamming again? Was he claiming her merely in order to get her released? But how could such a lie, if it was a lie, possibly win her freedom?

Tripple allowed that he should have acknowledged his daughter from the first. It was a source of hideous shame to him now that he had not. His conscience pricked him night and day over it. It was because he had neglected to give his child a name that she had ended in this disgraceful situation. It was his fault she was here, for he had not only raised her as an orphan, but he had also schooled her in the art of picking pockets.

Inhaling a moment, he heard the sounds of sobbing all around. He had never made an audience weep before, at least not with pleasure, and for a moment he forgot the climax of his speech. Then recollecting it, he faced the jury and pleaded with the good and upright gentlemen to consider this: If Rosa Divine was a pickpocket, it was out of habit, not malice. She would sooner pick a pocket to please a friend than to garner a shilling. Moreover, the poor girl had never known the genuine affection that only an acknowledged father can bestow, and therefore she might be excused if she overstepped the bounds of propriety from time to time.

At the conclusion of this speech, he swept a bow. The hand clapping that followed inspired the old actor to shed a genuine tear. He made as if to stride back to his seat, then stopped dead still. A tall figure appeared in the rear of the court and acknowledged him with a nod.

Following the direction of Mr. Tripple's popping eyes, every face in the chamber looked round.

When Rosa saw him, she felt the control go out of her. She stood up and searched his face as though it might supply some precious reassurance. What she saw as he gazed back at her was the deepest anxiety, and she found it unbearable.

As the door to the prisoner's box had not been locked, she was able to escape. Running past Viscount Sunley, she fled down the corridor and through the main door before the guards could stop her.

The moment she emerged onto Newgate Street, she was overcome by the stench of the prison. She came to a halt and froze as she heard footsteps. But when she listened again, she heard nothing, and a disappointment such as she had not known before overwhelmed her. What she had heard were not footsteps at all but the cherished memory of footsteps, the memory of Sunley pursuing her through the alley near a London playhouse.

Drained of energy, she leaned against a stone wall and closed her eyes.

"I believe I have found something in Surrey," said a low voice close to her."

She turned and looked at him.

"I have these—copies of the workhouse register," he said.

Rosa glanced at the papers he held in his hand. "It doesn't matter," she said. "What is the difference who hangs for picking Lord Pomeroy's pocket—Beckwith's daughter, Sukey Dawes's daughter, or Tripple's daughter?"

"It matters to you. I know very well it does. That is why I went to Surrey. I thought you would want to know the truth, one way or the other."

"I am resigned to never knowing. It was silly of me ever to want to know. I wish I had never asked."

He could no longer stand to see her huddled against the wall, so remote and desolate. Reaching for her gently, he tried to comfort her, but she held him off. "You must not, my lord."

"I'm afraid I must. I've missed you."

"You must keep your distance, sir. I am a nursemaid's daughter, that is, unless I am an old actor's daughter. Whichever it is, you cannot afford to miss me."

"I cannot afford to love you, either, but that does not prevent me from doing it."

Rosa pressed her lips together and stepped away. "Nor can I afford to love you. You may have a noble name, sir, but you are as poor as a beggar."

"I should say we suit one another very well, then."

"We must return to the court."

"Rosa, say you are glad I am back. Say you are not angry at me for staying away so long."

"They will be sending the guards for us in a moment."

"Well, then, I will say that I am glad to be back, and I am angry with myself for staying away so long."

"Please do not say another word."

"I love you."

"Especially not that word."

"Marry me."

Afraid of losing her resolve altogether, Rosa gathered her skirts and ran back to the court.

What greeted her as she opened the doors was the unexpected sight of Miss Grahame in the witness-box. She looked pale to death.

"Ah, the accused has returned," the judge announced to the assemblage.

Everyone looked at Rosa, who tiptoed down the aisle, went to the box she had lately vacated, opened the door, sat down, and closed herself inside.

In another moment, Sunley followed her inside the chamber and sat as near to her as possible. He was closely followed by five guards who announced to the judge that they could not find the prisoner anywhere. After waving them away in disgust, milord pleaded with Sir Solomon to get on with it.

"As you were saying, Miss Grahame, you read today in the newspaper of Lord Pomeroy's engagement to the Honorable Miss Fanny Nitney, daughter of Lord and Lady Nitney."

She nodded weakly and glared at Pomeroy, who slunk down in his seat.

"I knew then it was my duty to come forward," she said.

"The civic spirit seems to be epidemic in London," Sir Solomon observed. "Go on, if you please."

"I should like to bring an action against Lord Pomeroy for breach of promise."

An oath of indignation escaped Lord Pomeroy, while the gallery applauded, whispering it was high time he got his comeuppance.

Sir Solomon frowned darkly at the yellow-haired young woman. "Miss Grahame, you are here to testify in the action against Miss Rosa Divine. You cannot suddenly inject your own action here."

The judge, yawning behind his hand, rapped for attention. Calling the attorneys to him, he suggested that all parties concerned be brought near the bench. Rosa, Pomeroy, Sunley, the Grahames, Mr. Tripple, and Mrs. Dawes were each in turn escorted before the judge. Appraising them as they stood in a line, he said, "It appears we may be able to make sense out of this case after all."

All agreed that such a miracle would be welcome.

"If Miss Grahame will drop her action against Lord Pomeroy, Lord Pomeroy may drop his action against Miss Rosa Divine, or whatever she calls herself, and we may all go home."

Pomeroy and Miss Grahame glared at each other for a second.

"Surely you do not wish to grow old while this case is tried," the judge snapped.

Seeing the steely look in his eye, they both nodded their heads and sullenly agreed.

The judge smiled. "I have the notion that the Crown will not object to dropping the action."

Sir Solomon declared he would like nothing better than to see the charming Miss Rosalind Divine anywhere but in a courtroom. He then called upon his ancestors to bear witness to that.

Satisfied, the judge sat back in his chair. "Now, get out of here, all of you," he invited, and all parties in the case moved to obey.

"One moment, if you please," said the viscount.

"What now?" the judge snapped.

"I have some papers here which I beg you to read over."

Snatching them from Sunley, the judge read. As he did so, the others drifted round the bench again in curiosity. After reading for some time, he handed the papers back to the viscount saying, "That is edifying in the extreme. You may all get out now."

"But, milord, did you note the entries I marked?"

Seizing the papers again, the judge read, "Elizabeth Martin and infant. Sukey Dawes and infant." He thrust the papers back and said, "There, I have read them." He stood up to leave.

Refusing to take the papers, Sunley pushed them back and asked, "I beg your pardon, milord, but do you note any difference between the two entries?"

"The purpose of this court was to try Miss Divine, Viscount Sunley. These papers do not further the case."

"But you can distinguish between one entry in a register and another, I believe."

Snatching the papers from him, the judge slapped them down so that he might read them once more, which he did fiercely. He then looked up to pronounce, "There is no difference whatever between the entries."

Sunley bowed his head, grieved.

"Unless, of course," said the judge, "you are referring to the fact that Elizabeth Martin's infant was a girl while Sukey Dawes's was a boy."

Raising his head, Sunley smiled. "Thank you, milord. That was precisely the difference I meant."

◊ Epilogue ◊

The viscount surveyed the gloomy courtroom, empty now of litigants, complainants, interrogators, witnesses, judges, jurymen, and oglers. He folded his arms and regarded Rosa, who sat very still in one of the public chairs. Walking to her, he asked if she was ready to go home.

"Home," she repeated.

"The sight of you will restore my father again."

"Oh, but Lady Delphia, William. She is not speaking to me."

"You must learn what is the chief cure for all the wounds she fancies her dignity suffers. Pour the balm of money on them and they will heal magically."

"What about Sukey Dawes? Poor woman. It was for my sake she lied. She was afraid you were all a passel of parasites and leeches, only after the money I might get you."

"And she was not far off the mark. But Mr. Tripple has promised to look after her. I believe he means to take her to a play."

"Dear Tripple. I always knew he would claim me one day. It was brave of him to lie about it, and he did it very affectingly, I thought."

"If you are quite done worrying about everybody else now, I should like a little of your attention."

She stood as he drew close to her. The opportunity soon presented itself for her to touch her finger to his lip. "And to think I was a fine lady all along. How very strange."

With his mouth close to her ear, he informed her, "I knew who you were from the minute I saw you in a blanket."

She felt his breath warm on her neck. "You knew I was Beckwith's daughter?"

"I knew you were the woman I loved."

"Well, it's very nice to have all that business of mothers and fathers settled now. I vow, for a while I thought I should change my identity as often as I change my dress."

"I'm afraid I must ask you to make one more change, Rosa. Be my wife."

"I suppose that while I am in a changing vein, I may manage one more."

He kissed her forehead. "You haven't said you love me, you know."

"Well, I do love you."

"Then you will give me your hand in marriage, fair cousin?"

"Here it is," she said, adding, as he raised it to his lips, "and it will never pick any pocket but yours."